STRUCK BY LIGHTNING

By
Lizzie T. Leaf

Triskelion Publishing
www.triskelionpublishing.com
All about women. All about extraordinary.

Praise for Lizzie T. Leaf

"*Lizzie T. Leaf* has penned a wonderfully funny and heartwarming romance with enough heat to fog your windows! **Struck By Lightning** will keep you chuckling throughout at the antics of Bella's loving, yet controlling Italian family and Galvin's nutty immortal family. *Ms. Leaf's* characterizations are fabulous! You feel like you're living this book and thinking in Bella's head. This book is a knee slapping good time and I highly recommend it." –Holly, Euro-Reviews

"*Call Me* is a funny look at a virtual innocent learning the sexual ropes by telephone. ... **Lizzie T. Leaf** pens a honey of a tale, and I'll be looking for more goodies from her! 5 Angels" –Michelle, Fallen Angel Reviews

"*Boy Toy* by Lizzie T. Leaf will have you swelling with emotions, laughing at life in general and looking at younger men in a whole new light. Ms. Leaf paints a wonderfully sensual picture with her words and leads you on an adventure that I would not be surprised to find in my own "back yard." ... I hope to be given the opportunity to spend more time with more of her work soon." –Keely Skillman, eCataromance Reviews

Triskelion Publishing
15327 W. Becker Lane
Surprise, AZ 85379

ISBN 1-933471-85-9

Dedication

Thank you to Kristi for working with me on the edits. I was struck by edits and needed them.

To my critique partners, thank you as always for all of the suggestions, corrections and prodding.

Thank you to my husband for the time and support he puts into my efforts. You know I couldn't do it without you, honey.

A special thank you to Mike and his team at Channel 7 and Kathy at Channel 9 for allowing me to follow them around in my research to discover how things work behind the scenes in addition to all the information they shared with me on storms and weather patterns.

PROLOGUE

Azgard
Present Day

"I cannot understand this fascination you have with mortal women, Galvin. Surely you can find an immortal to your liking." Sif furrowed her lovely brow in frustration as she looked at her youngest son.

By the powers that be, he was a feast for the eyes even by the standards of the goddess. Strong and muscular in build, he had her pale blonde hair, shot with streaks of red inherited from his father, Thor. Why he chose to wear it in a short mortal style was beyond her. She preferred it longer, the way her husband wore his.

Galvin's dark blue eyes appeared to have the wisdom to see into the windows of the soul when one met his gaze, which Sif tried not to do often. She attributed this ability to his grandfather, Odin, along with several other attributes inherited from him. Of course, Odin paid dearly for the wisdom with the loss of an eye, but her baby boy's legacy included much of the knowledge and abilities his grandfather now took for granted.

"Mother, I know you'd like me to settle down and

produce grandchildren for you to bounce on your knee, but the immortals with whom I come in contact…" He paused. Galvin knew what he had to say was not going please his mother.

"Yes." Sif looked at her son expectantly.

"Well, in truth, they bore me. They can only talk about what deity did this, or what herbal remedy to use to prevent that or even more boring, all their talk of casting spells. They are minor immortals with no real capabilities or strengths of their own." Galvin paced in front of his mother.

"Given the might that is yours, do you need a wife to have powers?"

Galvin stopped pacing. "Exactly my point. Why do I need a wife with power, given all of my abilities? Selecting a wife from the earth realm would be of no issue."

Sif realized her error and tried to recover. "Son, you do need a wife who is aware of your strengths. How can you expect to hide them from a mortal? She wouldn't understand."

"The mortal I chose will be strong and intelligent. I will be able to share everything about myself with her. Instead of being frightened, she will find my aptitudes a challenge. She will help me to find ways in applying my powers for the good of all." Galvin gave her the wicked smile Sif found so hard to resist.

She tried another tactic. "I'm sure your father would arrange to send you to Mount Olympus to check out the immortals there. I know he doesn't condone the interaction of the godly realms, but he would make an exception in this matter. Why don't we ask him to talk with Zeus? After all, Zeus is your godfather and has said many times to Thor and Odin how much he enjoys your visits."

"No. My mind is made up about this, Mother. I would think your being a fertility goddess, you would want me to procreate."

"But, with a human? The child will be a…a half-blood." Sif wrinkled her perfect nose. "There are enough of those running around due to the lascivious escapades of the gods like your grandfather. Not to mention the depraved Gods of other Realms, especially those Olympians." Sif shuddered at the thought.

Many mortals bore the blood of the gods and were not aware of it. They only knew at times things happened to them or were created by them that others didn't experience or couldn't do. Some ended up in what the inhabitants of earth called mental institutions. Sif sighed out loud. The thought of this fate befalling a grandchild of hers was more than she could bear.

"Mother." Galvin kissed her cheek. "I can read your thoughts you know. Any child I create with a mortal woman will know its father as well as its mother. We will be husband and wife and our child will know love. I take precautions when I have the need to fulfill my carnal desires with an immortal. I promise the same with a mortal."

Sif heard voices coming down the hall and patted her son's arm. "You have always been my most reliable son."

"And your favorite. Do not forget that." Galvin kissed her cheek again.

"Ah, Sif, here you are."

Thor entered the room with Loki on his heels as usual. Sif's posture straightened as she looked at the trickster. How the son of a giant and giantess could be considered a deity was beyond her, but it wasn't her place to question these things.

"Sif, your hair looks especially lovely today." Loki tipped his head in greeting.

"Thank you, Loki." She fixed a smile on her lips. Understanding his dig, she chose to ignore it. Protocol required her to accept his presence, but she would never forgive this creature the loss of her beautiful hair. No matter how fine the gold he had the dwarfs spin to replace her own hair it was not the same. How Thor forgave him so readily would always be a mystery to her. Males, whether immortal or mortal, would always be beyond understanding.

"I see our youngest son is here, too." Thor's eyes came to rest on Galvin. "What news do you have for us? I hear you have been locked away with the lovely Siera for several days. Did you come to share the news of your impending nuptials?"

Sif found herself unable to restrain a gasp. "Nuptials? But, I thought —"

"Mother, my father is jesting. It must be the company he keeps." Galvin shot a dark look toward Loki. "No, Father, I have no such news. Just the opposite I am afraid."

"The opposite. What does this mean?" Thor's brow furrowed in puzzlement.

"I have been sharing with Mother my desire to seek a wife in the mortal world."

"*What?*"

Sif knew Thor's shout had been heard on earth, but would be shrugged off by the mortals as thunder.

"A mortal wife. Such nonsense. To take a pilgrimage to earth and sow a few wild oats is one thing. In fact your grandfather encouraged me to do it in my youth. To go there in search of a wife that is ridiculous. Immortals do not lower themselves to marry a..a..a human." Thor spat out the word as if it left a bad taste in his mouth. "Galvin. Be reasonable here. Mortal women are only good for dalliance, not commitment by one such as yourself. You are the son of Thor, grandson of Odin the Powerful One and Jord, the Goddess Earth. The most gifted of my sons."

"Father, I am well aware of my heritage. I am also an individual with a mind of my own. I need a wife who will give me more than sexual stimulation. The available immortals are a bunch of spoiled, self-centered females who hold no interest outside the bedroom."

"Why would one need the interest of a female outside the bedroom?" Loki murmured.

Hearing his remark, Sif shot The Lord Jester a look of contempt and turned her attention back to Thor and Galvin.

Fortunately, Thialfi, Thor's loyal servant, distracted Loki. "What is it, Thialfi? Can't you see we're busy here?" he bellowed, but allowed the thin man to whisper in his ear.

Sif watched her two men stand eye to eye. Understanding of why Thor's mother, the Goddess Earth, fought to bring life back to her son after he ingested the venom of the Midgard Serpent's breath flowed through Sif. She loved her husband, even with his legendary temper, but her son's pain she did not tolerate well.

If she had to choose between her husband and her son, to her there was no choice. This was the child of her heart, possibly, because he came to her so late in life, when she thought there would be no more. She watched as her baby prepared to do battle with his father. There would be no question of where her loyalties lie.

"*I forbid it!*"

She flinched at Thor's thunder. Even Loki jumped. Only Galvin seemed unmoved.

"I am past the age of your forbidding me to follow my desires, Father." His voice remained calm.

Sif noted the twitch in the muscles of Thor's cheek and knew what would come if she didn't stop it. The two men who mattered the most to her would be throwing lightning bolts at each other at any moment. She stepped forward and pushed between father and son.

"Stop it, both of you. This is no way for Gods to behave." She shoved the two apart.

Galvin stepped back and took a deep breath. "You are correct, Mother. Thank you for saving me from going against my father. I would hate any harm I do to him."

"*Harm to me?*" Loki grabbed Thor by the arm in an attempt to restrain the Thunder God's lunge toward his son.

"Wait, Thor. You have business to attend to. Your servant, Thialfi, has brought a message. It appears there is something happening on earth of which you should be aware." Loki waved his hand and a meadow surrounded by woodland appeared.

Four women held hands as they danced in a circle and chanted.

"By the gods, they are trying to conjure up an immortal." Loki laughed with obvious delight.

"Hmmm." Thor caressed his red beard, a habit Sif knew to indicate deep thought.

The four voyeurs in Valhalla watched as the circle broke up and the women stumbled out of the meadow.

"That felt positive," the one with the straight black hair said.

"Yeah. We've struck a blow for womankind," two of the others concurred.

The one with the curly dark hair frowned. "I agreed to go along with this nonsense because I'm as drunk as the rest of you. But, I'm not an idiot. I'd have a better chance of being struck by lightning than finding an immortal."

Sif watched as Galvin stared in fascination at the group below them. She shifted her attention to Thor and became concerned as a smile played across his lips. It could only indicate trouble.

"That can be arranged, my beauty." The Thunder God held his right arm out straight and released a bolt that headed toward earth.

CHAPTER 1

Isabella Girardi opened one eye and quickly shut it as the light in the dimly lit room triggered a bolt of pain through her head. "Shit." Fireworks exploded at the sound of her voice and she rolled over, worming her head between the two pillows on her bed.

She needed to stop drinking those damned blue martinis. Why did she let herself get caught up in the moment each time she got together with the girls? Any sane person drank one and called it good, but not her. No. They went down so smoothly, before she knew it her glass was empty and the little voice in her head, urged her to guzzle one more.

The phone rang and the Flamenco dancer in her head applied his taps with relish. Fumbling for the current cause of pain, she finally located it and slipped the handset under the pillows where her head was still buried. "What?"

"Aren't we Miss Sunshine this morning?" Mona Nichols chirped in her ear.

"Fuck, Mona. What the hell are you doing calling at the crack of dawn?" Isabella lowered her voice as her verbal response to Mona's perkiness created another explosion in her head.

"Darling, it's after one. As in one p.m. I'm calling

as a friend to make sure you're okay. That lightning bolt came pretty close to you last night. Are you sure you weren't hit?"

"Lightning bolt?" Isabella struggled to focus on what Mona rambled on about.

"Yeah. It really was strange since there wasn't a cloud in the sky. I have to admit it was pretty funny after we knew you were all right. Imagine, making a statement about having a better chance of being struck by lightning than of finding an immortal, then wham! You were almost struck by lightning." Mona started to giggle. "Do you think that ups your chances on meeting an immortal?" Her giggle changed to a roar of laughter, forcing Isabella to push the phone away from her ear.

"You were always too fucking cheerful when we were roommates in college and I see things haven't changed," Isabella wondered why she stayed friends with such a positive person.

"Ahh, come on Bella. Be a sport. If it'd been one of us you'd have laughed your ass off. Seriously, are you okay?"

"Other than the whole Army marching band blaring through my head, I'm fine. I vaguely remember some of it. Didn't we end up in Central Park doing a weird dance and this stupid chant thing?"

"Yeah. We were all too drunk to drive to Raine's suggested spot out in the country, so we compromised and went to the park instead."

Isabella hated Mona right now. She drank more than most of the group last night and yet, she didn't sound any the worse for wear today. But then, she'd always been like that in college, too. "What was it we were trying to accomplish?" *Besides a rotten hangover.*

"Raine came up with the brilliant idea we need to find an immortal male, since the men we get stuck with aren't meeting our needs. They're only interested in the under thirty bimbos with cup sizes larger than their IQs." Mona sounded happy to fill-in the blanks in Isabella's memory.

"Oh, yeah. Something about her grandmother's stories, shapeshifters and such shit." More of it was coming back to Isabella and she wasn't sure she wanted to remember. Talk about grown women making fools of themselves.

"Hey, a girl's gotta do whatever it takes. Our clocks are ticking here. We're all in our mid-thirties and not getting any younger. I wouldn't mind some gorgeous vamp putting the bite on me." Mona, as usual, laughed at her own humor.

Isabella pulled the pillows off her head and looked over at the clock on her nightstand. Mona was right about the time. Time? Was there something she needed to do? "Hey Mona, thanks for calling to check on me. You're a real friend, but I'd better get myself into the shower and see if I can accomplish a few things today."

"Okay. Do you want to go out tonight? There's a new club over on the Eastside. We could see what kind of action it has."

The woman was out of her mind. No way would she, Isabella go out tonight. Her body couldn't handle two nights in a row like last night. She wasn't twenty-one any more. "I'm going to pass, but thanks."

"Okay." Mona sounded disappointed.

Finally ending the conversation with Mona, Isabella headed for the bathroom, stumbling over something on the floor. "Damn. What the hell? Where did this book come from?"

Picking up the object in question, she closed one eye and attempted to focus with the other as she read the title. *"The Still Sexy Ladies Guide for Dating Immortals*. Crap. Mona must have helped me get home last night and left this as a joke."

Disgusted, she tossed the book on the dresser and winced as it slid down behind it, hitting the floor with a thud. "Screw it. I'll fish it out later. My head isn't up to bending down."

Continuing into the bathroom, she turned on the hot water and dropped her bathrobe to do her normal Saturday morning body appraisal. At thirty-eight, she admitted to a little more meat on her bones than in her college years, but that gave the illusion of more curves under her clothes. Okay, so her tits sagged a little bit, that's why she invested a fortune in her bras; in hopes the support would delay further deterioration of what she considered her best feature. Thighs showed a little cellulite, but not too flabby yet. Better spend more time in the gym.

She heard the phone ring and tested the water coming from the showerhead. It was probably another of her crazy friends checking up on her. The water still wasn't hot enough anyway, so she'd let whichever one it was know she still lived.

"Bella, honey. Where are you?" Her mother's voice vibrated in her head.

"I'm home, Ma. Where do you think I am since you called my home number?" Sometimes her mother was so dense.

"I realize you're home, dear and don't take that tone with me. I mean why aren't you here at the decorator store? You promised to help me pick out curtains for the living room today."

"Shit." This was the thing nagging at the back of her mind. She'd told her mother they'd pick out the curtains and then have dessert at Angela's favorite pastry shop a few doors down from the decorator's.

"Don't swear, dear. You know I don't like that. It's not becoming to a lady."

She could see the look of reprimand on Angela's face. Damn, the woman was good. She only had to use a certain tone of voice and Isabella felt like she was in the room. "Look, Ma. I'm getting a late start today. Why don't we do this next Saturday? I promise I'll be there with bells on."

"No. I'll wait." Angela gave a long sigh of resignation. "I have to get this done today. Your father and I have guests coming tomorrow, and you better be one of them. I can't have a house full of people thinking I have no taste. The windows are bare, except for the shades."

Great. She used the 'poor me, my daughter doesn't care about me' voice. Lord help her Jewish friends if their mothers were any worse with the guilt trips an Italian Catholic mother could lay on. "Okay, okay. I get the picture. I'll be there as soon as I can."

Damn, how did she forget the party tomorrow? Her parents were throwing a birthday party for her father's oldest brother. Another fun family event. A room full of pregnant cousins holding their bellies, while their mothers clucked sympathetically to Angela over poor Isabella's inability to find a man.

Isabella swallowed several aspirin before stepping into the shower. Drugs combined with the caffeine she'd pick up on her way to the subway might give her the strength to survive an afternoon with her mother. An afternoon spent with Ma while hungover was sure to give her a better appreciation of *Dante's Inferno*.

*****

The party was in full swing when Isabella arrived. Her parents came from families who felt it their duty to take the Bible literally and "go forth and multiply." Her mother's parents were blessed with six kids and her father's did even better with eight. The current generation seemed to have inherited the same philosophy. She counted at least seven female cousins with protruding bellies.

"Scary, isn't it?" Her brother Gino came in behind her.

"'Bout time you got here. I thought I was going to be thrown to the piranha alone. It's been a regular feeding frenzy up to now." Isabella hugged her brother and laughed. The two of them had to stick together since both were a disappointment in the area of marriage and reproduction.

"I wish Ma would get it though her head I'm gay and leave me out of the mating rituals she cooks up." Gino's voice reflected his frustration.

Isabella looked at her brother. His looks were the kind that made women's heads swivel when he walked by. Probably some guys, too. Gorgeous, tough, and dangerous with dark hair brushing his collar and the muscular body a long shoreman, or a body builder, would envy.

In fact, his build probably came in handy in his non-family approved choice of employment. He ran numbers, and Isabella didn't want to know what else, for Joey DeBenedetto, a known Mafia Don. Yep, one of Joey's boys was gay and Isabella often wondered how well it would go over if his working peers figured out Gino's sexual preference.

"Oh, Gino. It's just a phase. You'll grow outta it and give your Mama beautiful babies before she's too old to enjoy them." Isabella did a pretty good imitation of their mother's response when the subject of Gino's sexual preference came up which caused both to crack up.

"So, what's so funny?"

Thank heavens the noise level in the room was loud enough Angela's bat-like sonar didn't pick up the joke at her expense. "Nothing, Ma. Gino and I were talking about how it looked like a maternity hospital in here."

"You should be so lucky."

Angela shot her one of 'the looks' and Isabella mentally kicked herself. *Damn. Talk about sticking your foot in your mouth. Now, if she doesn't give the lecture to go with it I'll be home free.* No such luck.

"Bella, look at your cousins, blooming with the new life growing in them. When are you going to give up this career foolishness and find a nice husband?"

Career foolishness? She didn't think being named the top weather forecaster in New York State, not just the city, foolish. Isabella took her job as Head Meteorologist for KDWI Television seriously and wished for once, so would her mother.

"Your father and me, we're not getting any younger, and we want grandchildren to bounce on our knees." Angela sighed for effect and batted her wet eyes. "Do you know how much it hurts us to see all the grandchildren our brothers and sisters have and us without any?"

No, no. Not the tears, Ma. Please don't start with the tears. Damn, she hadn't been here fifteen minutes and things had already reached the tears stage.

A glance at Gino didn't help the situation. Her brother's face turned red from trying to hold back his laughter. She fought the impulse to poke him in the ribs when her mother took care of things for her.

"And, you." Angela turned to her only son and pushed her finger in the middle of his chest. "When are you going to find a nice girl and settle down? Find a decent job that's not going to end up getting you put in jail? Mark my word, working for Joey DeBenedetto is going to get you nothing but trouble."

"Ma, I told you a thousand times. I'm gay. I don't like women in that way. When I find a life partner, I don't think he'll be able to conceive a baby. So give it up already." Gino's chin jutted out in stubborn defiance just as it had since he was a little boy.

"Ahh, it's just a phase. You'll outgrow it."

Isabella didn't dare look at her brother in fear they'd end up rolling on the floor with laughter. She heard her father's voice calling for Precious, his nickname for Angela. The lump of gratitude she always felt when Lou Girardi saved her from a conflict with her mother clogged her throat.

"Precious, people are asking when Bruno is going to cut his birthday cake." Lou winked at his son and daughter as he led his wife away.

"Wow. Pop to the rescue again." Gino breathed a sigh of relief.

"Amazing isn't it. Pop never says much, but he sure knows how to manage Ma when it comes down to the wire." Isabella was sure the relief flowing through her body matched her brothers.

"He never gets the chance to say much. Ma talks enough for both of them. What never ceases to amaze me is how he still calls her "Precious" after all these years. If I were married to her I'd be calling her Pain in the Ass."

"Gino, that's not a nice way to talk about our mother." He was right though and Isabella admitted to herself if she'd thought of it first, she'd have said the same thing or worse. She loved her mother, but there were times, especially when she got on the grandchild kick, that trading her for anyone else seemed like a good idea.

"Here they are. My favorite niece and nephew."

Isabella smiled weakly at her brother as Aunt Rose, the wife of Angela's youngest brother Tony, swooped down on them, giving kisses and pinching cheeks, like they were still five-years-old.

"So, you find yourself a husband, yet?" Aunt Rose turned her round body to face Isabella.

"No, Aunt Rose. Can't say I have." Out of the corner of her eye she saw her brother start to ease away and brought to a stop by one of the claws Aunt Rose called hands. The woman's fingernails were a good two inches long. How she accomplished housework was one of the great mysteries Gino and Isabella spent hours discussing as children.

"You need to let me fix you up with my butcher's son." Rose never gave up in her efforts to fix-up her niece.

"You mean Tony Ramboni?" No way in hell would that happen. Isabella knew 'the Octopus' only too well from high school.

"Anthony. He's called Anthony now. His father's ready to retire and Anthony is going to take over the butcher shop so the business stays in the family." Rose's smile gave the plan her seal of approval.

"I'm happy for Anthony and his father, but the answer's still no." Anthony, Tony, or whatever he called himself these days was definitely in the right business. Isabella doubted he received many complaints from the pieces of meat he spent his day groping like he did from the girls in school during their high school days. He'd obviously made a good career choice.

"Such a shame." Rose shook her head sadly and giving up on Isabella focused her attention on Gino whose arm she still held in her grasp.

"For you I have such a girl." Rose relaxed her

death grip and her hand now lay on Gino's shoulder.

"Aunt Rose, I'm gay."

"Oh, pish-posh. You'll grow outta it." Like their mother, all the other women in the family considered Gino's statements of being gay a phase he was going through. The only one who didn't pooh-pooh his life-style announcement was Nonna Piccoli, Angela's mother, and that was because no one, not even Gino could muster the courage to tell her.

"Now this girl, she's new to the neighborhood so you can't have the pre-conceived ideas like Miss High and Mighty," Rose shot a dark look at Isabella, "does about the boys I try to fix her up with."

Isabella watched Gino's eyes glaze over as he steeled himself for what was to come. She slipped away as Aunt Rose launched into the virtues of her latest discovery for Gino. True, she did feel a little guilty, but that dissipated when she recalled he'd tried to disappear when it was her on the grill.

"I must be living right. My favorite weather forecaster is here." Jimmy Congnomi tried to plant a kiss on Isabella's lips, but quick action on her part only got him a cheek.

"Hello, Uncle Jimmy." Isabella removed his hand from her ass. She never understood how her father considered this man one of his best friends. It would help if Jimmy tried a couple of those new-fangled ideas now popular, like taking a shower and washing his hair. The man oozed oil from the pores on his face and his hair always looked like it'd been dipped in olive oil, plus he omitted an odor she couldn't identify. Combined with his playing grab-ass since she turned eighteen, being alone with him became a challenge she never allowed to happen. She counted her blessings once again that this man wasn't really a blood relative.

"What? You don't sound too happy to see your old Uncle Jimmy. You getting too big for your britches with all the awards you're winning down at that television station?"

"Thank you for noticing the awards." Isabella removed his hand from her waist.

"Who couldn't help but notice the way your father goes on about them? You'd think he was proud of you or something." Jimmy's grin showed off his tobacco stained teeth.

"Oh no." Isabella raised a hand to her mouth and widened her eyes in a look of dismay. "Uncle Jimmy, I forgot. Pop was looking for you earlier. Did you connect with him?" She watched as Jimmy searched the room for her father. "I think he may be in the kitchen."

"Thanks, kiddo. I'll go see what he wants." Jimmy tried to steal another kiss, but Isabella dropped her napkin and bent down to retrieve it in an avoidance maneuver.

Glancing at her watch, she groaned. She'd been here less than an hour, but it felt like an eternity. Another scan of the room and her eyes landed on the one thing Isabella feared. There were a lot of things that annoyed her, a few she didn't care for, and some she tried to avoid, but only one really terrified her. Grandma Pia Piccoli.

Whenever she thought about it, Isabella's ears still rang from the boxing they received when she told her grandmother this was America and she should learn to speak English after being chastised for not addressing her grandmother in Italian.

No doubt about it, Nonna Piccoli was one tough cookie. Even her five sons trembled when she erupted with one of her infamous temper tantrums. The only one who seldom received her ire was Assai, her baby daughter and Isabella's mother. Angela's older brothers translated their sister's nickname into English and now all the family, including Isabella's father called her Precious.

Everyone, that is, but Nonna. Angela was still her little Assai.

Well, may as well go and greet the old witch, Isabella decided. No way to avoid it. Her mother would have a cow if she didn't speak to Grandma.

"Ciao, Nonna Piccoli," Isabella used her limited knowledge of her grandmother's native language in an attempt to start the conversation smoothly.

"Ciao, Bella. What's a madda you. You eyes, they red." The old woman focused her beady stare on Isabella, dissecting her inch by inch.

"Nothing, Nonna. I'm fine." Just like the crone to notice the lingering affects of Friday night's partying.

"You still on the telabision?"

"Yes, Nonna." Man this conversation was going no place fast. Thank heavens her mother burst through the kitchen door singing off-key and carrying a birthday cake containing so many candles Isabella was sure a fire permit was required to light them.

Everyone in the room joined in singing Happy Birthday to Uncle Bruno, who sat at the head of the dining room table like a king waiting to receive his subjects. Once the candles were extinguished and the cake distributed, the old man attacked the mountain of gifts that were put in front of him. Isabella wasn't sure what to get him so she'd picked up a gift card for his favorite bakery.

"Can we talk?" Gino appeared by her side.

"Sure, what's up?" Her brother's face bore more emotion than usual. A blank face was a requirement for his job and he'd become adept at it.

"Not here. Private." He took her hand and started working their way though the mob of relatives.

They slipped down the hallway to his old bedroom which Angela turned into what she now called her private retreat. Gino sat down in a delicate chair that Isabella worried might collapse under his weight. She selected the recliner her mother used for watching her soap operas and taking catnaps.

"Are you going to keep me sitting here in suspense or tell me what's on your mind?" Isabella wanted to know as she watched her brother fidget.

Gino got up and went to stand by the window. After staring out for a couple of minutes he turned to face his sister. "You know Anthony, the one Aunt Rose was trying to set you up with."

"Well, yeah. I went to high school with him."

Gino fidgeted with the blind cord. "Oh yeah, I forgot you were a year ahead of me. Well, you see, it's like this." He paused to clear his throat. "We've been seeing each other for the past three months or so."

"What? Oh. My. God. You're telling me The Octopus is gay." Isabella burst into giggles. Wiping the tears from her eyes she started to speak and another roar of laughter escaped instead.

"Yeah. He sorta was back in high school, too. He, ahem," Gino cleared his throat. "He was my first, and I was his."

"Holy shit. You mean you lost your virginity to that creep." Isabella was dumbfounded.

"Oh, he wasn't so bad. Just confused, like me, about the whole sexuality thing." Gino turned beet red. "We only did it the one time, and then we both tried girls. He lasted with them longer than me." Gino turned to stare out the window again.

"You see, we ran into each other a few months back when I went to collect a little debt owed to Joey from this guy who hangs out at the same bar Anthony does. We started talking, and one thing led to another and…well, it's to the point he says he's ready to come out of the closet if I'll move in with him."

"Oh, I see." Isabella was at a loss on what to say beyond that comment. Her brother needed her support and she searched to come up with something to help.

"How do you feel about him? Are you ready to make a commitment, and what if it doesn't work out? Will he hold coming out of the closet against you?" She could envision the scene if the relationship failed.

"That's part of the problem. I like him, but I'm not in love with him. I'm trying to find a way to let him down easy." Gino started to pace.

"Stop." Isabella stood in front of her brother to block the pacing. "You can't be concerned about letting him down easy here. If you don't want to make the same kind of commitment, you need to be honest with him." Even a dirty little weasel like Anthony Ramboni didn't deserve the repercussions of coming out of the closet about his sexual preferences and then getting dumped.

Gino placed his large hands on Isabella's shoulder. "I know. I've been telling myself the same thing, but guess I needed to hear it said by someone else. Especially my big sister." He pulled her into an embrace and squeezed.

When they returned to the party, the guests were starting to leave and Isabella saw this as an opportune time for her to make an escape.

"Now, Bella. You come to dinner Wednesday night. Okay." Angela slipped an arm around Isabella's waist, which made it impossible to escape without an answer.

"Ma, I can't. I'm working. Remember, I do the six o'clock weather."

"Yes, I know and the eleven o'clock too." Angela sighed her best martyr sigh. "No wonder you eyes are red. You never get enough sleep. Okay, then we'll make it Saturday night. And Gino, you come too."

Brother and sister exchanged glances of defeat. If they didn't come their mother would hound them until she wore them down. Each learned a long time ago...just do it, and be done with it.

"Saturday night it is. See you then." Isabella kissed her mother's cheek and planted a quick peck on her brother and father before making a strategic retreat out the door.

She heard Gino as the door closed. "Okay, Ma. I'll

be here. What time?"

    Isabella quickly forgot her family as she headed for the subway. Her focus now was on tomorrow and work. The one sanity factor in her life.

CHAPTER 2

"Good morning." Kyle Morgan greeted Isabella as they squeezed onto the elevator. "Sweet Cheeks," he whispered in her ear as they were pushed closer together by the entry of additional people.

"Morning." It took all her self-control to even respond to the despicable anchorman for Channel 12 News. She wouldn't have bothered answering if they'd not shared the confined space with any number of people who'd like to spread the news of a feud between the station's top anchor and weather person. Pushed up against him now, she could detect the outline of an erection as he pressed harder against her butt cheeks.

Escaping from the mass of humanity as quickly as she could when the elevators doors opened at her floor, Isabella felt Kyle on her heels.

"You know you want me, baby," he leered as he came up beside her.

"Yeah, about as much as I want a case of the clap." She made a sharp turn and headed toward the weather pod, which thankfully was on the opposite side of the newsroom from his.

"I see our favorite news letch has been whispering words of endearment to you again." Sandy James, the weather intern, laughed when Isabella threw her purse on the desk and continued to mumble under her breath.

"How Joanne Kent can stand to have that creep touch her is beyond me." Isabella's skin still crawled from where a part of Kyle's body came in contact with hers.

"There's a good case of two people deserving each other if you ask me." Sandy wasn't a fan of either of the nighttime news anchors. "They're so in love with themselves that an affair between them makes sense. They don't have to bother with telling the other how beautiful they are. The one I feel sorry for here is Sam Kent. He doesn't seem to notice his wife and her co-anchor are boinking their brains out almost in front of him. Talk about in your face."

"Yeah. Know what you mean." Isabella didn't rate the station manager her most favorite person, but even a brown noser like Sam didn't deserve Joanne. The affair between her and sleaze-ball Kyle gave the office gossips a field day and made her husband the laughing stock of the newsroom. The only time the two were discreet in the carrying-on was when Sam was around or they were out in the public arena. After all, they had to keep up that public image.

"Then again maybe his nose is so full of shit from having it up the new owner's ass he can't smell news anymore." Sandy wiggled her eyebrows at Isabella.

"You're awful." Isabella giggled, but Sandy's wicked sense of humor was one of the things she liked about her, along with the intern's brilliant mind. She needed to figure out a way to keep the young woman on the team when her internship ended. Everyone depended on her now and all of them would feel her loss.

"Oh yeah, the radio station called. They're ready for you to do your bit over there when you want to call in, and speaking of Sam, he wants you in some kind of meeting in his office at three." Sandy handed her the weather projections from the National Weather Bureau and spouted off a list of additional reminders.

Glancing at her watch, Isabella decided to utilize the thirty minutes available before she made the command appearance in Sam's office to accomplish a couple of things on her list. "Okay, I'll call the radio station now and record their weather spot. That'll leave me with a few minutes to record a couple of blurbs for tonight's weather forecasts."

After a hectic half hour, she made her way through the newsroom to Sam's office. Passing the news team's pod, Kyle Mason directed a wink and leer her way, which earned both of them a seething glare from Joanne Kent.

Isabella almost felt sorry for the woman. It must be tough carrying on an affair with the biggest womanizer in the city right outside your husband's office door. Then again, Joanne was a major bitch who never missed the chance for a dig when they were alone in what passed for their makeup room. Now that she thought about it, the cheating slut needed a dose of arsenic more then she needed sympathy.

"Come in, come in." Sam's door was open and he called out to Isabella. "Close the door and take a seat," he indicated the only empty chair since the other two chairs crowded around his desk contained male bodies.

How lucky can I get? She thought when her eyes met those of Leif Moultar, or Mr. Albino as she referred to the station owner in moments of frustration. "Good to see you again, Leif." The man's blank expression didn't change when he nodded his acknowledgment of Isabella's comment. His pale skin, white blond hair and iceberg eyes creeped her out the first time she met him and continued to do so.

Repressing a shudder, she turned her glance from the man who signed her paycheck to the person in the chair next to him. She caught her gasp before it escaped. Sitting before her was the best piece of eye candy she'd seen in a long time...possibly ever.

Even sitting, she could tell he was a large man. The suit jacket stretched across his broad shoulders and tapered down to a slender waist. The sleeves appeared to barely contain the biceps that threatened to rip the fabric covering them.

She was a sucker for a strong face, especially one with a cleft in the center of the chin. The blue eyes reminded her of a pool of water, calm and deep, but the thing that made her fingers itch was the hair. Barely brushing his ears on the side, the long blond top, shot with streaks of red and copper fell to one side of his forehead and over an eyebrow. She wanted to reach out and brush it back just to see if it felt as silky as it looked. Women paid good money for hair that color.

"Isabella? Are you feeling okay?" Sam looked at her with concern.

"Great. Never better." She quickly recovered from the zone she'd drifted into while her eyes devoured the stud-muffin.

"Good. I want to introduce you to your newest team member. This is Galvin Haldor." The blond hunk stood and held out his hand.

Isabella reacted automatically, placing her hand in the one extended toward her.

"Nice to meet you, Izzy." Galvin's smile revealed a dimple in his right cheek.

The deep, rich voice combined with the lethal smile sent shivers down her spine. "Me, too," she mumbled. Then it hit her. He called her Izzy. Who the hell did he think he was? Nobody called her Izzy since Gino tried it when they were kids and she busted his nose.

New team member? Where did Sam get off hiring someone for her department without bringing her into the decision? Nope, this wasn't going to work. She wasn't some teenager who went ga-ga over a drop-dead, gorgeous male.

"Sam, don't you think you should've brought me in on the interviewing and hiring decisions for my department? After all, I am the Chief Meteorologist." She glared across the desk at the station manager daring him to dispute her.

"Well, you do have a point, Isabella, but this was an opportunity we couldn't let get away." Sam squirmed uncomfortably in his chair and glanced at Leif. "You know we're in a ratings war here and Leif...ah, Mr. Moultar knows Galvin's father, and when they were talking..." Sam ran his finger under his shirt collar in an attempt to loosen it. "Well, he found out that Galvin was looking for a job and thought he was exactly what the station needs. We know you draw a strong male group, but with Galvin here on board, it would increase our female demographics."

Isabella heard Sam's audible sigh of relief when she turned to face Leif Moultar. "You felt it was your place to make this decision without consulting me?"

The pale eyes reflected the emotion of a hunk of steel. "When it's your signature on the checks, then you can make any decisions you want." His voice dripped the same ice reflected in his eyes. "No, I didn't feel the need to get your approval."

Isabella took a deep breath to gain a moment to control the rage flowing through her veins. She could end up unemployed if she wasn't careful. The impulse to tell Leif where to stick his job subsided and reason took over once again. She'd just bought her apartment when the building converted to condo units and the down payment took all her savings. The last thing she needed right now was to put herself in a position of no income, desperate enough to take any job offer.

"You are correct, Mr. Moultar. You do sign the checks." She bit hard on the inside of her cheek to keep from adding it would be her reputation on the line if his brilliant idea didn't work.

Directing her attention to Galvin, Isabella indicated her defeat with a tip of her head. "Okay, Mr. Haldor. You can start tomorrow. Be here by two and we'll begin your training."

"Why tomorrow? I'm available now." Galvin

grinned and she felt her insides melting.

"I'm not ready for you. I need to get a training program outlined and right now my focus is getting prepared for the six o'clock news."

"I don't think Galvin will require much in the way of training." Leif Moultar chose to step in again on behalf of his protégé. "He can start now. There is no need to delay."

"Fine," Isabella fired back. She hated losing control and she hated the stilted way the station owner always talked. Right now, she despised everything about Leif Moultar, but especially his power over her life.

Isabella stood and headed for the door with Galvin directly behind her. Outside of the prying ears of Sam and Leif she turned and faced him. "Let's get a few things straight. I'm the Chief Meteorologist at this station and you follow my instructions."

"Whatever you say, Izzy." Galvin grinned.

"To begin with, don't call me *Izzy*. The last male who did that ended up with a broken nose." Isabella figured it was none of his business it was her then six-year-old brother.

"Like I said, whatever you say." Galvin said and followed her toward the weather pod. "Izzy," he mumbled under his breath.

*****

"You sent for me, Sif?" Loki hesitated at the door of Sif's private quarters.

He considered himself the king of pranks, but it

wasn't beyond others to try and pull one on him from time to time. Sif never asked for his company these days. The woman carried one long grudge. The little thing with the hair was one of his better tricks. Too bad she didn't see the humor.

"Yes, Loki. I did." Sif turned from the window where she'd been looking out over the city. "I need a favor from you." Her eyes met his for the first time in eons.

A favor…from him? Oh, my, my. This could give him a way to achieve redemption in her eyes. When he was honest with himself, he admitted he missed his friendship with the goddess and longed to have it back.

"Ask, and I shall do my best to see that you receive." Loki knew he'd move heaven and earth to do Sif's bidding even if it went against Thor's wishes.

He did owe Thor for taking away the snake venom and releasing the chains which bound him to the boulder, but he was not nearly as much fun as Sif. When he spent time with Thor, he also contended with Thailfi. Thor's loyal servant was a constant shadow, hovering in the background. Enough to get on a guy's nerves, which Loki knew was Thailfi's intent.

"I want you to go down to earth and keep an eye on the situation in which my son has become involved. Learn more about this mortal woman in whom it appears Galvin is interested, as well as her family." Sif turned back to the window. "For once, Loki, try not to make any trouble that will cause pain for my son. Do you think you can do that?" She faced him again and this time he felt her gaze prick his soul.

"Yes, for you I will control my urge to create discord."

"Thank you." Sif's sad little smile left Loki with the hope she too remembered the friendship they once shared.

*****

Galvin watched the ease with which Isabella prepared for the evening news and weather. The woman knew her job and did it well. She plotted the printouts of various weather fronts on paper, instead of relying solely on the information from the National Weather Bureau. Smart and beautiful, the combination presented a package that greatly interested the deity. His respect for her increased by the minute as he watched her juggle her job and the people involved in pulling it all together.

"Did you get that?" Isabella's face bore a look of exasperation.

Her question caught him wool gathering over what he'd like to do to her outside the newsroom where work didn't consume her. Then again, clearing a desk and taking her right here also appealed.

"Sorry, I missed the question. Could you repeat it?"

He watched her mouth tighten and heard a small sigh. "I said I prefer my staff plot out the local weather using the information we have at hand, instead of depending on the NWB. National is great for some things, but they're not local and we know what's happening here more than they do." Isabella pushed back a dark curl that fell across her eye. "Do you know how to do manual plotting or is that a class you missed in college?"

Galvin didn't take the class, but he'd be an idiot to miss the sarcasm in her voice. "I'm sure I can handle the plotting without an issue." He didn't need a piece of paper or satellite feeds to tell him about the weather.

"Good. Let's see what you can do then. Put together my forecast for the six o'clock news. I'll check it when I get back from doing more radio spots." Isabella pointed to the printouts on the desk and walked away.

"Whatever you say. After all, you're the boss. *Izzy.*" Galvin stared after the departing form before tackling his assigned task. If she thought she could get the best of him, then she'd better think again. He'd cut his teeth on controlling weather and predicting it on earth would present no problem.

"You're really trying to get under her skin, aren't you?"

Galvin turned to find Sandy standing behind him. "No, not really. Just trying to establish the alpha order here."

"Alpha order, my ass." Sandy burst out laughing. "What do you think you've joined here...a wolf pack? If you don't stop testing her, you're going to find yourself out on the street. Isabella doesn't take crap from anyone."

"We'll see about that." Galvin turned back to study the papers spread out in front of him.

"You don't know what the hell you're doing, do you?" She peered over his shoulder.

"I know weather, but maps are not my strong suit." Galvin admitted.

"Here, let me show you." Sandy pulled a chair over and sat down beside him. "See, what you're doing here is tracking the weather fronts."

"Yeah, but that's what we have here from the National Weather Bureau." Galvin pointed to the computer screen.

"True," Sandy agreed. "The problem with accepting their forecasts at face value is like Isabella explained earlier. They're not here. We start with a model in raw form, that way we have fewer biases which may not take in variances such as local inversions."

"Inversions?" Galvin didn't know the term. Mortals used strange names for simple things and this was probably another example.

Sandy fixed him with a hard look. "How in hell did you get this job? It's obvious you don't know jack shit about weather forecasting."

"I know weather." Galvin shrugged his shoulders. "And my father knows Leif."

"Don't make a statement like that to Isabella. She's worked too damn hard to have some upstart roll in and try to lord it over her because his father has pull with the station owner." Sandy shot flames in Galvin's direction.

"She went to college and studied weather. I'm not trying to take that away from her." Galvin met Sandy's glare.

"It goes beyond graduating with a degree in Meteorology. She also has her CCM, and that's not pulled out of a Cracker Jack box."

"CCM?" Another term Galvin found unfamiliar.

"Certified Consulting Meteorologist." The intern shook her head. "Amazing all you don't know. It requires at least five years experience on the job and passing a hard-ass test."

"I think I get the picture." Galvin nodded. "I admit I have a lot to learn about the way you do things here. Will you help me?" He smiled at Sandy and used the look that worked best with his mother, the 'I've been a bad boy' expression.

Her frown turned into a slight smile and then she laughed. "Okay, but listen up good. You want to map over…"

They'd completed the mapping when Isabella returned and Galvin handed her the maps. "Okay, let's head over the studio," she said after a quick scan.

"I'm covering the morning shift tomorrow, also. I want you to come in so we can get you trained on setting the time lapse cameras." She continued to walk, barking out expectations of what she demanded of her new employee. "You'll probably end up covering the morning shift in a few weeks and will also work with our email." Isabella paused before an unopened door and turned to face Galvin.

"I don't expect any more from my people than I give, but I give one hundred and ten percent. Do we understand each other?"

Galvin nodded. "Understood."

They continued into the studio. Galvin found the size of the studio surprising. It looked bigger on television.

"That is Robo Control." Isabella pointed toward a large raised desk with a man sitting behind it. "The cameras are controlled from there. That eliminates the need for individual camera operators." She waved at the three cameras in front of the news desk, which the man behind the control desk manipulated.

Walking behind her, Galvin admired the slight sway of her bottom in the snug fitting black skirt. His interest in Robo Control was next to none. The woman giving him the tour, now that was a different story. Everything about her interested him, not just her sexy body.

"Here is where I do the weather forecast," she walked over to a large green screen. "I have the monitors on either side to let me know where I am on the map. The engineer in the control room inserts the images viewers see on their television screens at home. Magic to the outsider." A tiny smile played across her full mouth. "Any questions?"

He caught a whiff of her perfume and inhaled, committing the scent to memory. It was her; light and airy with a hint of something he couldn't define, other than Isabella.

Galvin urged his male member to lie down and play nice. "No, I'll just watch and absorb."

"Take a seat in one of those chairs." She pointed to a row of folding chairs along the wall facing the news desk.

"Isabella, you're on in five. Let's do a mike check." The director of the evening news handed her a small black box and moved in to attach something to her lapel.

Galvin watched Isabella pull her jacket up and reach around and clip the box to the back of the waist of her skirt, then smooth the jacket down.

"No butt shots," she called out to the man in the camera control booth. "This thing makes my ass look even bigger than it is."

"Whatever you say, Isabella. The last time was an accident." The cameraman laughed and gave her a lewd wink before she went over to take her seat behind the news desk.

The anchorman sitting beside her leaned over and whispered in Isabella's ear. Whatever the man said didn't set too well from the body language she projected and his female co-anchor didn't seem happy either.

Interesting, Galvin thought as he observed the mortals. Izzy, what goes on here? Are you involved in a triangle?

"Ready on one," the director called out. "Three...two...one."

The director pointed to the three people behind the desk and all smiled into the camera, the best of friends.

"You're amazing, Izzy," Galvin murmured watching her relaxed manner on camera in a situation that was definitely strained off camera. This gave him a new of appreciation for the woman who interested him on more levels than the strong physical attraction existing between them. Yes, definitely a woman of many layers and he wanted to discover them all.

CHAPTER 3

"I don't care if you disagree." Isabella folded her arms across her chest and glared at Galvin. The man was on the job less than a week and a miracle occurred. A miracle in that she didn't lean over and wrap her hands around that strong neck and strangle him. "I'm in charge here and we do things my way."

"Okay. But, I'd like to point out that you were wrong on your projections yesterday." Galvin held up his hands to indicate surrender.

"No weather forecaster is right all the time. Today is a new day and I say there's a sixty percent chance of thunderstorms and that's the number we're going to use." God, she hated it when he used that face, the 'oh, I'm so sorry, forgive me' face she'd seen him use on Sandy too many times this week. She saw how the intern tripped over herself in an effort to help when he used it and it almost made her want to agree to anything he wanted. Almost, but so far she'd been able to resist. After all, she was a woman of the world, not a young co-ed trying to impress the big man on campus.

"If you enjoy being wrong, go ahead and put out that projection, but I say we're not going to have rain today." Galvin sat back in his chair and smiled.

Isabella took three deep breaths as she watched the cocky smile spread across his full mouth and light up his eyes. She resisted the impulse to reach out and brush back the shock of hair that constantly fell across his forehead. If she did that, then it would tempt her to run her hands over the shirt and down the well-developed chest to the waistband of his pants. Then she'd have to struggle with the belt that held the pants in place, denying her view to something she thought about way too much. The heat forming between her legs brought her back to the present.

"I'll take my chances." She turned and stalked out of the weather pod, but not before she caught the knowing look Sandy directed her way.

Was she that easy to read?

She fought hard to forget the dreams that haunted her nights. The ones in which she escaped into a world where her image wasn't a priority and she could give in to her lust for Galvin Haldor. *So what if he is the most interesting man you know. He's also the most irritating. It's only lust that makes your heart do little flip-flops every time you brush against him or he smiles at you.*

Last night's dream was especially memorable. She'd been alone in the newsroom when he came in and pushed everything off her desk. He set her on the edge and pushed up her skirt. His fingers slipped under the silk barrier of her panties and massaged her sex. For the first time in her life she experienced an orgasm resulting from a dream.

"Ah, Sweet Cheeks, just the woman I wanted to see. We need to talk." Kyle Morgan blocked her path.

"Not in the mood, Kyle. Let me pass." Now a dream about this one was a regular nightmare, she thought as she tried to step around him.

"Come on baby, don't be that way." Kyle moved with her and cut off her escape.

"What the hell do you want?" The men of this world really were getting on her nerves. Raine's immortal idea sounded better all the time.

"I just want to caution you about the stud you've added to your weather stable." Kyle reached out and took her arm when she tried to walk in the opposite direction.

"Kyle, I'm not even going to acknowledge your idiotic blithering and ask what you're talking about." She pushed his hand from her elbow.

"Tell the pretty boy to stay away from my woman."

"Excuse me. Your woman? You *actually* have a woman?" Isabella couldn't resist the dig.

"You know Joanne and I have a thing." Kyle adjusted his tie and smirked.

"Oh, how interesting, and here I thought she and Sam Kent were married. Must have gotten the wrong information." Isabella didn't try to suppress the giggle that slipped out.

"Yeah, well they have problems. They may not be married much longer."

Isabella watched as Kyle scratched his balls before he slipped his hands into his pockets and proceeded to toy with them. There was no understanding some people's taste. Granted Sam Kent could be dull, but how Joanne could prefer this crude, obnoxious jerk was beyond her. The stupid woman should focus her energy on the husband who adored her.

"Make sure you tell the weather stud not to dip his wick in my pool. Do I make myself clear?" Kyle leaned forward and hissed into her ear.

Holy Mary and Jesus. He actually expected her to deliver a warning to another man for him. This day couldn't end soon enough to suit her.

"You listen to me, Mr. Morgan. If you want the weather stud to keep away from 'your woman'," Isabella wiggled two fingers on each hand to emphasize her sarcasm, "you tell him. I don't deliver messages that are stupid to begin with and especially ones sent by an idiot, to boot." The look on Kyle's face when she released her parting shot improved her mood tremendously. Looking directly at his crotch she'd said, "And, another thing, no one enjoys watching you play pocket billiards."

*****

"Bella, you're late and you're wet." Isabella's mother wore her best dress and pearls.

Isabella groaned to herself, her mood sinking lower. Just what she suspected. Her mother was trying another fix-up.

"You're the big weather person. Couldn't you tell it was going to rain?" Angela reached over and squeezed water out of Isabella's hair. "Go get a towel and the hair dryer. They're in my bathroom. Fix yourself up."

"Why, Ma? The family's seen me looking like this and worse." Like she didn't know there would be a nice Italian man sitting there when she walked into the living room.

"We have company. Your brother is here and a pretty young woman friend of his." Angela shooed her in the direction of her parent's bedroom.

A pretty young friend of his meant a female in her mother's eyes and she didn't see Gino showing up with a girl.

Maybe the man Ma browbeat into coming tonight didn't make it, but it sounded like whatever unsuspecting female her mother managed to convince did though. Poor Gino. If possible, he hated these evenings more than her.

The sleek straight hair she walked out of her apartment with was now a thing of the past. Laying the hair dryer down, Isabella pushed at the ringlets that now framed her face and used her fingers in an attempt to bring more order to the riot of curls. Feeling the soft silky stands, her mind wandered to hair of gold, shot with streaks of copper and red. Her fingers itched, just as they did each time she saw the lock of hair that seemed determined to fall into Galvin Haldor's eyes, the urge to touch almost impossible to control.

If Leif Moultar wanted to hire the son of one of his friends, why on earth did it have to be one who looked like a Nordic god? Her hands tingled when she envisioned them touching and caressing every inch of that luscious body. The wide shoulders, the broad chest, the tapering waist down to the... Heaven save her from the fascination she had with Vikings and Nordic mythology since she was a young girl.

Isabella shook her head and saw large, lust-filled

dark eyes staring back at her from the mirror. She needed to focus on the fact this man drove her insane with his constant challenges of her decisions, not how much he reminded her of the Viking she'd always dreamed of carrying her away. She turned from the mirror to go meet tonight's fate.

Laughter directed her toward the kitchen. Good grief, it sounded like Gino laughing. He never enjoyed these functions. His norm was to spend the evening wearing a look of such martyrdom; it put Angela's best efforts in that department to shame.

Her light mood evaporated when she entered the room. Her mother forgot to mention the male guest for this evening. Thank heaven she was able to stop the groan that almost escaped.

"Bella, come meet our guests," Angela motioned for Isabella to join the group gathered around the island in the center of the kitchen.

"This is Jane Smith," Angela smiled and patted the arm of the young blonde woman beside her. "Don't you think she and Gino look good together?"

Isabella wasn't too sure about that since Gino stood down at the end of the island in an animated conversation with their father and the other new face in the group. Given her brother's dark hair and olive complexion, he'd definitely contrast with Jane's light blonde hair and white skin. Insipid flitted through her mind when she searched for a word to describe the pale creature in front of her.

"Gino, Lou, stop bothering Tom and let him come meet Bella." Angela instructed the men in her family.

Isabella watched as all three males moved in

unison closer to the women. Good Lord, it looked like her mother finally reached the end of her Italian stable of singles for both her children.

"Tom Waters, this is our Bella. I know you've probably seen her on television." The pride in Angela's voice surprised Isabella. Pride over her career wasn't something she heard conveyed by her mother very often.

"I sure have. Great to meet you, Isabella. I count on you to help me plan my day with your weather projections." Tom smiled, displaying a gap in his white teeth. "I think I'm going to have to get a new television set though. Mine doesn't do you justice."

She felt the blood rush to her face. Excessive compliments always made her uncomfortable. Isabella took in the red hair, freckles and blue eyes of her date for the evening. The skinny body was given ballast by the huge ears that stuck out from his head. She felt herself responding to the gap-tooth grin and thought how much he reminded her of the puppet Howdy Doody she'd studied in Broadcast History during her college years.

Ma couldn't have gotten any further from the Italian bloodlines she usually focused on with tonight's fix-up selections if she'd put an ad in the paper. This gave a strong indication of how determined Angela was in getting her children married.

"Tom's a financial advisor. He works with his father who helps us manage our money." Isabella knew this was Angela speak for; Tom has a job and money.

How the hell was she supposed to respond to that

little tidbit? "Great. Always nice to keep it in the family." She felt like an idiot and Howdy Doody's face reflected the embarrassment she felt at her inane remark.

"Here, Sis." Gino placed a glass of red wine in her hand. "Drink up. You're behind." She gulped down the contents of the glass without coming up for air.

"Gino, no. She needs to eat. You know Bella can't handle wine on an empty stomach." Angela slapped his hand when he reached for the bottle to refill Isabella's glass. "Here, make yourself useful. Take this bread to the table."

Gino rolled his eyes at his sister and disappeared with the basket of bread.

Her mother handed her the salad. "Take this and I'll bring the Chicken Cacciatore. Okay everybody. Dinner's ready. Take your seats."

Good heavens her mother put name cards out for the seating arrangements. The woman was obvious in her determination that the fix-ups get to know each other, with Gino seated beside the ghost and Isabella's name card next to Howdy Doody.

Isabella didn't think things were going the way her mother wanted. Gino barely talked with poor Jane. Instead, he spent dinner talking with everyone else at the table, especially Tom who sat directly across from him.

She tried to draw Jane into the conversation, but the meek young woman would only duck her head and smile, after answering yes or no to Isabella's questions. Finally, Isabella gave up and devoted her efforts to the rest of the group.

"Bella, you want to help me with dessert?" Angela stood and started to clear the table. A knot formed in her stomach as she thought about the real meaning of help with the dishes. She envisioned a turkey on a spit rotating round and round as it roasted. Her mother had a way of bringing that picture to mind any time she wanted 'a talk', no matter how she got the message across. The bottom line was the person selected to help ended up getting grilled and unfortunately as far as she was concerned, Isabella usually got the honor.

She gathered up the dishes around her and followed her mother into the kitchen. God, she loved the way everyone else sat and didn't bother to help with clean up. You'd think Jane would at least get off her dead ass and offer to pitch in. Instead, she continued to sit like a lump on a log, eyes downcast while toying with the spoon on the table in front of her.

Relief at Gino's alternative life style flowed through. He could have ended up with someone like Jane to contend with at every family get together.

"Bella, so how do you think this evening is going?" Angela stacked pots and pans in the dishwasher as she started the inquisition.

Good grief, Ma was blind if she needed to ask that question. Talk about being out of touch with reality. "I don't think Jane and Gino have much in common to be honest with you, Ma."

"I guess you're right. She doesn't seem to talk much and you know with our Gino, a girl has to have lots of personality to get his attention." Angela stopped talking for a moment and seemed to mull over the situation with her baby boy and her latest attempt to steer him toward the altar, and then shrugged.

She shot a wicked grin in Isabella's direction. "What about you and Tom? Now there's a man with personality."

No denying that. He and Gino blabbered all evening. She'd even discovered things about her brother's hobbies she never knew under Tom's questions on books and movies. "He seems like a nice enough guy."

"What do you mean nice enough? He's crazy about you. Didn't you hear him say how beautiful he thinks you are and he watches you on television?" Her mother pulled the best coffee service out of a cabinet and set the cups and saucers on the tray, making sure to leave room for the dessert she'd be dishing up.

Angela was wearing her rose colored glasses tonight, if she couldn't see the obvious between her and Tom. "Yeah, but there's no chemistry there, Ma. We don't have much in common. He and Gino seem to have more of the same interests."

"Wash your mouth out with soap if you're suggesting what I think you are." Angela placed her hands on her hips, an indication of preparation for battle.

"What? I'm just saying Tom and I don't have much in common. I hate the movies he and Gino were talking about, you'll never catch me on the back of a motorcycle, and the books he reads would put me to sleep in under a minute."

Looking at her mother's face, it hit her. Oh my gawd, for a mother in denial over her son being gay,

Angela certainly made the quick leap there mentally, even while denying.

To avoid her mother's glare, Isabella walked over and opened a window and heard the strains of Wagner's *Ride of the Valkyrie*. She smiled, envisioning her grandmother sitting in her favorite chair while the waves of music washed over her. How such a stubborn Italian adored a German composer's opera that focused on Nordic gods when everything else in her world focused on things Italian always amazed her.

"Why didn't Nonna come to dinner tonight?"

"You know Mama. She lost interest the minute I told her our guests weren't Italian." Angela peered over Isabella's shoulder at the light in what had been the garage before the conversion to an apartment to house her mother. "Maybe it's a good thing we fixed up the garage. That noise she calls music would drive me crazy if I listened to it all the time."

Isabella laughed at her mother's description of the opera her grandmother listened to daily. Angela had never learned to appreciate classical music and Isabella found it interesting that the love of music was the only connection she shared with her grandmother.

"And, she's so stubborn. Do you know she still insists on taking a walk every night before she goes to bed? That's why your father got that noisy little dog to go with her." Angela shut the window to block the rain, which started to come down again.

Stubborn? Had her mother *looked* in the mirror lately?

At least they'd managed to avoid coming to blows

over Gino. Ma needed to accept Gino's choices or spend the rest of her life telling everyone, but mainly herself, he was a confirmed bachelor who never found a woman good enough for him. Who knew what it would take to bring Ma into the real world. Probably the same thing it would take to put Nonna in touch with it...a force stronger than anything on earth so far.

"Have I told you about our new team member?" Isabella took a glob of frosting off the double chocolate cake Angela started to slice for dessert.

"No. So you got another intern like that girl...what's her name...Sandy?" Angela paused and looked at her daughter.

"Nope. A man." *A very hot man at that.* "Seems our illustrious station owner decided the son of a friend needed a job and he was given to me to turn into a weather man.

"Hmmm." Angela swatted at Isabella's hand when she reached for more frosting. "Tell me about him. What's he look like? Is he good looking?"

Thanks heavens she didn't make the hot man comment. "He's okay. Tall, blond with reddish streaks in his hair. Blue eyes and..." Isabella felt the tingle in her body she got every time she thought about Galvin Haldor for long.

"And?" Her mother looked at her strangely.

"Oh, he definitely has a face made for television. He's also got the cocky attitude to go with it. He'd probably make a better news anchor than weatherman." Isabella chuckled at the idea of Galvin giving Kyle Mason a run for the position. Talk about a battle of egos.

"So, he doesn't have a degree like you got? You know the weather thing?"

"Meteorology." Isabella answered absent-mindedly. She tapped her lower lip with her fingers. "You know, I'm not really sure what his degree is in." Now that she thought about it, Sam never responded to her request to see Galvin's employment application and résumé. The hiring of Galvin Haldor painted a strange picture and she wanted to get to the bottom of it. Definitely a puzzle and she loved to solve puzzles.

"It's pretty obvious he's never reported the weather before, but he keeps insisting he knows weather. Must have been born with the knowledge." The two women shared a laugh at that idea.

Angela picked up the tray loaded with coffee cups and cake and instructed Isabella to grab the coffee pot while she used her hip to push the swinging door open into the dining room.

"You two sounded like you were having too much fun out there." Gino said when Angela set the tray on the buffet and started to hand out dessert. "I told Pop one of us needed to go out and see what you were up to." Gino speared a bite of cake before his mother could set the plate in front of him.

"Don't be so greedy," she chided. "Our guests will think you were raised without manners. I promise you he does have them, he just chooses to forget the way he was brought up."

Angela directed her comment to the table, but Isabella knew it was meant for the timid woman now sitting beside her when Angela patted a thin shoulder as she set a slice of cake in front of Jane.

Delivering a dark look in Gino's direction, his mother fired off another shot. "Must be the company he keeps that causes him to forget how to behave."

"Ah, come on Ma. Don't knock my friends. Most of them were brought up good Catholic boys just like me." Gino's attempt to defend his friends while consuming another bite of cake ended with him choking and Tom pounding him on the back.

Amazing how she now sat beside Jane, who if possible, became quieter and her brother now occupied the chair next to Tom. Nope, this evening wasn't going according to her mother's plans. Too bad for Gino that Tom wasn't gay and something could result out of this evening for one of them.

Tom started the evacuation when he stood to say his goodnights and thanked her parents for a wonderful evening. He kissed Angela's cheek, "And you fed me a meal better than I can get in any restaurant."

While her mother basked in the glow of Tom's compliment, Isabella saw it as an opportune moment to make her escape too, and moved in for hugs and kisses from her parents.

Even timid Jane mumbled a soft goodbye. When Tom offered her a ride home, color rushed to the white cheeks and Isabella saw potential for the woman. Give her a makeover and some assertiveness training and the girl had definite possibilities.

After hugs and kisses for her parents, she moved in for a squeeze from her brother and Gino suggested they walk to the subway together. Turning she found herself looking into Tom Water's eyes and returned his infectious grin.

"Good luck with your business, Tom. You and your father keep making lots of money for my parents."

"We'll do our best. You keep winning awards on your weather broadcasting."

Both acknowledged with a quick nod of the head her mother's efforts for a connection on a level more than friendship wouldn't work for them.

*****

A lone figure stood in the shadows of light across the street. In his need to see how Isabella spent her evenings out, he followed her when she left her apartment. When an older version of her opened the door to the unassuming house that was her destination, he concluded she'd be spending the evening with her family.

Still he stayed at his post and the rain helped him remain unobserved while he lingered. The few mortals who did pass were more concerned with getting in out of the wet, than giving him more than a glance...with one exception.

An old woman and her yippy dog came around the corner when he'd been lost in thought. They'd stopped directly in front of him, the dog yapped so hard it actually bounced itself backward on its skinny little legs. He and the dog stared at each other for a minute and he got the dog's message...my territory. Each then became determined to establish alpha male dominance. It became obvious to Galvin he needed let this piece of skin and bones know where the power lay. He was surprised when the creature lifted its leg and proceeded to mark his shoes.

When he looked up in disbelief, Galvin locked eyes with the old woman. A slight smile played across a mouth that from the down-turned corners looked like it didn't smile much. The expression on her face seemed to say, *"I know who you are."*

She and the dog continued on their walk when Galvin bent down to wipe his shoe. He admired the animal with the body of a toy, but the heart of a warrior.

A short while later he found himself humming along to the strains one of his favorite pieces, *Ride of the Valkyrie,* as they floated through the air.

The door across the street opened. His vigil came to an end. He watched a laughing Isabella link her arm through that of a large dark haired man and laugh up at something he said.

Galvin felt his groin tighten with need while his heart pounded with anger. If only she'd laugh like that with him. He resisted the urge to catch the couple walking ahead of him and punch the man who made his heart's desire laugh in that way.

Realization slammed into the pit of his stomach like Thor's hammer. What he felt for this woman wasn't just lust. He was falling in love.

CHAPTER 4

Galvin watched the news team seated behind the desk. He wasn't sure what took place out of his sight, but he knew Izzy well enough now to tell from the slant of her eyes something made her very unhappy. He recognized the fake smile she put on each time the camera panned in on her. Once someone else became the focus of a headshot, she clamped her lips into a tight line and directed a scowl toward Kyle Mason sitting beside her.

"Isabella, give us a final rundown on what to expect tomorrow with the weather. Shall we start bringing our raincoats and umbrellas to work as normal procedure since you seem to be a little off on your forecasting?" Joanne Kent's voice dripped sweetness as she leaned forward to look past Kyle and smile at Isabella.

"Might not be a bad idea, Joanne. It appears my crystal ball is on the blitz." Isabella responded in a similar saccharine voice.

The director pointed and started to lower each of the four fingers she held above her head as she counted down. "Over in four, three…"

"Goodnight everyone and thanks for joining us here at 12 News. We look forward to seeing you again tomorrow night." Kyle flashed his veneered smile into the camera and the rest of the group seated at the desk said goodnight.

The director gave an all clear and Isabella jumped up from her chair. "You slimy son of a bitch. Why don't you crawl back under the rock you slithered out from under?" She glared down at Kyle Mason who remained seated.

"What the hell is going on here?" Joanne sprung from her chair and stood on Kyle's other side glaring at Isabella.

"Why don't you ask this piece of crap you seem to think is so perfect?"

"Now ladies," Kyle tried to stand, but ended up back in his chair with a push from the hand each woman had on either of his shoulders.

"Shut the fuck up, Kyle," both women yelled at the same time.

"Uh oh, cat fight." The director stood beside Galvin. "Sure wish I could get video on this."

"Your man, here," Isabella spit out the words like they left a bad taste in her mouth, "is well known for not keeping his hands to himself, but now he's developed a case of roaming feet. He's been trying to creep up my skirt with his toes most of the evening." She and Joanne stood nose to nose while Kyle sunk down into his chair.

"I don't believe you." Joanne stepped back and smoothed her suit jacket down over her stomach. "He's told me how you've been coming onto him."

Isabella put one foot forward and found Kyle's chair blocking her progress. Galvin started toward the set when the director grabbed his arm.

"She has to fight her own battles. You'll make matters worse if you get in the middle of it. This has been brewing for a long time."

"Believe what you want, sister. Given the fact that you're stupid enough to get hooked up with an idiot like this," Isabella pointed down at the cowering Kyle, "right under your husband's nose, then I figure you're about as bright as he is. Listen to his lies and pray you don't catch something the way he so generously spreads himself around." She turned and stormed out of the studio.

"I'd better go calm her down." Galvin slipped around the director and took off in pursuit of what appeared to him was an Isabella out to make trouble.

"Izzy." Galvin caught himself after he called out the nickname she hated and hoped the infuriated woman didn't hear the slip up. "Isabella, wait up."

She stopped suddenly and Galvin plowed into her back. He reached out and caught her and managed to keep them both from falling.

She whirled around and faced him. "What do you think you're doing?"

"I'm trying to calm you down before you do something you'll regret." Galvin resisted the urge to pull her into his arms and kiss her until she forgot her anger and everything but him. It upset him to see her unhappy.

"Regret something? What do you think I'm going to do?"

"I think you're heading for Sam Kent's office intent on telling him about the relationship a lot of people assume his wife has with Kyle Mason." Galvin folded his arms across his chest and waited for her response.

Isabella chewed on her bottom lip for a moment before answering. "Don't you think someone should? He needs to know he's being cuckolded and people are laughing behind his back."

"Have you caught them in the act, or are you basing your knowledge on the gossip which seems to run rampant around here about everyone?" He knew from the look on her face he'd made his point.

"No, I've never seen them in action. Their relationship's been part of the rumor mill for months. Much longer than normal for the gossip of the week." She drew herself into a defensive pose. "People are laughing behind Stan's back and I think he should know."

"Mortals," Galvin coughed to cover his slip. He'd better be careful about the words that slipped out of his mouth in addition to using the stilted speech of the immortals. "People always seem to want a scapegoat, don't they?"

Before Isabella could respond, an out of breath Sandy rushed up.

"Hey you guys, I've been looking for you." The intern seemed frazzled as she approached, which was out of character for the calm blonde.

"What's the problem?" Isabella started to walk as Sandy left her no choice when she grabbed her arm and proceeded toward the weather pod.

The Doppler has been going crazy. This is turning into one weird summer. I never studied about weather like this around here." Sandy frowned. "Would you believe the potential for a tornado has been picked up? Radar shows lots of rotation in the cloud formations south of the city heading this way. We got a call from someone reporting they saw a funnel drop out of one for a few seconds."

"Tornados can appear anywhere. All it takes is the right conditions." Isabella studied the radar on the screen with a riot of red and orange colors reflecting strong weather patterns. "Though I have to admit it is unusual around here."

Unless you have a Thunder God playing games, Galvin thought. A visit to his father was in order. Thor enjoyed tinkering with weather patterns for his own entertainment and probably more so than usual since he could turn it into what amounted to a chess game with his son.

A face to face with his father might not be a good idea. They always found a way to unleash each other's tempers and when their stubborn streaks kicked in each of them became rigid in their demands. Maybe he should talk to his mother instead. Her ways of getting Thor to do her bidding always eluded Galvin.

"Galvin." Isabella said something to him and he'd missed it.

"I'm sorry. Did you ask me a question?" He knew from the glare directed toward him he'd once more endeared himself to her.

"When we have serious weather issues going on it is part of your job to stay on top of them, not go off in dreamland." The look shot his way would have frozen the water shooting from a geyser.

"Sorry, it won't happen again. Please, repeat what you said." She was correct, but he hated to admit it, even to himself when she used that tone of voice.

"I said we need to issue a tornado alert."

Great. He'd have to disagree with her again. Thor wouldn't do anything so foolish and turn a tornado on New York City, yet he couldn't tell her that. Once he gained her trust and developed a relationship built on more than arguments and lust, then he could share his true identity. For now he'd just have to do battle to save her from herself.

"I don't think that's necessary." He looked at the radar and tried to appear to study it. He hoped he could focus hard enough to move the clouds and decrease the danger. Dealing with Thor's anger over his interference in his father's game was a piece of candy compared to the wrath he'd have to face from the whisky eyed woman beside him. Thor would have calmed down by the time he saw him.

"Listen, mister. I will not endanger the lives of thousands, maybe millions of people in an ego battle with you."

Galvin loved the way her sherry colored eyes spit fire when her anger reached peak level. "I'm only saying we need to wait a few minutes. It's almost midnight. How many people will be aware of an alert anyway?" He watched her take a deep breath and prepared for another blast directed toward him.

He quickly pointed toward the radar screen. "See, things are already calming down." Where only a few minutes before a mass of colors existed, now only a few blips indicated adverse weather. His focus diverted the most dangerous storm out of the area.

"Things don't feel right here." Isabella shook her head and looked at the screen again. "Storms don't dissipate that quickly, especially one of the magnitude we were watching."

Something in her gaze made Galvin anxious. She stared at him for what seemed an eternity.

He noticed Sandy standing by his desk, her head moving back and forth, as she looked at the two of them like someone engrossed in a tennis match.

Finally, Isabella dropped her eyes. "I don't know who you are, Galvin Haldor, but I'm going to find out. Rest assured of that."

*****

Isabella stretched and ran her fingers through her hair. "I'm out of here. You coming, Sandy?"

Galvin watched Isabella fish her purse out of the drawer where she kept it, along with her stash of junk food. She'd chatted with the intern all evening, while she barely answered his questions after their earlier dispute. The need for a quick visit to Azgard became more urgent in an attempt stop Thor's interference. The Thunder God's games made it difficult to form the connection with Isabella his heart wanted.

"No, I want to check out a couple of things before I pack it in. You go ahead. I'll be fine." Sandy buried her head back in the book in front of her.

"I'm ready. I'll leave with you." Galvin received no acknowledgment of his offer and Isabella waved at Sandy on her way out.

"I'll walk with you to the subway." Galvin followed her toward the elevator and watched as she hit the button to bring it to their floor. He hoped having time alone with her would give him an opportunity to learn more about her. Yes, she was hot, but a lot more made up what he was coming to know as a complex woman.

Tired of the silence between them he asked a question. "What do you do for fun when you're not consumed by work?"

Her scathing glare didn't stop him from continuing. "I enjoy music and reading."

Isabella pushed the button again and didn't respond to his questions. Maybe she was justified in being upset with him, but she could at least be civil and respond if only to tell him to shut up.

"Do you like to read, dance...stand on your head?" He saw her lips twitch in what may be a smile. Okay, she enjoyed humor. Maybe he needed to use more of that. "How about singing in the shower? I bet you're a karaoke fan."

A groan escaped and definitely a smile with it.

"No. If you heard me sing, you'd know why. I like to read, especially mythology. And I love music."

Ah ha, finally she talked to him "It appears we have some things in common. I love mythology and what is life without music, especially classical."

"Stop trying to make nice and leave me alone." She pounded on the button again in an attempt to bring the elevator to eighteenth floor.

So much for conversation.

The elevator doors opened and when they entered,

she distanced herself to a far corner of the wood paneled car and stared down at her shoes.

The woman was enough to make any man, be they mortal or immortal, insane. Friendly conversation was not going to happen tonight. He sighed.

It might be a good time to point out how rude her behavior in the newsroom had been earlier. "You really do make a lousy boss." He almost laughed when her head shot up like a cobra ready to strike. That probably wasn't the best opener for a conversation on her management style.

"I think—"

The elevator jerked to a stop before he could find out what Isabella thought. A quick glance at the control panel told him they were stuck between the sixth and seventh floors. The lights flickered twice and then blinked out. The only light in the elevator came from the glow of the dim emergency globe in one corner.

"What the hell?" Isabella glanced around the darkened space her eyes round with panic.

"I think we're stuck between floors." Galvin had seen her mad on numerous occasions, but fear never entered the picture until now.

"Then get on the phone and have someone get us unstuck." She pressed against the wall.

Galvin picked up the phone and found it dead. "The phone's out, too."

"You did this. How did you do this?" Isabella's voice held a hysterical edge.

"Hey, I'm as much at a loss here as you are. What's your problem?"

"I hate being confined in small spaces."

He didn't know that about her. Even given all his powers, he'd never realized the strong, beautiful and confrontational woman he was coming to love appeared to suffer from what humans called claustrophobia. There were times when being a god was no better than being a mortal. He reached out and pulled the shivering woman into his arms and held her close.

"It's going to be all right, my love." Galvin delighted in finally having her in his arms. His hands roamed over the luscious body he craved. The outline of her curves against his palms as he caressed down her sides were better than his dreams.

By the heavens, he must watch using terms of endearment. Thank the gods she in her fear failed to notice. He needed to go slow and not alienate on any more levels than he already did. She snuggled closer against him and he fought to hold back the growing thickness in his male member, not wanting to spoil the opportunity handed to him to hold her.

Isabella pulled back. "Thank you. I'm all right. Just lost it for a minute." She gave him a shaky smile. "When we were kids my brother and I used play in the attic at my grandmother's house. One day we were playing hide and seek and I hid in a trunk and couldn't get out. It took my family hours to find me and since then I can't stand being confined in small dark spaces."

"Everyone has their fears." His fear was the thought of never having her, but he knew this wasn't the time to share it.

He felt her push against his chest with her hands

in an effort to get him to release his hold on her. Their lower bodies pressed closer together and the secret he tried to hide became obvious. She looked up at him and he saw the fear replaced by confusion. He lowered his head and claimed the full, pouty mouth he longed to kiss.

She resisted at first, her lips tighter than a virgin's thighs on her wedding night. A slow softening allowed him to slip his tongue in and touch the tip of hers. She tasted of sun filled meadows and ripened fruit.

A sigh of surrender escaped her perfect mouth and she too, gave into the chemistry that existed between them from their first meeting. Her hands caressed his back, slid downward to his waist and lower still to squeeze his bottom. She ground herself against his hard maleness, to the point of delicious pain.

"Enough. We can't do this." Isabella jerked away.

Okay, things were going too fast for her and he needed to slow down. "It's alright. We don't have to do anything you don't want to do." He stroked her cheek with the back of his hand. "I'd never force you to do something against your will."

Eyes the color of sherry studied him. "We could be discovered any moment." She chewed on her bottom lip and glanced frantically around their small prison. "Could you just hold me for a minute?"

"Sure." He held out his arms and she stepped into them, resting her head on his shoulder.

"There is an attraction between us, isn't there?" She snuggled closer to his neck.

The ache of his hard cock left no doubt. "Yes," he

whispered against her hair.

Isabella tilted her head back and her eyes met his. "I've wondered what it would feel like to kiss you since the day we met."

"Was it what you expected?" His voiced sounded strained to his own ears.

"Yes, and then some."

Her head tilted back in an invitation for another and his mouth lowered toward hers. "Are you sure?"

"Yes."

Their lips were so close he felt the vibration from her whisper. He crushed her mouth with his and pulled her against him.

Once again, Isabella's hands began an exploration of his body, spurring him to allow his fingers to roam over her, touching and caressing.

He pushed aside her jacket to gain access to the buttons on the satin blouse under it. In his attempt to unfasten the tiny discs, his fingers trembled like those of an adolescent mortal when faced with their first conquest.

She smiled. "Allow me."

Deftly she accomplished what he labored to do and exposed the sheer lace bra underneath that held the full breasts that tantalized him the past few weeks. Galvin felt he should pay homage to their beauty as one did a goddess. He leaned down and proceeded to plant kisses across her chest.

"Wait." Isabella pulled back and worked to get out of the jacket and blouse.

"Allow me to help." He slipped the clothing off, dropping them to the floor. One hand unhooked the bra, which denied him access to her rosy nipples. He added the flimsy piece of lace to the pile of clothing on the floor beside them and bent down to claim his reward.

Isabella's hand worked through his pants, rubbing, squeezing and teasing the erection she found there. "I want you," she gasped. "Here. Now." Her hands worked to pull down his pants' zipper.

She wanted him. Should he share in words how often he thought about a moment like this? True, it never included them trapped in an elevator, but the end result was the same. Him exploring her body and burying his passion in her and driving her as insane with desire as he was.

He pulled them away. "Better let me do that so we don't have an accident that would result in me being no good to either of us."

She laughed and pulled up her skirt and tore down black lace panties. His breath caught when he realized she wore a garter belt and stockings. He didn't think there was any way he could become harder. Who knew the sight of where the stockings ended and the creamy bare thigh traveling up to her sex could give renewed energy to an already rigid cock.

He let his pants drop around his ankles and lifted the woman who caused him so many sleepless nights recently and braced her bare bottom on the brass handrail of the elevator wall. He placed his swollen manhood against her wet entry. Pausing, he counted slowly to ten in an effort to slow his aching need. If he slammed into her the way his throbbing penis demanded it would be over in seconds.

"Yes, oh yes." She sighed when he slipped into her heat.

He held her soft ass in both hands and pumped deeper with each stroke. Her muscles tightened around his shaft and her fingers dug into his back, alerting him to her impending climax. He thrust again and took them both over the edge.

Galvin's explosion ripped through his body when Isabella's muscles convulsed around him and his knees trembled from the intensity of the release. He now knew what the mortal men he'd overheard in the men's room meant when they talked about a full body orgasm. Panting, he leaned against her, not wanting to withdraw from the delicious warmth.

They looked at each other and laughed.

"I don't think I'll ever think of elevators in the same way again." Isabella placed her forehead against his.

He laughed and kissed her nose. "That makes two of us."

"Hello, is anyone in there?" The pounding on the elevator door from below alerted them of their discovery and that the little world they created was going away...

"Yes. We are here. There are two of us." Galvin winced. He'd slipped back into the formal speech used in his world. "We're fine." In fact, he'd never been better.

In a mad rush, they searched for their discarded clothes before they faced their rescuers. Isabella reached up and wiped lipstick from his mouth. He reached over and smoothed her hair as best as he could. The elevator whirred into action and the doors opened to expose them to several curious onlookers.

*****

"Man, Mr. Loki. We can sell this tape to one of those exposé magazines or television shows for a boat load of money, or even do our own website." Norman, the security controller for the night's camera span waved his boss over for a closer look.

"Even with the dim light in the elevator you can still make out it's Isabella Girardi getting it on with one of her team, don't you think?"

Pleased at his ability to stop the elevator between floors without affecting any other part of the building, Loki didn't appreciate the security guard's suggestion to capitalize on someone else's work.

"No, I do not think so, Norman." Loki ran his hand across the forehead of the security guard and took the videocassette from the recorder. "Sorry, but it is best you do not remember any of what you saw this evening."

Loki let himself out of the security room feeling safe with the knowledge Norman wouldn't remember his being there either.

CHAPTER 5

Isabella threw the spoon and empty container in the sink in disgust. Her breakfast consumption of a full quart of Mocha Java Chip ice cream did nothing to cool the heat that raged inside her each time she recalled last night's elevator sex with Galvin Haldor.

His hair was softer to the touch than she imagined all the times she'd resisted the urge to reach out and brush it back from his eyes. The lips more kissable and every inch of his body she'd explored, better than any of her daydreams.

She loved the look in his eyes when she raised her skirt and he discovered a garter belt held up her stockings. Her decision several summers ago to switch from panty hose during the summer had been a practical one. The stockings were cooler and having less heat trapped around her private parts had cut down drastically on her bouts with yeast infections, or crotch rot, as she and her friends had called it in her college years.

The feel of his hard organ pressing against the entry of her sex created a sensation rushing through her beyond her imagination. Their heated coupling left her wanting more. The need to explore his body at her leisure. Touch, feel, taste...devour...just like a quart of ice cream.

"Galvin Haldor is without a doubt the most frustrating male I've ever met," she announced to the ice cream carton in the sink. Yet, there were times she saw gentleness in his eyes when someone asked for his help, and dammit, she wanted to have that look directed toward her.

"Instead, here I stand talking to an empty container and crabbing over losing a night of sleep."

Sleep last night was non-existent. The few minutes she managed to drift into a light doze filled with dreams of Galvin and she woke shaking with desire. Then, instead of her exhausted body seeking much needed slumber, her mind relived her ass braced against the handrail in the elevator while Galvin plunged into her again and again.

"Man, you got it bad." She woke with a listless desire to do nothing, not even eat, usually her favorite thing on a lazy Saturday morning.

She pulled on her sweats and tried to muster up enough energy for a trip to her favorite coffee house where she loved to read the paper over a steaming latté as she munched on the muffin of the day, but even that held no appeal.

Finally, she turned to her solution for all problems. Ice cream. Today that brought no satisfaction either. Isabella paced the apartment like a caged animal, faced with a long Saturday afternoon and evening looming before her.

Well, she'd just be damned if she was going to sit around the apartment like a love sick teenager waiting for the latest crush to call. "Okay, enough of this. He's good looking and so are a lot of other guys. There's nothing special about this one." She tried to ignore the little voice in her head that whispered, *are you sure?*

Good grief, she'd spent the morning talking to herself, out loud. "It's more than his drop dead gorgeous body. His sense of humor is great, when he isn't being a pain in the ass. And there's no doubt he's very bright because his challenges keep me on my toes. You also have to give him a plus mark for his love of music."

Music appreciation, the one thing she had in common with her grandmother. The old woman reined terror on her family, but classical music put a soft dreamy look in her eyes. Isabella knew anything that accomplished that had power and she came to understand it, too.

"Don't forget the mythology thing. Any male who is into that couldn't be all bad." There I go again, talking to myself. "I've got to get out of here."

Isabella changed out of her sweats and into jeans and tank top. Standing at the door, she commanded the telephone to ring before she made her exit. Instead, the few minutes of silence resonated through the apartment. "Idiot, you know he's not going to call." She slammed the door behind her and put the key in the lock when the shrill peal of the phone grabbed her attention.

Relief flooded her and she fought the door to get it open and made a mad dash to answer.

"Hello." Damn, she didn't want to sound so breathless when he called.

"Bella, you didn't call to say when we're going

shopping." Her mother's voice sounded perturbed like it always did when she missed one of their meetings. Part of Isabella's regular Saturday routine included spending time with her mother. Today wouldn't be a good day to spend an afternoon listening to Angela expound on the joys of marriage. Not what she needed given how tired she felt, both physically and emotionally.

"Ma, I'm not able to have lunch with you today. I have to go down to the station and work on a couple of things." Okay, so now she'd stooped to lying to her mother.

"Bella, I count on these lunches. They're the high-point of my week."

Heaven help her. Angela pulled out the guilt trip card she always used when things didn't go her way, but today even that wasn't going to work. "Sorry Ma, but with all the weather anomalies we've been having the past couple of weeks I've got to go in and see if I can spot a pattern here." Well, that's what she ought to do instead of mooning over the sexy body and the driving thrusts of Galvin Haldor.

"Maybe you can come over for lunch tomorrow. We haven't seen you since you were here for dinner a few weeks ago."

"Ma, I had lunch with you last Saturday."

Ignoring her daughter's comment, she continued. "Your father misses you." This was Angela-speak for, "I'm losing control here".

Low blow, Ma. Using Pop to make me feel worse. "Sorry, no can do. I'll take you and Pop out to lunch next week." Isabella knew she needed the whole weekend to work out her feelings over what happened with Galvin

She spent the afternoon and early evening dropping off and picking up dry cleaning, grocery shopping and doing laundry. Isabella settled down for an after dinner snack...a quart of ice cream. Maybe Peanut Butter Passion could accomplish what this morning's offering hadn't been able to.

Tuning into Channel 12 news Isabella sat back ready to critique Galvin's first solo appearance on the Saturday night weather.

"Tonight we have a new member to our weather team." The anchor turned to face Galvin. "Join me in welcoming, Galvin Haldor. What do we have in store for us weather-wise tomorrow, Galvin? Hope it's good since my family and I have plans."

She rolled the first spoonful of dessert around in her mouth, letting the peanut butter and cream coat her taste buds. Better than sex, she told herself and held onto that thought until the camera switched over to Galvin.

Once again she found herself back in the elevator, pressed up against the body of the man whose face she devoured now. The thought of critiquing his weather performance flew out the window. The only performance she could focus on definitely scored a ten plus.

The image of their hastily gathering discarded clothes, pulling them on over bodies damp with sweat before the elevator door opened came to mind. *I'm sure people got an eyeful when we stepped out. Our clothes probably would have looked better if we'd slept in them, especially mine.* Her cheeks flamed at the recollection of her mussed hair, rumpled suit, and the wetness trickling down the inside of her thighs.

Wonder what they thought about seeing the person they invited into their homes every week night walking off an elevator looking like she'd been rode hard and put away wet.

No, that wouldn't get her another award for best weather forecasting, but she could give one for the hottest sex she'd ever experienced. "Hmmm, wonder if sex in an elevator qualifies up there with the Mile High Club?" she asked the television screen.

"Shit." Isabella paused with the spoon mid-way to her mouth with last glob of fat and calories. She tried to determine if the need to throw-up came from polishing off her second quart of ice cream of the day, or from the memory of the security camera in the elevator.

*****

Loki turned the videotape over and studied the case. The security guard did have a good idea when he suggested creating a website. The fun he could generate with it. What Norman called money didn't interest him, but the idea of creating mischief, now the entertainment he could have... No, he couldn't let his thoughts go there. He could never win Sif's trust again if he gave into the temptation to create havoc for his own pleasure with her son as one of the stars on this film.

He was happy with his prank in stopping the elevator. The idea to tamper with the elevator popped into his head and he had reacted impulsively. There was nothing wrong with wanting to see what would happen to two volatile personalities trapped in close confines for a period of time. He did not anticipate the effect it brought about and the coupling that resulted from it.

His abilities did come in good stead here among these people in the way he could manipulate not only their lives, but also the equipment they relied on so heavily. Not turning off the power to the other elevators and the rest of the building made it appear an electrical problem occurred with the one car. This would keep the service people perplexed for days. Turning off the phone in the elevator was another brilliant idea.

The best thing to do was destroy the video before temptation became too much and he did something he would regret. Maybe what he needed was to visit Sif. Yes, a quick trip to Azgard would keep his goal foremost in his mind. He didn't want to spend the next thousand years getting the cold shoulder from Sif. He hated to admit he needed anything from anyone, but he needed her friendship.

*****

"You look much too serious for such a pretty lady." Galvin observed his mother for several minutes before speaking.

Sif turned and laughed. "My son, how I have missed your teasing."

"How go things in Azgard, Mother?" He kissed the offered cheek.

The goddess frowned. "Galvin, you're picking up the slang the mortals use. You know how that annoys me."

He laughed and reached out to smooth the wrinkle on his mother's brow. "There are times, Mother, we could benefit from being less formal here in Azgard and especially in the halls of Valhalla. We can learn a few things from the mortals."

"My son," Sif appeared to pause in thought. "Never mind. It is good to see you. The halls of Valhalla lose some of their glow when you're not here as does our home."

"Mother, we know there are more than enough deities here to keep the hall glowing." Galvin laughed. "Is Loki ill? Surely he keeps things lively with his pranks."

She twisted her hands before responding. "It appears Loki is occupied elsewhere."

How odd, he thought, seeing how agitated his mother became at the mention of Loki's name. He knew her dislike for Loki, but to demonstrate such anxiety at the sound of his name didn't fit her usual reaction. "Oh, what's he up to?"

His mother glared at his slip back into what she considered mortal speak. "I would not know. It is not my job to keep track of the Lord of Pranks."

"Did someone call my name?"

Galvin and Sif turned toward the speaker.

"Loki. What are you doing here? I mean, Loki…" She seemed at a loss for words.

"Sif, my dear. I needed only to rest my eyes on the most beautiful of women, be they mortal or immortal."

Loki bowed deeply before the pale woman.

"Master Trickster, have you been creating havoc in places other than Valhalla?" Galvin wasn't sure what transpired between his mother and the prankster. Obviously, something more than their usual conditional truce was occurring in front of him and it was frustrated him to not figure it out. He knew for sure any tricks the imp cared to pull would not take place within Sif's home.

"Havoc? Me? Surely you are mistaken, Galvin." A sly grin spread across Loki's face.

Galvin laughed. He enjoyed Loki and regretted the breach that caused his mother's coolness toward him, but cutting a woman's hair as a joke wasn't a good idea. "The only mistake anyone would make with you, milord, would be to not think you'd been creating trouble."

Reminding himself to speak in the more formal manner his mother preferred Galvin decided now would be a good time to bring up the reason for his visit. "It is good that you are here, Loki. I have come to talk with my mother about an important matter and possibly you can help too."

He saw the look of interest in Sif and Loki's eyes.

"Do not keep us in suspense, son of Thor. By all means share with us this matter." Loki encouraged.

"I seek your help in controlling Father's tendency to meddle." Galvin saw perplexed looks appear on their faces.

"Meddle how, Galvin?" Sif asked.

"Father has been playing games with the weather in the New York area. I know it is because I am working in the weather room at the television station that he creates the storms unusual for the region." Galvin sighed when he saw the blank look on his mother's face. "He amuses himself by my having to contradict Isabella on weather predictions."

"Why would your father do such a thing? Surely, he has better matters to attend to than create havoc for your situation. This is the type of thing Loki would do." Sif turned to face the Lord of Mischievous.

"Not me. I am completely innocent of this." Loki held up his hands in defense of the accusation.

"Mother, be realistic. Yes, this is the type of trick Loki would enjoy, but he does not have the power to change the weather." Galvin smiled at the thumbs up Loki flashed him. "This is Father's doing. He is creating anomalies in the normal conditions of weather for this area."

Loki rubbed his chin and paced and Sif wrung her hands in agitation while Galvin watched them digest the accusation. Loki stopped and spoke, "Are you sure these anomalies, as you call them, are not being brought about by what the mortals call global warming?"

"If that were the case, Loki, do you not think it would be affecting more than just the region where I am? No, I think it is Father. Thor is trying to prove he is in control whether I am here in Azgard or in the human world."

Galvin turned to face his mother. "So I ask again, Mother, will you help? Will you have Father cease with the games? If I approach him it will turn into an argument."

He watched her mull over his request and saw her internal war play out in the expressions that danced across her face.

"I will keep a close eye on what your father is up to. If I learn he is doing this, then yes, I will confront him. We both know that with Thor you must have all of the facts or you lose the battle before it begins."

She smiled at her youngest son. "Now, tell me about what else has been happening with your entry into the world of the mortals.

"I promise to tell you more when I return, Mother. Today I must hurry back as there are unfinished things to which I need to attend." Galvin placed his hands on her shoulders and kissed each cheek. "Do not look so sad. I will come for a long visit shortly."

"Galvin, I will walk with you to the exit. We can discuss ideas on how to handle Thor and I will share them with your mother." Loki said as he fell into step beside Galvin.

Taken aback he nodded in agreement. Loki's offer of assistance in going against Thor came as a surprise. He'd been devoted to the Thunder God since Thor freed him from the chains that secured him to the boulders under the dripping poison of the snake.

Once they were out of Sif's view, Loki stopped and placed a hand on Galvin's arm bringing him to a halt.

What now? Galvin wondered. "Why are we stopping, Loki? I really must go."

"Here." Loki reached into his jacket and pulled out an object. "I think you may want this."

Galvin frowned and took the box handed to him. "What is this?"

"It is the film of your...shall we say elevator experience." Loki smirked.

"What? How did you get this?" Galvin's eyes narrowed and his face flushed with anger. "What have you been up to, Loki?"

"I assure you, Galvin, you should be grateful that I happened to be in the right place at the right moment. Otherwise, this video would have been sold to the highest bidder. A lot of people would pay big money to find a personality such as Isabella in such a compromising situation." Loki met Galvin's glare before he continued. "You seem to have forgotten, the mortals have security cameras everywhere."

Loki turned and took several steps and then stopped. "Say: *Thank you, Loki,*" he called over his shoulder.

Dazed, Galvin responded to the departing back of the Lord of Chaos, "Thank you, Loki."

*****

"What did the two of you decide is the best way to approach Thor?" Sif asked when Loki returned.

"He still thinks the best way to handle Thor is through you."

"Very well." Sif bowed her head in concurrence. "I shall see what I can do, but enough on that for now. Tell me what you have found out with your trip into the mortal world. What is this woman like that seems to have captivated my son's interest so strongly?"

Loki paused and mulled over how much to share with Sif. "She is very intelligent and has strong ties to her family as does your son to his. In addition she is beautiful and strong-willed." He smiled as he recalled some of the confrontations between Isabella and Galvin.

"I see. She offers a challenge to my son then." Sif drifted around the room picking up various objects and putting them back down. "He loves a challenge." She frowned. "This is not good. Tell me about her family. What do know of them?"

Once again, Loki thought over how much to disclose. "Her family originates from Italy."

"Ahh, close to the region of the Greeks. Then they are familiar with Zeus." Sif looked even more interested.

"Yes, they are familiar with what the mortals refer to as folklore about Zeus and Mount Olympus but put no stock in the tales. The grandmother is also a fan of an opera written by Wagner, or at least one of the pieces in it. She plays *Ride of the Valkyrie* often."

"Really. That is one of my favorites, too."

"I know, as well as your sons," Loki said, but he didn't share with Sif that it became Pia Bartolo's favorite after she had an interlude with a handsome Nordic man in her younger days. The young stud was actually Odin disguised as a mortal when he sought amusement during one of his visits to Zeus. Disguised as a bird of prey, Loki accompanied Odin on his walks through the hills of the countryside and witnessed his meeting with the beautiful Pia.

Oh yes, he recognized the pictures of the younger version of the old woman that she kept scattered around her apartment. He slipped in while she was out on one of her nightly walks after the encounter between her and Galvin. Loki kept vigil the evening the son of Thor stood sentry outside the family home to spy on Isabella.

Loki laughed. "Yes, I think you and the grandmother would get along famously."

"If Galvin's interest in her granddaughter continues, I may have to visit her."

Not much surprised Loki, but Sif's indication she would venture into the mortal word did shock him. Sif never ventured from the safety of Azgard.

"You look like a brisk breeze would knock you over, Loki. Get on with your story before you faint. Tell me about the rest of her family." Sif sat down in an overstuffed chair.

Regaining his composure, Loki continued. "The woman's mother is manipulative. She will use whatever means she feels will work to bend her family to her desires."

Sif's eyebrows shot up into her hair of gold that fell across her forehead in soft bangs. "Do tell," she muttered.

"The father is a nice man who only wants what is best for his family and there is a brother who..." Loki coughed.

"Yes?" Sif prompted him to continue.

"Who has a preference for men over women," he finished with a smile.

"Interesting, but understandable. That sort of thing is strongly condoned in the mortal worlds over which Zeus reigns. I especially recall a place called Rome where that practice took hold and of course,

Greece." Sif returned his smile.

"Continue to keep me informed of the progression of my son's relationship with this woman." Sif pushed herself out of the chair and smiled. "Things may become interesting for both of us Loki."

"I am sure they will." Loki took the offered hand and kissed it. "I'm sure they will become most interesting before all is settled, my friend."

It *will also be most interesting to see what Galvin does with the video. Will he destroy it or share it with Isabella?* Loki headed back to the mortal world to see.

CHAPTER 6

Isabella studied the dark circles under her eyes and the pinched, drawn look of her face. She resembled a caricature of a raccoon. In the glare of the florescent bathroom light, she didn't look like a woman making the ascent to forty, but more like one that rolled up that hill a long time ago.

Another night of no sleep didn't help her mental state either. After she recalled the security camera in the elevator yesterday, she'd gone into the office to figure out what would be the best way to get access to the tape.

Saturdays were pretty low key with one weather person and the skeleton newsroom crew who worked the weekends keeping tabs on what happened in the city and around the world. If anything major broke, they called in reinforcements to help out.

"Hi, John."

The weekend weatherman was a 'keep to himself' personality, only animated when he faced the camera. "Hi Boss, what brings you in on a nice Saturday like this?"

Good grief, even John was going to be chatty today. From Sandy or one of the other weathermen, she expected conversation and an endless quiz on why she wasted her time coming in on a dead Saturday and making her regret she did.

"Thought I'd stop by and see if anything new is going on, plus I need to get some paperwork out of the way." *Liar, liar, pants on fire.*

"Everything's quiet. Looks like we're in for sunshine all day." He gave her a smile that could have passed for a grimace and returned to studying his weather maps and forecast reports from the National Weather Bureau. He took preparation for his spots on the six and eleven o'clock news seriously.

Isabella went through all her manuals on the building's security not finding anything of use. Slipping into Sam's office, she rummaged through any book that mentioned security and sighed in defeat. The last book she pulled out confirmed her worst nightmare. Cameras were everywhere, including the elevators.

Someone in the security room always watched the bank of screens in front of them to which the cameras fed constant views of all the activity in the building. The only ray of hope centered on the way in which the footage was shot. They didn't have enough monitors to accommodate all the views at once and switched back and forth between areas, unless something critical happened that necessitated constant observation.

How long were they stuck between floors? Sliding the foundation soaked sponge over her face in an attempt to even out her skin tone; she calculated the time frame in her head. "Let's see, we left the office after the eleven o'clock news and I got home around, oh crap. What time did I get home?"

She lost track of time while they indulged in the attraction that sparked at their first meeting and how no idea how long they were trapped in the elevator car. Not long enough, her treacherous body cried, each time she thought about it.

A loud sigh escaped. "Maybe the guard didn't have the screen up," she said to the reflection in the mirror as she applied more concealer in an attempt to mask the dark circles under her eyes.

"They only keep a constant view if there's an issue and what would you do if an elevator became stuck between floors with people in it." She threw the tube of makeup down in disgust. "Fool, fool, fool!" she shouted to the wide-eyed woman who stared back. "I need to talk to someone other than you."

A call to Mona resulted in the answering machine picking up. Mona never crawled out of bed before noon on Sunday and should be home. This was her recuperation day from her weekend of partying. No pickup told Isabella that Mona must have gotten lucky on her Saturday evening prowl and was getting her rest in someone else's bed. Well, maybe not rest.

She didn't want to discuss this with Raine or Holly. They were friends and she liked them, but they didn't understand her the way Mona did. Maybe because she'd been a friend with Mona since junior high and they'd spent their college years together as roommates.

Who else could she confide in? "Gino!"

She'd always been able to talk to her brother. Chances were good he would be home and surfacing about the time she made it to his place. Energized with the knowledge she'd be able to pour out her soul to her brother spurred her into action.

An hour later, Isabella stood in front of her brother's door armed with two grandé lattes. She needed the caffeine to help her focus and if she knew Gino, he'd need it to pry his eyes open from his late night of hitting the gay bars.

After leaning on the doorbell several times she wondered if a phone call first would have been the wiser thing to do. Maybe he wasn't home either. Just as she turned to leave, she heard the rattle of locks being opened on the other side.

"Good morning, brother dear," she called when the door began to crack.

"Good morning, sister dear, and what the hell are you doing here?" A large hand reached out to relieve her of one of the cups she held in each of hers. "Thanks for thinking of me."

The sun's reflection off a diamond bracelet encircling his left wrist blinded her. "Nice bling," she said as she looked up.

Stunned, Isabella stared. Her brother stood in front of her encased in a cloud of pink chiffon. The filmy negligee covered a matching pink satin gown, which flowed to the floor. "Oh, my," escaped her lips before she could stop the words from flowing out.

Gino stepped aside and motioned her to come inside. "You didn't know?" He blushed as his sister appraised him.

"No. I mean I know you're gay, but you never mentioned cross-dressing." She gulped. "I didn't know you were into that."

"I haven't announced it, if that's what you mean. I like to wear women's clothes. It helps me get in touch with my softer side." Even surrounded in a halo of pink, Gino looked anything but soft while he glared at her with a hand on one hip and the other paw clutching the coffee she'd brought him.

Okay, so her brother liked feminine clothes--and eye shadow, he wore plum eye shadow... and it made his eyes look larger. The lipstick...now she wasn't so sure she liked that shade on him and good lord...obviously, those slippers were custom made. Somehow, she didn't think men's size thirteen pink satin slippers with fluffy feather trim were a stock item.

"Hey, far be it from me to slam your choice of dress, though you may want to rethink that shade of lipstick." Nope, she definitely didn't like it on him, she decided while pushing him out of her way to access his lair.

Gino watched her with narrowed eyes and then grinned. "I should have known you could handle it. Come on, I'll heat our lattés up a little with a shot from the pot of coffee I just brewed."

Looking past her brother into the small kitchen, she saw the table set for two, which wasn't unusual since Gino always kept placemats on the small round table. What caught her attention were the flowers and the place settings that obviously anticipated someone else for breakfast. Or would it be brunch given the time?

"Expecting company?" she commented when they passed the table.

"Not exactly." Gino did the squirming thing with the ball of his foot he couldn't control when he was uncomfortable. She watched the feathers float around the pink satin shoe and caress his hairy ankle. All the fluff looked anything but delicate on a foot the size of which any good Yeti would be envious.

"Not exactly? Honey, either you are or you're not." Enough of the evasive answers from the man in pink. For cripes sake, if she could make such a quick adjustment to his wardrobe he could at least stop with the word games.

"Well, I'm not exactly expecting company because –"

"Dear, do you know where I put my..." the question from the man standing in the door leading to the bedroom trailed off as he stared at Isabella.

"Holy Moley," Isabella didn't know if her heart could take any more shocks today. The sight of her brother in pink chiffon startled her enough, but Howdy Doody clad only in a towel wrapped around his thin waist took things too far.

"I uh...uh..." Tom's face matched the color of his hair. "Hi, Isabella," came out in a squeak as he clutched the towel in his effort to make sure it didn't come off.

It appeared that their mother finally made a match in her continuous efforts to find a partner for her children; only Isabella didn't think this was what Ma had in mind.

Freaking amazing and she thought her problems would create havoc with their mother. At least her hot elevator copulation was with a member of the opposite sex.

"Tom, what a surprise."   Talk about an understatement.

She gazed back and forth between her brother and what was obviously his latest flame. "I didn't know you were here." *But, dense one, you should have picked up on the signs Gino had a visitor.*

Gino walked over to stand beside Tom. "Love, maybe you should put on some clothes and we can all sit down and talk over a cup of coffee."

"Excellent idea." Tom made a hasty retreat into the bedroom.

"When…how…I mean what the hell did I just see?" *Shit, open mouth, insert foot.*

Isabella took a deep breath. With any luck, she'd be able to put together a coherent thought at any moment. "Okay. I noticed you two hit it off at dinner when Ma did the big fix up, but I had no idea you'd hit it off to this extent." Where did she set her latté? She desperately needed caffeine to lift the fog from lack of sleep and the never-ending surprises she'd encountered since she arrived at her brother's. "I mean…" She inhaled deeply in hopes the additional air into her lungs would help her focus, "I thought Tom was straight."

"Yeah, well, life holds surprises for all of us." Gino bustled around the kitchen working on breakfast preparations, putting a basket of muffins on the table to go with the butter and honey he'd already set out. "Why don't we wait for Tom? It would probably be better if we explained together."

"Fine." Isabella considered asking Gino to change

into something less pink, and then decided what the hell.

"Sorry I took so long." Tom appeared in jeans and a pink Ralph Lauren t-shirt which amazingly enough didn't clash with his red hair.

Okay, maybe he was gay. At this point Isabella didn't think anything else would surprise her.

"Everybody sit down." Gino added another place setting and poured steaming coffee into the three cups, the cold lattés now forgotten.

"Look, Isabella," Tom paused as if gathering his thoughts. "I…we didn't mean for you to find out like this."

"That's right, Sis." Gino reached over and squeezed Tom's hand in a show of moral support.

"Hey, no problem. I'm the one who came over unannounced and crashed your party."

She tried to laugh and found her cheeks still tight with tension. "You two are going to have to help me here." She saw the look that passed between the two men. Would she ever have someone in her life that she could exchange a glance with and know what they were thinking?

"I mean, Tom, I thought you were straight."

Tom shrugged his lean shoulders. "I did too. But when I met Gino over at your folks' house that night I felt a connection like none I'd ever experienced."

Gino reached over and stroked Tom's cheek. "Yeah, I knew from the moment I met him this guy was special and if I could only have him in my life as a friend, well, then I'd take that. I figured I'd have to settle for doing the manly-man things with him. You know...ball games and such."

"Anyway, the next morning we ran into each other at the grocery store. We started talking," Tom flashed a grin in Gino's direction, "and as they say the rest is history. The more time we spent together, the more I came to realize my feelings for Gino weren't just those for a buddy."

"Yeah, I'd already laid it on the line with him on who I am. I told him I was gay, but still have a lot of guys who are just pals. But, I knew I'd have to do battle with myself to accept him as a friend anytime we planned something."

Tom laughed and winked at Gino. "And we've planned things every night since then. We celebrated my landing a big account a few nights ago and a couple of bottles of wine did a lot to release my inhibitions."

"So what did you do?" Isabella discovered she was curious in spite of herself.

"I told Gino I though he was pretty damned hot." Tom blushed.

"And I told him how I really feel. One thing led to another and we found out we're perfect for each other. We just wanted to enjoy the, shall we say glow, before we told anyone." Gino gave a sad little smile to Isabella. "You know Ma is going to have an absolute shit fit."

"Safe to say that's an understatement." Isabella nodded her head in understanding. "Yeah, telling her and Nonna will be a real treat. I don't blame you for putting it off as long as possible. Pop will be able to handle it better than those two."

The group grew quiet, each lost in their own thoughts. Isabella's heart ached for her brother. She knew his lifestyle couldn't be easy on him given their family and add in his job situation...well she wasn't too sure how Joey would view having an out of the closet gay on his payroll. She didn't know a lot about the views of the underworld when it came to individuals who chose an alternate lifestyle.

Gino broke the silence. "Sorry to put so much on you today. Not only do you have the secret of our relationship to keep, but my love of women's clothing."

The words popped out before Isabella could stop them. "I think the most surprising thing is you're the one who's a cross-dresser. Sorry, Tom." She clamped her hand over her mouth to stop the verbal diarrhea since each statement was more ludicrous than the one before.

"No offense taken." Tom winked over the top of his cup.

Laughing, Gino pulled her hands away. "Ah, Sis. Stop and think back to when we were in our early teens. Remember how you couldn't find a sweater or a new eye shadow for days, and suddenly they'd appear out of the blue."

"Yeah, come to think of it I do." Isabella's eyes narrowed and she studied her brother. "You rat. You mean to tell me you took them."

"Guilty. At least until I got too big for the clothes and didn't really care for your taste in eye shadow."

"Tom, how do you feel about Gino's cross-dressing?" She met Tom's look square on.

"Hey, if he enjoys it, then more power to him. I'll have plenty of ideas for special occasion gifts ,won't I.?" Tom fingered the chiffon of the negligee Gino wore.

"Good point." What the hell. They were happy. A lot happier than she'd be for a long time, especially since she let Galvin Haldor get under her skin. "I'd better be going and let you two enjoy what's left of your day."

"You haven't said why you came over in the first place, Bella."

Now that Gino's secrets were out in the open, he must have realized how unusual it was for her to show up at his door unannounced on a Sunday morning.

"It's nothing." All the humiliation and frustration of the last thirty odd hours came rushing back. She'd been able to forget them in the surprise of finding her brother dressed like a woman and the discovery of the situation between Gino and Tom.

"Don't think so. `Nothing' wouldn't have brought you over here today." Gino's look challenged her to deny he was right. "Our Sunday connections are usually at our parents doing one of Ma's command performances."

"Maybe I should excuse myself so you two can talk." Tom started to get up.

"No. Wait. After all, whatever I share with Gino, you're going to find out about anyway. We may as well save him the trouble of repeating it." Isabella chewed on her bottom lip and fought back the tears that burned her eyes.

Tom relaxed in his chair and he and Gino waited

for her to share. "Okay, but you guys asked for it. It's not smartest thing I've ever done." Where to begin?

"I got it on with a member of my weather team."

Gino grinned and leaned forward. "Not the end of the world. Just tell the guy you made a mistake and it can't happen again."

"If only it were that easy." Isabella squirmed in her chair, hating to divulge the full extent of her stupidity. "We were in an elevator, stuck between floors."

Her brother shook his head and laughed. "So, did you just make out?"

"No, it went beyond making out. We did it right there in the elevator while waiting to be discovered." She buried her head in her folded arms in an attempt to hide her embarrassment.

"Boy, Sis. You know how to fuck up worse than me. What the hell were you thinking? You know they have security cameras everywhere now." Gino shook his head.

Lifting her head, she met her brother's gaze. "That's the problem. I didn't think...I reacted. I have the hots so bad for this guy my brain shut down and my hormones kicked into overdrive." Her lips pressed into a thin line and she blinked hard to keep back the tears. "I told you, it's the stupidest thing I've ever done."

"Okay, calm down." Tom hadn't said anything while Isabella told her story. "Did you try to get the tape?"

Isabella sighed. The man obviously didn't have an idea of what he was saying. "How in hell am I supposed to get the tape from Security? Walk in and ask for it?"

"That's probably the best way." Tom wiggled his eyebrows at her. "After all, you're the big television news person. Asking to see the video of people trapped in the elevator would make sense."

"Except for one little thing. The privacy of the people trapped, plus I'm weather, not news. Since I'm one of the people involved and the situation isn't exactly one I want to draw attention to, if by some miracle it got missed, I'm probably better off waiting to see if there's any fall out."

"I could steal it." Gino pulled off a piece from a blueberry muffin and popped it into his mouth.

"Steal it? That's brilliant, little brother. Just what I need. To give more fuel to all the scandal sheets so they can have a field day. I can see the headlines splashed across every rag in the country, 'Top New York weather forecaster caught in sexual compromise and gay cross-dressing mafia brother fingered stealing video.' No. Thanks, but no thanks." She gasped, wanting to bite her tongue on the mafia remark, "By the way, does Tom know your current employer?"

Gino shrugged. "Yep. Can't keep something like that a secret." He looked across at his lover. "He's not too happy with it and we're looking into other avenues of employment for me. Maybe I'll go back to school."

"Well, praise the Lord. Mama won't stop dancing for weeks when you accomplish that. Thank you, Tom." She blew him a kiss. Poor guy's ears couldn't get any redder.

"Anyway, no theft. That's worse than Tom's

brilliant idea."

"Hey, just trying to help." Tom made a face and stuck out his tongue at her.

"Whatever you do, don't take lessons from Gino on how to help. You just heard his genius mind at work."

"It was only a suggestion." Gino looked hurt.

"I know." Isabella punched him on the shoulder. "And I love you even if it's about the dumbest idea from you, since we were kids."

"Really, guys, I have to go. I'll head home and see if my answering machine has a whispery message from some guy wanting me to make a money drop in exchange for the video footage he has on me making like a bitch in heat, while trapped in an elevator with a hot stud."

Picking up her bag, she walked to the door and turned to receive her brother's hug.

"Nice purse." Gino caressed the Versace leather.

"Don't even think about it." Isabella sheltered the purse protectively under her arm and kissed her brother on the cheek and waved goodbye to Tom.

Outside in the summer heat she squared her shoulders and made her way to the subway stop determined to face head-on whatever fate awaited her. The worst-case scenario, the tape got released and she became unemployed when the station exercised their morals clause.

CHAPTER 7

Galvin decided the visit he made to Azgard to seek his mother's help was the right thing to do. Sif obviously talked with Thor since there'd been no more strange weather events. He wished he could fix things with Isabella as easily.

Watching the video Loki had given him, Galvin relived each exciting moment of what happened in the elevator. They went at each other like a couple of rutting deer in the small confines of the walled space. The sparks shooting between them caused him to realize this was the first time he'd created lightning bolts with anyone, other than the moments of temper he experienced with his father.

Yet, she ignored him since their arrival at the office. She was cool and aloof. Did she find their encounter exciting? Her actions gave no indication they'd indulged in the best sex he for one, had ever had.

Okay, enough of this game of silence. I'm going to ask if it was as good for her as it was for me.

Isabella jumped when Sam came up behind her and said, "Isabella, I need to see you in my office."

She looked pale when she came to work earlier, but now her face almost matched the white blouse she wore. Galvin saw the deep breath she took before she followed Sam to his office. His stomach twisted knots and he wondered if Isabella experienced the same sensation.

Did someone expose them and if so why didn't Sam call both of them into his office? Who knew what really happened? *Loki.* Did Loki make a copy of the video before he turned it over to Galvin? If the Lord of Pranks pulled one of his tricks, he would have to answer to him.

Calm down, Galvin told himself. Don't make the human mistake of jumping to conclusions. Wait and see what happens. He tried to read Isabella's body language through the glass that comprised Sam's office wall next to the newsroom. Not closing the blinds was a good omen.

Galvin watched Isabella stand and walk to the door where she paused and continued to talk with her boss. Color returned to her face and she appeared calm. Gavin exhaled in a loud swish.

"What's with you today?" Sandy, the nosey weather intern, bounced over to his desk and propped against a corner.

"Nothing. Why do you think there is?" Galvin quickly learned to be careful around the ever-vigilant young woman. She observed too much and at times, if he didn't know better, he'd swear she could read minds. She was a mortal with what they called "intuition". If he investigated her background, it wouldn't be at all surprising to find out that somewhere in her family, a liaison between an immortal and one of her ancestors resulted in a contribution to her family tree.

"Hmmm." She pinned him with her hazel eyes before continuing. "Yeah, you're feeding me the same line of bullshit that I've gotten from Isabella all day. For two people who have no problems you both are acting really strange."

"How so?"

"Well, you've been lost in thought since you came in, and boss lady," Sandy indicated with a nod of her head toward Sam's office, "has been jumpier than a cat thrown on a bed of hot coals. She acts like her paws have been burned." She laughed at her little joke.

"Guys, we have a request from Mr. Moultar which came through our fearless station manager."

Thank the gods she didn't hear us, Galvin thought when Isabella's sudden appearance caught both he and Sandy by surprise. "And what might that be?"

"It seems Leif Moultar has taken more interest in his ownership of the station, especially the weather area." Isabella frowned at the thought of Moultar's attention to her domain. "He thinks some of the unusual occurrences we've experienced recently are only an indication of things to come. I don't know what advanced radar system he's using, but he told Sam we're probably going to see storm situations this area seldom experiences and we better be prepared."

Galvin groaned to himself. His father, the Thunder God, must have paid a visit to Leif and told the lesser immortal what fun he was having playing games with his son. Moultar was always a strong admirer of Thor and before concluding he would have more power in the earth realm, he followed the mighty god around much like an adoring puppy. He probably saw this as a way to become involved with his hero's antics. Hopefully, this happened before Sif talked with the Thunder God and there would be no weather anomalies to worry about.

"Did he give any indication on how we're to prepare for the unknown?" Sandy looked as disgusted as Isabella's tone indicated she was.

"His main focus is if we should have storms that offer tornado potential, we need to be ready to do a storm chase."

"Are you shitting me?" Sandy fell into her chair. "He expects us to become friggin' storm chasers? Doesn't the idiot know how dangerous that is?"

"He thinks it would be good for ratings to have us gallivanting around the countryside and doing live remotes in the storm areas." Isabella's eyes narrowed. "Station owners always come up with brilliant ideas to improve ratings, but they don't consider the difficultly involved for the people who have to enact them."

"If he wants to get his ass hammered by hailstones or sucked up in a tornado, then send him out there if conditions develop." Sandy's suggestion on what Leif should do lost some of its initial heat. Galvin detected a touch of interest at the idea in her voice.

"What about you, Galvin?" Isabella turned to him. "You haven't said anything since I dropped the bombshell from our fearless leader."

"More like brainless leader," the intern mumbled loud enough for Galvin to hear.

Yawning to hide the smile that threatened to escape, he threw in a stretch for good measure. "I think what happened the other day was a freak incident and we have nothing to worry about. No need to get our adrenalin pumping before something happens."

"Just like a man to be proactive." Sandy grinned and threw a wadded-up ball of paper at him.

"Weather patterns are back to normal for this time of year. Maybe Galvin's right. We'll keep an eye on conditions and if a cycle develops of continuous storms like last week, then the possibility of at least going out of the city on a storm chase exists." Isabella appeared to have settled the way to handle the directive in her own mind.

"A storm chase in Central Park would be easier on the bottoms than a long car ride out of the city." Sandy laughed once again finding humor in her statement.

"We'll do what we need to do." Isabella's determined expression left no doubt about her feelings. "Got it?"

"Got it," Sandy and Galvin responded, though neither jumped for joy at the decision.

That's not all I've got, Izzy. Galvin knew he needed to make a decision on what to do with the video Loki had given him. Should he destroy it or give it to Isabella?

*****

Isabella shut the door behind her and leaned against it in an effort to keep the world at bay. Hell day ended. Her nerves were raw as she waited for the proverbial shoe to drop and she jumped anytime someone approached her desk.

Visions of word getting back to Sam about Friday night's elevator quickie danced through her head. Her boss inviting her to pack up her desk and not let the door hit her in the ass on the way out would be certain if he found out.

Yes, 'quickie' definitely described what had transpired. Now, more then ever she wanted to savor every luscious inch of Galvin's magnificent body. Thinking about him, her treacherous mind recalled the feel of his hard cock pounding into her while he held her butt cheeks propped on the cold brass handrail. Damn, she was horny and she needed to take care of the problem. Breaking out the Rabbit for a quick battery operated fix should do it.

She shrugged her tired shoulders and winced at the tightness under her shoulder blades and up the back of her neck. Maybe a shower was a better idea. She could take care of two aching areas of her body by that method.

The pulsating water plummeted across her tense back as she lathered her body with her favorite body wash. Hands caressed her skin, sliding over the slick surface. Her nipples ached and she pinched and pulled on the rosy buds, allowing the sensation of pleasure to spread through her body.

"Ohhh, feels so good."

Fingers stroked and teased their way down, stopping to circle her belly button before going further to stroke her trembling thighs and then parting the slip of hair that covered her most private part. Inserting one, then two digits, she allowed them to explore her heat before slipping them out, letting them rub the swollen nub of her clitoris. Her breath came in fast pants and her knees wanted to collapse as her body turned to mush.

"Oh my." The intensity of the orgasm left her stunned and she leaned against the shower wall. When she thought her legs could hold her, she stumbled out of the shower, grabbed a towel and wrapped it around her body, her mind returning to her earlier problems.

Things at the office were pretty normal. Joanne snubbed her and Kyle the Letch made his usual pass. Everything was ordinary except for one minor detail...Galvin. She played it cool and ignored him, but he went out of his way to be nice and not having their usual confrontations made her want to be with him more than ever.

Okay, so she got a little excited when Sam called her into his office. She thought for sure her ass was grass and out on the street. But he only wanted to tell her Leif Moultar said things were going to heat up weather-wise and she and the weather team should be prepared to do storm chases this summer. Now how did he know that? It wasn't like every rich, albino looking station owner knew about weather patterns and storm chases?

"He's weird." Isabella shuddered at the thought of his cold pale blue eyes.

The loud rumbling from her stomach alerted her to the fact she'd not eaten anything since breakfast. If she focused on something other than sexual hunger, maybe her body would cool down. Give it real food to cool desire and tonight's intake wouldn't be ice cream. Enough of stuffing her face with fat calories that only increased the size of her behind.

An inventory of her refrigerator revealed a sad head of lettuce, a shriveled tomato, eggs and a block of cheese with mold starting to grow on one end. Okay, if she cut the moldy end off the cheese and shredded the rest she could whip up an omelet with the eggs. She took a single slice of bread from the loaf she kept in the freezer and ignored the quart of ice cream that called her name.

She devoured the cheese omelet and toast and felt much better. *Now chill out for a while and you'll be fine.* A burp escaped as she pushed back from the table. Laughing to herself, she recalled the burping contests she and Gino used to have as kids and how their mother yelled about them.

She fought to keep her mind off Galvin Haldor since thinking of him fueled her body's need to have his arms around her. *Stop it; don't go there. Get your bathrobe on and find a mindless movie to watch until you can sleep.*

The doorbell pealed strains of *"Are You Lonesome Tonight"* through the apartment as she shut off the hairdryer. "Damn, you Gino. Why did I ever let you talk me into installing that stupid thing?" She never ceased to flinch each time someone came to the door and pushed the button.

Isabella struggled into her bathrobe on the way to the door. She peered through the peephole, which gave her the vision of a shoulder clad in a blue shirt. Keeping the chain in place, she opened the door as far back as it would go.

"So, are you?" asked the visitor through the cracked door.

Holy shit. "Am I what?" Isabella managed to squeak out.

"Are you lonesome tonight?" Galvin laughed at his little joke.

Tomorrow she would kill her brother for the stupid door chime, but for now, she smiled at Galvin's play on the song title. "Why should I be lonesome? I happen to enjoy my own company."

She barley heard Galvin's response through the door. "I enjoy it too."

Isabella's heart skipped a beat at his words.

"Are you going to let me in or do I stand out here and have a conversation with you that we share with your neighbors? The lady down the hall just stuck her head out and I think she's listening."

Crap. Mrs. Lawson has ears Dumbo would envy, Isabella thought as she envisioned her nosey neighbor's ears flapping to not miss a word of what transpired down the hall. "Okay, give me a minute." She closed the door and took off the chain before opening it again to let in her visitor.

"Don't you know anything about manners?" She grumbled when Galvin stepped inside. "People are supposed to call before they show up unannounced, especially at this hour of night...or should I say morning."

"Sorry, where I'm from we don't stand on such formalities," Galvin's blue eyes traveled over her from head to foot. "I have trouble winding down after work and thought you might suffer the same affliction."

"Yeah.   Well, it's frigging one o'clock in the morning and you should've called."   She grudgingly motioned him toward a chair.   "What can I do for you now that you're here?"   *Ooops, bad choice of words.*   She saw the lust that flickered in the depths of his eyes and caused them to deepen to a darker blue.   "I mean, why did you just decide to drop by?"   She saw Galvin pull an item from his pocket.

He studied it for a moment before handing it to her.   "I though you would be interested in knowing where this disappeared to."

Puzzled, Isabella took the dark case from him.   "A video?   What do want me to do with this?"

"You can watch it if you want."   Galvin coughed slightly before he continued.   "You may not need to since you were in the original version, shall we say."

"What..."   It hit Isabella like a hammer between the eyes.   "Oh my gawd, where did you get this?'

"Let's just say a friend thought the record of our Friday night adventure would be something we didn't want splashed across tabloid headlines."

"True."   Relief surged through Isabella and her legs would no longer support her.   She plopped down onto the sofa behind her.   "Oh, my."   Her heart pounded in her ears.   She could think of nothing else to say while she tried to quiet the roaring in her ears. Here in her hands lay the evidence she'd spent many sleepless hours thinking about.

"Feel better?"   Galvin sat beside her on the couch and reached over to massage her neck.

"Much."   Her pulse began to slow down and the

pounding surf in her head subsided.

Galvin's hands were magic. His fingers pushed down the collar of her bathrobe, leaving her neck bare and working on the tension in her shoulders. The pain from the stress of the past few days began to melt as he released the knots across her back with his manipulations.

"I'll give you until morning to stop that." She sighed in bliss.

"If I have until morning for that, how long do I have for this?" Galvin turned her head toward him and his mouth captured hers.

Desire shot through Isabella's body, every nerve ending raw. "Forever," she moaned and leaned against him. *Why, oh why did she want this man so much?*

His lips played along her jaw line, nibbling and kissing. Then his mouth claimed hers again and their tongues fenced, each trying to explore more of the other's mouth, before he withdrew his and licked the outline of her lips.

One of his large hands moved from her shoulders and slid down to her waist and untied the belt holding her bathrobe closed. He laid his body back on the sofa with her pressed on top of him, his erection contained by his jeans, pressed against her bare body. Isabella rocked slowly, enjoying the sensation of little sparks shooting through her.

"Stop. Be still for a minute." Galvin held her hips with his hands to quiet the undulating motion of her against his erection. "Even immortals have limits."

What did he say? Her sex-dazed brain affected her hearing. It sounded like he said something about immortals. The almost constant state of arousal her of body the past few days became more intense and clouded her thinking. God, she needed a real orgasm, not a self induced one.

"We need to get you out of these clothes." Isabella swung her body around to allow room to start the undressing process of the man creating her frustration.

She pulled his shirt out of the tight jeans and with trembling fingers unbuttoned each button. She rejected Galvin's efforts to help with a slap on the hand. His shirt spilled open and Isabella kissed the nipples on his muscular chest, teasing each to a tiny bud.

Her focus then became the belt. Once that obstacle was out of the way she'd gain entry to the compound and her prize.

Galvin reached down, and insisted on taking the needed measure to get the belt free of the buckle and proceeded to unzip the jeans. The boxer shorts he wore reminded her of a tent with a pole in the center, leaving no doubt of the state of his arousal.

Isabella grasped the band of the offending underwear and worked them down over his hips. The weapon on which she'd impaled herself on a few nights earlier now danced before her face. Galvin's fully erect penis weaved before her like a snake responding to a charmer, more impressive than she remembered.

Never being one to turn away from temptation of this magnitude, she captured the twitching organ in one hand and brought her mouth to its tip. Her lips slipped down the shaft to where her hand cuffed the bottom and she willed her throat to relax. She'd given many a blowjob through the course of her dating years, but none of her prior recipients came close to this man in size and she couldn't take in the full length.

'Niccceee," Galvin hissed.

Isabella stopped her efforts and looked up. She tossed back the mass of curls that fell over her face and smiled, glad to have a moment to rest her jaws. "You like?"

"Oh, yes. Like doesn't come close to describing the way it feels."

Speared on by Galvin's remark, she returned her attention back to the pulsing cock in her hand. He bucked when her teeth traced a path back up the route her lips had gone down while her hand grasped the base of the straining sugar stick.

"Enough." Galvin reached down, put his hands under her arms and pulled her toward him. "I want inside of you when I seek my release."

Twisting, Isabella positioned her body and caught his hard shaft between her thighs. "I think you'd better do it soon because I need a little release myself," she bit his lip to reinforce her words.

Galvin lifted her hips and with a sure shot impaled the arrow into her hot depths, holding her in place while he took two deep breaths.

Heaven. Isabella knew she'd died and gone to heaven when he started to move and her body responded with volition of its own. She bit into Galvin's shoulder to muffle the scream that came with her release. The need to bite surprised her. Pain with sex was something she never considered, but she enjoyed putting the bite on him.

Instead of pushing her away, he appeared to welcome her teeth sinking in his skin and he latched onto her ear with his lips, nipping the lobe. Isabella felt his body spasms join hers and they plunged into the brink together.

Gradually, Isabella became aware of a ringing sound somewhere in the room, taking a few seconds to identify it. "Damn, who the hell is calling at this time of morning?" She pushed herself to a sitting position still straddling Galvin and could feel him twitch inside of her. The phone stopped ringing.

"Hope we didn't wake the neighbors. I don't need the condo association ragging on me for disturbing the peace with screams of ecstasy."

Their shared laughter came to an end when the ringing started again. "Whoever it is, they're most definitely persistent." Isabella felt Galvin slip out of her as she lifted off the couch to find out who was so determined.

She stifled her initial response to answer with 'what the hell do you want,' after a glance at the caller ID. For someone from the station to call two hours before the weather shift started meant trouble. "What's up? Okay, I'll be in shortly."

Isabella hung up the phone and turned to Galvin. "I have to go into work. It looks like a major storm is on the way and they're going to need my help in getting out the updates." Not giving him a chance to respond she sprang into action.

If she hurried, she would be at her desk in less than an hour. A blast of wind pushed against the windowpanes in the bedroom as she entered and the window creaked sending a shiver down her spine.

Pulling out the clothes she needed, it occurred to Isabella she had no more idea of what the future held, either for the weather or her relationship with Galvin Holder, than Gino did of getting their mother to accept his relationship with Tom.

CHAPTER 8

Isabella sloshed though the melting hail and stepped into her condo building's lobby. Frank, the doorman, sucked in his protruding stomach to make room for her while he held the door from the inside so he wouldn't get his feet wet.

She leaned against the wall while the elevator took its sweet time to descend to the bottom floor. A glance down at her size nines told her to kiss this pair of Manolo Blahnik heels goodbye. The sexy shoes were made to show off her legs to their best advantage, not to slop though three blocks of slush.

Saturday night seemed a lifetime ago when the phone call from the night crew interrupted the afterglow that existed from a fantastic session of lovemaking with Galvin. The frantic station employee called in the morning weatherman, but insisted Isabella get in as soon as possible. By the time she arrived, reports were flooding in from all over the region of heavy thunderstorms and even a waterspout reported in the harbor. Thank heavens it retracted back up into the clouds before it hit land or caused any major damage to the boats out on the water.

That was strange also, and something nagged at the back of her mind, but she'd been too busy to follow-up on the feelings then and too tired to think about it now.   All her instincts told her Galvin somehow played a part with the things happening, but then again, she did have an active imagination.

Bracing against the hard surface of the wall allowed her to relax just enough for exhaustion to win and she closed her eyes in surrender.

"Ms. Girardi," The doorman held the elevator door open.

"Sorry, Frank. Guess I dozed off." She pushed away from the wall and prayed she didn't fall asleep on the tortoise ride to the eighth floor. The slow elevator system had caused her to hesitate on purchasing when the building's owner converted it from rental units to condos, but a quick check of the real estate market convinced her, slow elevator or not, purchasing was a deal she couldn't pass up.

"Weather's been a might strange the past couple of days, for sure. Must be tough on you." His smiled conveyed sympathy for her plight.

"Strange is an understatement. When was the last time New York City had to bring out the snowplows to clear away three feet of hail?" She punched the magic number that would take her to her apartment and sleep. Momentary regret on buying surfaced as the elevator crept toward her floor, but when she was tired everything irritated her.

Once inside her apartment Isabella started peeling off clothes, dropping them like bread crumbs on the way to the bedroom.

"Ahhh," she exhaled a sigh of relief and stretched her exhausted body under the covers. Sleep, blissful sleep she promised her tired aching carcass.

An hour later Isabella's exhausted brain refused to shut down and she stared into the dark. How could she drift off leaning against the wall while waiting for an elevator, yet here in the comfort of her own bed sleep eluded her? Weather events from the past two days surged through her mind, but the primary reason for not getting to sleep was Galvin Haldor.

He'd gone with her to the station, but he seemed withdrawn. When the camera crew picked up the waterspout and did a live feed into the newsroom, he'd stared at the monitor for several minutes. They all did, though Galvin focused intently. He didn't respond when someone asked him a question and when the swirling dervish pulled back up into the clouds he visibly relaxed.

Odd. A lot of things about Galvin were odd, including her need for him. Even when she wasn't around him, her body craved his touch much like a wino craved the next drink. Visions of his blond hair falling across his forehead into his eyes floated before her. She touched her fingers to hungry lips and remembered the taste of him when his mouth claimed hers.

In frustration, she threw back the covers and padded to the bathroom where the nightlight saved her from facing the glare of the bright overhead lights. The bottle of melatonin surrendered its last pill of the homeopathic sleep wonder and she downed it with a gulp of water from the faucet, not bothering with a cup.

A search though the top of drawer of her

nightstand produced the Rabbit, her tried and true vibrator. Isabella slipped the soft vibrating gel shaft between her legs. It became the hard spear of Galvin's cock sliding into her and the gelled ears were his fingers tickling her clit.

Her daydreams of dominating the situation kicked in and she controlled Galvin and the release of their passion. The orgasm came quick and intense. She turned off the vibrator and dropped it to the floor and rolled over, cuddling the extra pillow against her. Finally, sleep pulled her into oblivion.

*****

Galvin sat at the kitchen table in the tiny apartment he'd chosen to establish his lifestyle in the mortal world. Efficiency was the word the landlord used to describe it and efficient definitely fit. A couch doubled as a bed, a table which you could barely squeeze two chairs around and a minuscule kitchen with a few shelves, a single cabinet, a hot plate on the counter, a sink smaller than a wash basin in the men's room at the television station covered the basics along with a tiny refrigerator that held a day's worth of food.

Humans would find it strange if they didn't receive answers to their questions about his living arrangements and he didn't want to deal with trivial issues such as where he lived. Thus, he rented small and cheap to cover the address information he listed when the Human Resources Manager gave him the reams of paper to fill out. Fortunately, his family contacts were extensive and the information fed back to the HR Department covered voids in his limited earth-bound life.

Turning the waterspout back to the heavens took a lot of effort and he noticed Isabella shoot him a strange look once he'd accomplished it. Distracted by another super cell building to the west of the city she didn't pepper him with the questions he picked up racing through her mind. There were situations in which being an immortal god came in handy, even when he suppressed his abilities.

He needed to center on his father now, not on Isabella. Thoughts of her distracted him from the problem with Thor and his meddling. The Thunder god enjoyed his games and Galvin's profession in this world seemed to bring out his father's competitive streak.

The trip back to Azgard and the halls of his parent's home to talk with his mother didn't produce the results Galvin hoped for. Either Sif had not yet talked with Thor or if she had, then his father chose to ignore her suggestion. Thor's temper and stubbornness were things legends were made of.

"Galvin." Startled at hearing his name called, he turned to find Loki standing beside the refrigerator.

"Do you have any bottles of the water the humans call beer?" Loki buried his head in the refrigerator.

"When did you develop a taste for drinks of the human world?" Galvin studied the Lord of Pranks who stood before him with a disappointed look at not finding the desired beverage.

Handsome didn't describe the deity in either the mortal or immortal world. In his natural form, Loki's black eyes sparkled with mischief when happy and shot fire when angered. The eyebrows perched above the dark orbs always wore a quizzical arch, which drew one's attention even more to his distorted face. The punishment, when chained to three boulders for angering the other gods, did nothing to improve a homely appearance. The venom secreted by a serpent placed above his head left scars. They would have been worse if not for his faithful wife Sigyn who held a bowl over the Sly One's head to catch most of it. Her quick moments of emptying the vessel allowed some of the poison to drip on his skin which has resulted in the red marks he still carried as a brand of his sentence.

From his study of the history of this world they both traveled in now, Galvin read stories comparing Loki to another force of darkness, Satan. Give him a pair of horns, a tail and a pitchfork and the little god could probably pass himself off for the Son of Darkness.

"To what do I owe the honor of your visit, Loki? Did my mother send you with news on her talk with my father?"

"I would think by now you figured out the results of your mother's conversation with Thor. No, I came to tell you of my talk with your father." Loki's eyes clouded for a moment with what appeared to be indecisiveness.

"Yes," Galvin encouraged.

"Like you, I saw an increase in the adverse weather patterns for this area and paid a visit to Sif. She spoke with Thor and much as I anticipated, he did not appreciate her interference. Your mother was very upset and asked if I would try."

Galvin watched his guest investigate the apartment, picking up an item to examine before placing it back and moving onto another as he continued his story.

"Thor appeared in good humor when I came upon him. He spent the morning riding through the heavens on his chariot and practicing his throw of his hammer Mjollnir. Thankfully, for you he chose another part of the skies for this practice." Loki stopped his wandering and held up his latest item for appraisal. "What is this?"

"That is a Palm Pilot. It is used by humans for many things." Galvin laughed at the perplexed look on Loki's face before explaining further. "They keep their appointments there and check what is called e-mail from their computer. Some even use them to talk to each other and send pictures."

"Ahhh. This world is so complicated these days." Loki put the device down. "Now, of what was I speaking?"

"My father spent a pleasing morning and you found him in good humor."

"Yes. Combined with his excellent lunch he was in an exceptional mood. We discussed mundane issues until the conversation worked around to you." The deity paused again.

Galvin watched closely. He understood Loki's hesitation to betray Thor's trust. The Thunder God released him from a slow death decreed by the council of gods and then convinced the other gods to accept him back into Azgard. Then again, loyalty was never

Loki's strong suit.

"Your father resented your mother's plea on your behalf and has become convinced that you are too much of a...what they call in this world, a Mama's Boy. He has decided to test you and see of what you are made."

The attempt to avoid conflict with his father backfired. Galvin realized too late, he should have personally confronted Thor and asked him to discontinue playing with the weather patterns.

"Does my father intend to continue his games?"

"He no longer considers it a game. The opposite can be said now. His intent is to unleash adversity like this area has never seen before. I came to warn you and allow you time to garner your strength to battle him. You will need all you can muster to resist against what he has planned." Loki discontinued his investigation of the objects in the apartment and now paced back and forth.

"He has put on the belt Megingjard to double his already considerable power." The pacing stopped and Loki met Galvin's look. "For this test you will need to draw on all the strength passed to you not only from Thor and Odin, but also any that runs in your veins from your grandmother, the goddess Jord. The heavens will see an event seldom observed and earth will long remember the storms created so that the Thunder God can test his son. Or as the mortals say, 'hold on to your hats, folks, the fun is about to begin'." Loki's laughter echoed through the tiny room long after he disappeared without even a good bye.

*****

Amazing how much better twelve hours of sleep made you feel, Isabella thought as she stretched before throwing back the covers. There'd been no dreams either, at least none she could remember. Fully awake now it became evident a mad dash for the bathroom was needed.

Next, she padded barefoot into the kitchen to fix coffee. While the coffee brewed, a quick search through the refrigerator and freezer netted a frozen bagel, which she popped into the toaster. She'd pick up something more on the way to work.

The toaster dinged its alert and she checked the bagel, once again pushing down the lever to achieve the level of crunchy, she preferred. The carton proclaiming it low fat cream cheese barely contained enough to smear on the top of the toasted bread and she added a glob of strawberry jam.

Inhaling deeply before she took her first sip of the brew, she let the aroma flood her senses. The smell of coffee always titillated her more than the taste.

The memory of her two intense encounters with Galvin sent what was becoming a familiar tingle through her body. She consumed the last bite of bagel and started to choke, her throat closing when her stimulated mind recalled the unprotected sex.

"Dear God in heaven, how could I have been so stupid?" Protection never once entered her mind when Galvin's hands touched her body. The Queen of Protection, dethroned by genitals that developed a mind of their own when a hunky Viking touched them.

"Okay, calm down. You're on the pill so pregnancy doesn't enter into the picture. But, the reason you're always so cautious about using condoms is disease. Consider the source here. This guy didn't seem to be...what? What doesn't he seem to be other than...someone you can't keep your hands off of at any presented opportunity? Shit!" Isabella's good humor and appetite disappeared and she welcomed the sound of the ringing phone.

"Sandy, glad to hear you're still one of the living." They all were dead from exhaustion after the long hours at the studio.

"You may not be so glad when I tell you orders from the powers that be have come down. We're supposed to take a couple of vehicles from the station car pool and head out of town. Looks like there's another storm developing which can lead to some interesting weather according to Sam who got the word from Leif Moultar. It's supposed to make the last one look like a blip on the horizon." Sandy didn't have the usual chipper lilt in her voice.

"How the hell does Leif Moultar know? Since when did he become a weather man?" Isabella bit down on the inside of her cheek to maintain the control she felt slipping away.

"Guess when you own a television station you become a weather genesis by osmosis." The sour note of Sandy's tone let her boss know the weather intern wasn't impressed either.

"Okay. Call in the rest of our team and I'll be there as soon as I can get it together. What does one wear on a storm chase?"

"Go for something practical, especially shoes, and sexy since I'm sure you'll be on camera and don't want to disappoint your male fan base," Sandy giggled.

"Yeah, right. See you shortly." Isabella hung up and ran for the shower.

Surveying her wardrobe while she dried off she pulled out a pair of jeans. "Screw sexy. If I'm going to end up mucking around the countryside I'm going for comfort." She pulled on sneakers and a v-neck tank top over which she tied the matching cardigan around her neck.

"Shit, shit, shit." Just what she needed. To have a man, who could barely spell weather, tell her a major storm was coming.

Then throw in being trapped in car beside a man who takes her breath away during said storm chase and life couldn't get much better. Did she need the closeness of Galvin for hours on end while they bounced around the back roads outside the city? No, not on an emotional level, but she did need to keep an eye on her newest employee and would be in the vehicle that contained Galvin Haldor. Lust factor or not, she needed to observe this man under stress conditions. So far, other than chest puffing with his comments about knowing weather, she didn't see a lot to qualify him to be part of the weather team. It was too bad, because the more she found out about the kind of man he was in other areas; the more she cared about him.

"Damn." This weather forecasting job just became much too complicated.

CHAPTER 9

Isabella glanced over at her passenger who had a death grip on the armrest of the four-wheel drive vehicle they'd received from the station. "You're going to leave indentations if you don't relax. Friend of your father's or not, Leif Moultar will probably charge you for the damage."

"You drive like a mad woman, you know that?" Galvin released his hold and glared at her. "When did you learn to drive...last week?"

"Hey, remember you're talking to a city girl here. I didn't learn to drive until I was in college and my driving instructor was my boyfriend of the moment." She shot a grin at Galvin. He needed to know there'd been other men in her life. "His father also drove Formula I race cars, so guess you could say I learned to drive for a racetrack.

"Which this isn't." Her companion mumbled.

A quick look in the rearview mirror told her the van with all the tracking equipment and the rest of the crew was having no trouble staying with them. Sandy won the toss with the two men for the privilege to drive the white beast at their last stop and Isabella's confidence in the woman's ability to stay with her, proved accurate.

"Sandy doesn't seem to have any trouble keeping up, so it can't be that bad."

"She's as crazy as you are." Galvin glanced over his shoulder. "You two are scary. Both of you have one-track minds when you focus on something and right now it's speed. Do you not...don't you realize you can be hurt if you crash."

This comment earned him a demonic laugh. "Why do you think I like her so much? Hey, if we have to go on this storm chase I want her covering my back. And speaking of storms, we could be injured or killed chasing storms too. When it's your time to go, then poof...you could be hit by a bus while crossing the street." The man beside her needed to learn to relax and live a bit more.

As for Sandy, she may not have her degree yet, but there was a lot more working for her than a piece of paper reflected. She was a quick learner who thought outside the box, something Isabella prided herself on being able to do. If things got tricky, she wanted someone like that backing her.

Galvin Holder didn't prove anything to her other than his ability to make her scream with passion and he seemed terrified of a little speed. As for the rest of the weather team...nice guys, but rigid in their thought process.

"Sandy, what are you guys picking up on Doppler?" Moultar somehow managed to get one of the station's vans completely outfitted for storm chasing in a matter of days. There was even a vortex probe mounted on top. Given the national weather map predictions, the director there would tell Albino

Man the investment in all the equipment was a waste of his money since this region didn't get storms to warrant such extravagance.

The real truth though, the information from NOAA, the National Oceanic and Atmospheric Administration in Washington, DC, where the maps were prepared, could be as accurate as throwing dice. She knew they couldn't be relied on for precision in local areas less than one hundred miles across since the local atmosphere flows changed things drastically. Sometimes she thought they'd do better with a crystal ball or Ouija board.

"Things look good so far," Sandy reported over the static of the walkie-talkie system they were using to stay in communication. "Only a small front showing about fifty miles northwest of here."

"Great, we'll head in that direction." Isabella handed the map to Galvin. "Here, make yourself useful and find what road we need to take."

She appreciated the beauty of the landscape as they made their way in the direction Sandy's group found activity. Growing up in the city, she'd never spent much time immersed in nature. A visit to one of the parks sprinkled like islands through out the miles of steel and concrete was her idea of a day in the country.

"Isabella, things are heating up," Sandy's voice crackled on the communications device.

"Great. Are we heading in the right direction to intercept?" Isabella saw nothing but sunshine and blue skies. Not even a cloud in sight.

"Yep. Doppler indicates thunderstorm activity

intensifying. Right now, it's ordinary storm activity. Nothing to indicate tornado activity. Strange we're only seeing cirrus clouds."

Isabella thought the same thing as she glanced at the thin white streaks against the blue sky. She glanced over and saw a frown on Galvin's face. "What's wrong?"

"Something doesn't feel right." He placed his hand on the ceiling to keep from hitting his head when the vehicle landed after coming over a hill.

"Makes you think of a roller coaster ride, doesn't it?" Isabella said when the SUV set down with a thud after sailing over another of the rolling hills on the road they'd taken a few minutes earlier.

"I would not know. I have never ridden on one of the contraptions." Galvin's voice took on the formal tone Isabella knew indicated his irritation.

"We'll have to take care of that then, won't we?" She threw a grin his way.

"Isabella. Isabella." Sandy's excited voice broke though the static of the walkie-talkie clenched in one of Galvin's large hands.

"What's up?" She hoped only hoped her voice patched through to the van better than the reception she and Galvin received in their vehicle.

"We're picking up a super cell! The probe is going crazy in collecting data and radar looks like a paint ball war with all the colors exploding. You should see something when you crest the next hill."

Chiding herself for being more absorbed in the man in the passenger seat next to her than keeping an eye on the clouds, Isabella cast a seasoned eye to the sky. When had the high, thin Cirrus streaks been replaced by the puffy white cotton ball Cumulus clouds?

They crested another hill and the bottom of the marshmallow forms in the sky came into view, reflecting dark and ominous below the fluffy caps.

"Do we have rotation?" Isabella yelled into the walkie-talkie Galvin held for her. She couldn't detect rotation or a wall cloud at the base of the monstrous storm formation covering the sky in front of them.

"Yes. Rotation is occurring. There's strong upper level winds and swirling lower." Sandy's voice held the same excitement Isabella felt flow though her.

"What do you think?" She asked Galvin as they progressed toward the dark clouds.

"I think we should turn around and forget it." Galvin eyes stayed focused on the sky.

Was he nuts? She'd never come this close to a super cell, not even during the summer she'd spent in Tornado Alley while attending school. Just her luck it was a relatively quiet summer for storm activity and a few insignificant thunderstorms was as good as it got.

"No way. We're here to report on storms and that's what we're going to do." She snatched the walkie-talkie from Galvin's hand. Meteorologists didn't run from their dream come true.

Splats of rain hit the windshield. She downshifted to drop the speed of the SUV and peered at the darkening skyline.

"Galvin, use the camera. Since we're lead vehicle maybe we can get some shots the cameraman in the van won't. I'm going to pull over and we'll do a live feed."

A look of disbelief passed over his face before Galvin silently pointed the small video camera in front of him.

Braking quickly, Isabella barked into the radio, "Stopping here for a live feed. Be ready to roll." She jumped from the vehicle as soon as it came to a halt.

"Let's get your microphone on," Sandy yelled as she bounced out of the van.

Wired, Isabella faced the cameraman while fighting to keep her hair out of her face.

"Change positions," Sandy directed. "We can't see you, just a curtain of hair." She screamed in an attempt for Isabella to hear her instructions over the howling wind. "Here, let's tie your hair back with this." A rubber band fluttered in her hand and she pulled the swirling mass of curls behind Isabella's ears and secured them.

"This is Isabella Girardi, coming to you from outside the city. What you see in the distance is a major super cell. This storm has all the ingredients to produce a tornado which is not an element of nature we see very often in this area."

Out of the corner of her eye, she saw Galvin standing with his feet apart and directly facing the storm. He appeared intent on the horizon; the wind whipped his clothes, molding them to his body. The lock of hair she always wanted to brush back now slicked against his head by a raging blast of air.

Suddenly, things became still. The wind disappeared and the dark sky began to lighten.

"What the..." the cameraman didn't finish his

statement, only shook his head in disbelief.

"Storms around here are really unpredictable, aren't they?" Galvin joined the small group who stared at what were now ominous-looking bubble-shaped clouds.

To the untrained eye, these could look frightening, but Isabella and Sandy exchanged knowing glances. They may get a strong thunderstorm from the Mammatus clouds, but the danger of a tornado was over for now.

"Looks like we're in for rain," Galvin observed with a chuckle. "Shall we call it a day?"

Isabella studied the rumbling clouds before responding. "Let's check out radar, Sandy." The two women headed for the van, neither responding to Galvin's suggestion to head back to the city.

"Good thing we didn't get the live feed to the station she wanted," the cameraman commented as he packed up the equipment.

"If we didn't have a feed why were you filming?" Galvin asked.

"The station was taping to air later, or if we did pick up a funnel cloud they would have interrupted the soap opera in progress. Man, cutting in on one of the soaps isn't something you do without good reason. The switchboard lights up like the Fourth of July fireworks."

"Amazing." Galvin shook his head and watched the two women approaching from the van.

"We'll cruise around for awhile," Isabella announced. "This storm is passing through quickly and I want to see if anything develops after it."

Climbing back into the vehicle she didn't speak to Galvin for several miles. "You know, strange things happen with the weather when you're around. If I didn't know better, I'd swear you're some kind of weather shaman or something." She bit back the nervous laugh that accompanied the statement. Yes, she meant it as a joke, but deep down a part of her wondered.

The scientific part of her brain refuted where the dreamer portion of her mind wanted to go. She was a scientist for crying out loud, not some silly schoolgirl who lived in fantasyland, she told herself.

"Not me." Galvin leaned toward her and grinned. "You must have me confused with the Thunder God, Thor."

"Something like that." Thor, one of the Nordic mythological gods. Sure, he existed and pigs could fly, too. One thing that did exist though was her lack of knowledge on Galvin Haldor's background. "You know, you've never told me where you went to school. Do you have a degree in meteorology?

"I've gone to many different schools and studied various things." He smiled at her. "No, I don't have a piece of paper that says I'm a meteorologist. I know weather though. You could say I trained at my father's knee."

The "I know weather" answer drove her crazy. She fought the urge to stop the car and strangle him. The part about his father was new though. She'd see if he'd expand on that. She cast a hopeful glance in Galvin's direction. "Your father is a meteorologist?"

"He doesn't have a degree on the subject either.

You could say it's a gift he has and chose to share with me."

Interrupted from a response by a squawk from the radio Galvin held, Isabella grabbed it and responded. "Yeah."

She came across abrupt in her one word acknowledgement to Sandy's attempt to reach them, but excused her rudeness because the man beside drove her insane with his cryptic answers to her inquiries. Come to think of it, he drove her crazy on all fronts, but the insanity that possessed her when they allowed their passion to explode fell into a different category.

"Thought you'd want to know we're picking up action again." Sandy lost the last coin toss and was now back to watching radar. "I'm pinpointing the direction now."

Isabella heard the rustle of paper and knew Sandy was checking her map. "Take a left at the next intersection and go about a mile then take the first right. If things don't change that route will take us in the needed direction."

Isabella felt Galvin withdraw into himself as soon as she started to follow Sandy's directions. She didn't have time for his moodiness and turned her attention to the weather ahead of them. The puffy Cumulus clouds built high into the sky, soft and white in their towering mountains while the bottom layer darkened.

"Oh shit." Rotation was visible to the naked eye and she watched in fascination as a wall cloud formed on the bottom, swirling down through the base of the thunderstorm.

"Man, this is like the mother of super cells," Sandy spluttered from the radio. "Damn, there's nothing but red and yellows reflecting on the radar screen."

The raging wind that only a moment before rocked the SUV, suddenly stilled. "Fuck, here we go again," Isabella yelled to Sandy. The stillness was different this time though. Her skin crawled in the eerie light around them, as everything grew quiet.

"Don't think so," Sandy's voice quivered.

The rain they encountered only minutes before turned to pea sized hail. The greenish color clouds boiled like a kettle of water on high heat. Isabella kicked the windshield wipers up to high as the size of the hail increased. A quick glance at Galvin told her he was useless again. *So help me, this is the last time I bring him on a storm chase.* In fact, maybe she needed to confront Moultar on letting him go. It was obvious he wasn't a weatherman and maybe if they weren't constantly fighting over the subject they could work on a real relationship.

"Look to your left." Sandy screamed through the static of the communication device. "Oh my God, look to your left."

A funnel dropped out of the sky and golf ball hailstones slammed the windshield. Isabella juggled the radio in her efforts to hold the steering wheel with both hand and keep them on the road.

Galvin wrenched the walkie-talkie from her and started shouting out instructions to Sandy. "Take the turn we just missed. Back off and get out of here. This is going to get nasty."

"What about you?" Sandy crackled back.

"We will take care of ourselves. I do not need to worry about you, too."

Isabella heard him slip into the formal speech pattern and knew he was agitated. Who the hell did he think he was shouting out instructions to her crew? Too many other things on the plate now to worry about who was in charge. Should she attempt to turn around? Too late. Another funnel appeared and the two swirling masses of debris drifted toward each other, and toward them. The noise level made her want to cover her ears instead of attempting to keep the SUV on the road.

"There's a bridge up ahead," she screamed at Galvin above the roar. "I'll turn around or try and make the cover of the bridge." She could at least buffer them from the pounding hail.

"Are you completely insane? He pressed his mouth against her ear and shouted. "Stop the car and get out. We don't have time to turn around and the last place we want to go is under the bridge."

She stepped on the gas, determined to make it to shelter when Galvin flung his leg across hers and stomped on the brake, stalling the vehicle.

"Damn you all to hell." She turned on him, teeth bared, like a caged wildcat.

"You're always so damned concerned about a meteorology degree. Didn't they teach you in any of those classes about where not to be in a tornado?" He reached across her and pushed on the door, which resisted.

The reality of his statement hit home. In her adrenalin rush, she'd forgotten the training drilled into her years ago. The last place they wanted was under a bridge or a tree.

She threw her shoulder into the door and with their combined efforts; they managed to force it open. A gust of wind ripped it from the hinges and she watched stunned as it flew upward into the darkened sky.

Debris assailed them. "Stay close to the ground. With any luck, there will be a culvert near the bridge. If not, lie down and stay flat. Follow me." Galvin grabbed her hand in his and they made their way along the ditch.

Luck was with them. The culvert stood high enough they could stoop and work their way into it. Isabella found herself glad she'd decided to wear sneakers for storm chasing, instead of the fashionable high heels she normally wore to work.

Galvin pushed her head down and shoved her into the opening where she made her way through the years of accumulated litter and dirt, which the storm turned to mud. Crouched in the mire, she maneuvered around to face the entrance and discovered Galvin wasn't behind her. Scooting back toward the opening, she screamed out his name, only to have the words pushed back down her throat by the roaring wind. The sound reminded her of jet engines out on the tarmac the time she did a broadcast from La Guardia Airport.

Tears stung her eyes, blinding her with the dirt the wind carried. The ability to breathe seemed to have gone, the air sucked out of her lungs. Did the atmospheric change create this or the fear that thundered through her heart because Galvin didn't respond? Did the storm carry him away? No, please God, no.

Suddenly, Galvin appeared and pulled her into his arms and she didn't care that their knees sunk into the muck. "It's okay," he crooned and stroked her back.

The tears that flowed weren't from the eye irritation caused by the storm. She buried her face in his neck and sobbed out the horror she'd felt at the thought of losing him.

The kisses he rained down on her face were softer than a spring breeze's caress and her body's response raged in conjunction with the storm outside. Only the two of them existed in their need for each other. If she could figure out how to get out of her jeans in this cramped environment, she'd add culvert to her growing list of unusual places for sex.

"Listen." Galvin whispered against her neck.

Silence surrounded them and she pressed her cheek against his.

"Did you hear that?" He cocked an ear toward the opening.

"It sounds like someone is calling us? I think it's Sandy." Isabella's face burned in humiliation. Once again, she'd become caught up in her passion for Galvin and forgotten the rest of the crew.

"Come on." Galvin took her hand.

Isabella adjusted her eyes to the blinding sunlight that greeted them.

Sandy, arms extended, rushed toward her and gathered her in a crushing hug. "Holy crap, I thought we'd lost you guys."

The blonde intern turned her attention to Galvin. "We got at least an F5 reading when the two funnels merged. I can't believe you survived a tornado with winds over two hundred and sixty miles an hour. That'll be a story to tell your grandchildren."

A stab of jealously flared in Isabella when Sandy planted a kiss on the lips of the man she now considered hers. They weren't to the point of thinking about children, much less grandchildren. But, maybe it was time to take this man home to meet her family.

"Most definitely. We all will." Galvin winked at Isabella.

"Actually we were pretty safe. We didn't even get close since you told us to take the turn you'd already passed. Storms of this type are really interesting." Sandy's excitement bubbled over. "One minute they're creating mass destruction and the next they're sucked back up into the clouds and the sun comes out. If it weren't for the damage left in their wake, you'd never know they'd occurred."

"Let's hope we don't experience any where the damage is more than trees and a bridge. Thank heavens we were in the middle of nowhere." Isabella's glance fell where the bridge once stood and followed the path of destruction, taking in the uprooted twisted trees on the edge of the meadow. She still didn't believe all of her training evaporated when faced with the chaos brought on by the storm, replaced by her natural reflex kicking in to seek shelter of any form.

"Well, I think it's safe to say you guys will be riding back with us." Sandy pointed in the direction of where they'd abandoned the SUV.   There was no vehicle.

"Can we go home, now?" Galvin asked, sounding like a petulant child.

Moultar will have to get the van detailed and file an insurance claim on the SUV, Isabella thought as she looked down at her mud crusted shoes and clothing. She pulled the blood soaked denim stuck to her right knee away from the skin. When did she cut her knee and what on? Given the mire in the covert, there was no way to tell. A little first aid administration would be in order once she got home. A slip of a dull knife three years ago resulted in a tetanus shot, so she didn't have to worry about that.

She watched the outline of Galvin's face in the fading light as the crew made their way back to the station. He seemed once again lost in thought.

How fragile life could be, she mulled. One minute you have eternity stretching before you and with the bat of an eye or one good breath, your life could be snuffed out. Maybe there were more important things than climbing the career ladder.

With that revelation Isabella Girardi came to the conclusion that family, even her crazy family were more important than she wanted to admit and that someday she'd like to have children of her own.

Now, she needed to determine what part the man sitting beside her played in her life and if the secrets he harbored would affect them.

CHAPTER 10

Galvin faced his father across the wide table. He did consider his decision to confront the Thunder God face to face, not making it in haste. He thought about it on the long ride back to the city and concluded nothing his mother or Loki said in their attempts to dissuade Thor would work. Only he, the Son of Thor, could end the games his father played with people's lives.

"You dare to tell me what to do." Thor's red beard trembled in indignation.

"Yes, Father. I do." Galvin held the glare from the older god. "Your boredom with life here in Azgard gives you no right to tamper with the lives of so many on earth in your efforts to show your son who is stronger."

Lightning flashed in Thor's eyes. "Do you admit my powers are greater than yours?"

Ego was another thing his father did not lack, Galvin knew, but to admit his powers were greater would be a lie. Through his blood ran not only the power of his father, but much from his grandfather, Odin, and his grandmother, Jord, the mother of all creation, thus his capacity far exceeded that of Thor on many levels.

"Father, I concede your control over weather is one of great power, but I feel when challenged as with the storm of yesterday my abilities answered."

Thor toyed with his beard, twisting the red hairs at

the tip of his chin. "You, the youngest of my sons dare defy me? Hmmm. I have always thought you too much of your mother's son to do this."

A glimmer of something Galvin never saw in his father's eyes when they set upon him replaced the lightning. For the first time in his existence, he felt his father respected him. Could it be in part because he managed to turn both storms Thor directed toward him yesterday?

If it were only a matter of the Thunder God playing games with him, it would be of no issue. It went far beyond that when it jeopardized the woman he loved, and he knew her feelings for him were becoming stronger and not based solely on the passion they shared.

He felt her agony when she thought him lost to the tornado and he came to her in the culvert after battling the storm. Yes, he tried not to use his powers when in her world, but his defenses were down after the war he had just waged against Thor. Her pain so strong he couldn't block it.

"Father, can we not call a truce? I realize you are unhappy with my decision to seek a wife in the mortal realm, but I am determined to at least make the effort. Your continued effort to thwart me will only extend my search."

The Thunder God played with the buckle on his belt, Megingjard, as he appeared to consider the words of his son.

"Very well." Thor unfastened the belt and laid it on the table. "I will return Megingjard to its place of safekeeping. Your mother and I only hope you return to your senses soon."

Galvin suppressed the sigh of relief that flowed through him. He would have continued to battle his father if need be, but not having to face the constant challenges Thor threw his way would free him to focus on his quest for Isabella. The decision on when to tell her who he really was also bore heavily on him and if he knew his love, the longer he delayed, the angrier she would be when faced with the truth.

Maybe Thor's agreeing to stop the games did not simplify his life as much as he initially thought.

*****

Isabella stole quick glances at Galvin throughout the day, receiving a wink and a grin when he happened to catch her eye. Man, oh man, could she have used him last night.

Once she got home and washed several inches of dirt down the shower drain, she attended to the cut on her knee. No telling what lay buried in the murky goop in the culvert.

The after effects from such an adrenalin pumping experience left her horny and restless. If he'd showed up at her door last night, she would have jumped his bones in nothing flat.

"Isabella, my office." Sam barely slowed down when he barked out the order on his way by.

"Coming." Isabella rolled her eyes at Sandy and flashed a grin in Galvin's direction as she followed the station manager.

The blinds to the office window were closed and

when she walked in, the ghostly form of Leif Moultar occupied one of the chairs in front of Sam's desk. Barely managing to repress the shudder that ran through her body every time she saw the man, Isabella nodded her head in greeting and took the chair Sam indicated.

"I've just been telling Mr. Moultar about the exciting adventure you and your team experienced yesterday, Isabella. He's very pleased with the coverage." Sam rubbed his palms together.

If he's so pleased why doesn't he say so himself? Isabella pasted a smile on her lips when she looked at the station owner. Iceberg eyes stared back and shivers played down her spine.

Moultar bobbed his head up and down as endorsement to Sam's statement.

Put him in the back of a car window and he'd make a great bobble head.

Isabella clamped down on the thoughts floating through her mind to stop the giggle threatening to erupt.

"Thank you, Mr. Moultar. Is there anything else I can do for you? I need to get back to filling out paperwork for the insurance company on the loss of the station's vehicle."

"Yes."

Isabella waited for him to continue. The silence stretched out so long she started to ask him if he'd be more explicit.

"I think Galvin Haldor's usefulness for the station has ended. You may terminate him." Two bottomless orbs of non-emotion stared at her.

"What?"   Anger bubbled up inside at the way Moultar dealt with employees.   "Let me get this straight.   You want me to fire someone I objected to being hired in the first place?"

"Letting him go shouldn't be a problem since you were against his hiring, then should it?"   The station manager looked down and studied his long slim fingers, flexing each, one at a time.

"I won't do it."   This was the last straw in the games this ego manic played with her staff.   It didn't matter that he wanted her to do exactly what she considered doing yesterday.

"Excuse me."   One of the hairs on his white blonde head may have moved he snapped his head up so fast.

"Now, Isabella, you're the department head and unfortunately letting people go when they aren't working out is part of your job."   Sam put in his two cents in an attempt to placate the situation.

"Yes, I'm responsible for letting people go when I don't feel they're doing their job, but how would Mr. Moultar know if Galvin falls into that category?"

"It does not matter."   Moultar stood up and walked to the door where he paused and turned back to face Isabella.   "Do it."   He dropped his parting words and left without giving her the opportunity to respond.

Rage filled Isabella and red spots danced before her eyes.   She came out of her chair intent on following the man who held her career in his hands and give him a piece of her mind.

"Isabella, no."   Sam blocked her way.   "No.   Sit." He pointed to the chair she'd just vacated.   "Don't give him an excuse to add you to the list."

"It's not fair, Sam."

"Honey, life isn't fair." He leaned against the edge of his desk, looking far older than his fifty years.

Pity tweaked at Isabella's heart. Did he know about the rumors flying around a bout his wife and her co-anchor? Looking at the tired man poised in front of her she hoped not. The station manager was a suck-up when it came to management and maybe a little dull, but overall he wasn't a bad guy.

"Go get it over with. Tell him where it came from if you want to." Sam waved her up and out of his office.

She took her own sweet time in getting back to the weather pod and knew her face was an open book when Sandy looked up and her eyes filled with alarm.

Isabella shook her head to tell Sandy not to say anything. "Galvin, can I talk to you?"

"Sure." Galvin leaned back in his chair, arms folded behind his head.

"Let's go into the conference room." The down side of the open pod arrangement was in a situation like this, when she needed to discuss a private issue with an employee. Locking themselves behind the closed doors of a conference room always generated rumors as to what transpired behind the glass walls. Speculation on the conversations was an office pastime and today they were probably right on.

Galvin followed her and closed the door behind him. "What's up? From the look on your face it can't be good."

"I've been told to let you go."

"Excuse me?"

"You heard me. I don't think I stammered. I have to let you go."

"Go where?"

He wasn't going to make this easy for her and she couldn't blame him. Joking wouldn't have been her way of dealing with being fired though.

"Go wherever you want to go. Just not here." The blank look on Galvin's face told her he wasn't joking. He didn't have any idea what she was talking about. What turnip truck did this guy fall off of?

"Galvin, I've been instructed to fire you. You no longer have a job here at Channel 12."

"Whose idea was it to fire me?" The dark blue eyes deepened and flashes of something that reminded her of lightening zapped in their depths.

"You? This is what you have wanted to do since the first day." He took a step toward her.

"Talk to Leif Moultar, the grand friend of your father. He says you're no longer needed here at the station." She'd just be damned if she would take the fall for this.

"I see." He stopped and studied her, giving Isabella the urge to squirm.

Galvin didn't say another word. He turned and left the office. She collapsed in a chair and fought back the tears that threatened to flow. "Breathe. Take deep breaths and you'll be fine."

When Isabella returned to the weather pod all signs of Galvin Haldor were gone. A stranger wouldn't know he ever existed. Now if only her heart could be wiped as clean as the desk at which he'd sat.

*****

Depression weighed heavy as Isabella made her way home. The spiked designer heels that she normally thought added a little sass to her step, contained lead tonight. Putting one foot in front of the other to make the trip from her subway stop took major effort.

"Good evening, Ms Girardi," the new doorman tipped his hat when he held the door.

Isabella attempted to muster a smile, but didn't venture to remember his name. That took too much effort.

Behind the locked doors of her condo, she collapsed on the couch; the pain acute to the point breathing took effort. She'd had her fair share of relationships through the years and the end of a couple left her sad, but this ache was ridiculous. Open-heart surgery couldn't hurt as much.

The door chimes sounded out the annoying strands of *Are You Lonesome Tonight* and irritating as it was, the effort to go to the door didn't exist. "Go away," she mumbled at the insistent sound.

The ringing changed to pounding as the determined intruder now hammered on her door. In frustration she stomped over and peered through the peephole. Whoever was making the attempt to crash her pity party stood out of her line of vision. She needed to do something about the arrangement of the security feature since this happen too frequently.

"What do you want?" She demanded.

"Izzy, open up. We need to talk."

"Galvin? Galvin, wait a minute." Her hands trembled in her attempt to unlock the barrier that kept them apart. The bolt finally released and she flung open the door.

Galvin didn't wait for an invitation to come in. He pulled her into his arms and pushed the door closed with his foot. His mouth claimed hers and her pulse beat erratically when his hands moved over her body in slow sensuous movements.

"I thought you were gone," she sobbed.

"Never. I needed to think and knew it best if I sorted things out before we talked."

"Are you still angry with me?"

"I was never angry with you. I admit to being upset when you told me, but my anger wasn't toward you." He nibbled her bottom lip. "Do you realize you always chew on your bottom lip when something is bothering you?"

"No." She buried her head in his shoulder; embarrassed her traits were so obvious to others.

Galvin laughed and claimed her lips again and slid his tongue into her mouth. He tasted of citrus and sunshine, igniting the banked fire inside her.

"I came over to talk with you." He pulled away and took her hand, leading her to the couch.

"Not now. Save the talk for later. Use it as pillow talk we women crave after a wild session of lovemaking." She turned and pressed her body next to his.

His strong hands on her shoulders pushed her back. "Are you sure?"

"More than sure." She wanted to drown in the dark stormy blue pools of his eyes.

A mutual reaching had them entwined on the sofa. Isabella paused only long enough to toss the pillows along the back out of their way to create more room.

Clothing became a nuisance. She rolled off the couch and began to tear the offending garments from her body. A glance in Galvin's direction told her he was of the same mind as his clothes flew in various directions around the room.

Maybe they needed to slow down a bit here. Their prior two couplings were quick and passionate, over much too fast. Instead of peeling the blouse off as she originally intended, she pulled it back onto her shoulders.

Her hips started to sway in a seductive manner, slow and easy. The blouse dropped down her golden arms, inch by inch. Free of its confines, she held the silky fabric in front of her, using it for a curtain, which she peeked around before tossing it aside.

Next, the straps on her bra slipped down one at a time. She reached around and unhooked it allowing her full breasts to spill free of their containment. A twirl around her finger and the lacy object landed against Galvin's face where he sat mesmerized.

Then, the skirt skimmed down over her full hips, followed by the panties she wore over a garter belt. The glint in Galvin's eyes led her to believe she wasn't the only one remembering the hot coupling in the elevator. Maybe she'd leave the stockings on.

Isabella strutted toward the couch, hips swaying. Galvin reached out and put a hand on either side of her waist.

"Come here. I have something for you." His voice sounded strangled.

She straddled his legs and eased downward to impale her hot sex on his waiting staff. "Yes, oh yes," she hissed.

Rocking back and forth Isabella quickly found herself on the edge of ecstasy. She paused, not wanting to achieve the ultimate goal just yet. The need to devour him was strong and she could understand why some spiders ate the male after mating. It wasn't out of maliciousness, but from the need to consume, to fill the void left once the act was completed.

"Let's move to the bedroom." Galvin's words were husky with desire.

Isabella slipped off and stood, offering her hand she led Galvin to the bedroom. He stopped her effort to lie down on the moss green comforter, instead slipping his hands around her waist and pulling her hips against his erection. There was no doubt in her mind he wanted her as much as she wanted him.

His hot breath on the back of her neck sent goose bumps flooding across her skin. Strong hands cupped her full breasts and his fingers tweaked the hard nubs of her nipples. The ache was exquisite and shot to her core.

A gentle pull turned her to face him and he eased her down onto the queen-sized bed. A moist mouth now replaced fingers on her nipples as his hands continued to cup her breasts. He suckled and nibbled the pointed tips until Isabella felt close to an orgasm without her female sex being touched.

"Please, oh please," she begged as she guided one of his hands down between her legs.

Wet with the lubrication of her passion, Galvin easily slipped a finger inside her and used his thumb to caress the exposed clitoris. "Galvin," she screamed his name when the first convulsion racked her body.

The spasms calmed to small tremors and Galvin replaced his finger with his engorged cock. She sighed with contentment when he slid into her hot vortex. "Yes, yes. Fuck me hard."

Complying, he thrust into her welcoming pussy again and again. She felt him tense and knew his release was imminent. Her fingers captured his nipples, squeezing hard as he shuddered against her.

"Wow," was the only comment Galvin could make. He cuddled her against him in the crook of one hand and stroked her face with his other hand. "You are amazing."

Isabella buried her smile against his shoulder. Amazing would be him, but let him think it was her.

"Izzy."

"Mmm" Consumed in the afterglow, the hated nickname didn't even bother her. She felt him shift his weight and opened her eyes.

"I am ready to tell you about me." The serious look on Galvin's face caused her heart to lurch in fear.

CHAPTER 11

Galvin watched fear play across Isabella's face. He only hoped it didn't change to disbelief or worse yet, disgust when he finished telling her who he really was.

"Okay." She sat up, her eyes never leaving his. "So, who are you? Or should I ask what are you? A mass murderer?"

Anxiety filled Galvin and the prepared speech he'd put together on his way over to Isabella's grew wings and flew from his mind like a bird. How could he explain without coming across insane?

The mortals of this time period believed the gods of old were legends. Those humans who did hold the ancient beliefs were rushed to what people called a psychiatrist. Some of who, in their infinite wisdom considered the treatment of such an individual a phenomenal way to expand their name in the world they shared with their peers. There were patients who ended up being institutionalized while the so-called doctor plied them with drugs for their delusions and then wrote papers for the medical community to absorb.

Now, he needed to convince the woman he was in love with of the reality of such a world. There were moments, such as this, when being a deity held no advantages. No longer able to still his restlessness Galvin removed himself from the bed in order to have space to move about.

"I know you're going to find what I have to say difficult to believe." He paused and raked his fingers through his hair.

Isabella sat on the edge of the bed watching, her fingers clutching and releasing the sheet, her eyes round with fear.

Galvin dropped to his knees in front of her and took her hands in his. They were clammy with moisture, betraying her anxiousness. He kissed each hand thinking how fragile they felt in his.

"Dearest, I'm not of this world." There. He'd said it.

A puzzled smile played across her lips. The urge to claim them with his almost overcame him.

"Not of this world. What are you saying? Are you from outer space? Don't tell me you're a Martian and you and your people have invaded earth." The idea caused her to giggle.

"Oh, if only it could be explained in such a manner. You would probably find it more believable." Galvin stroked one soft cheek, which created visions of rose petals in his mind. "My history is far more difficult for the people of your world to believe."

Then again, maybe not for all. Isabella and her friends summoned an immortal the night they did the dance and said their chant in the park. Inspired by this memory he decided to remind her of what she wished for that starlit night.

"Do you recall the night you and your friends

decided immortals were the answer to your problem of finding the right man?"

"How did you know that?" Isabella wrenched her hands from his grasp. "Who told you about a night of drunk partying with my friends?"

He could feel her frantic search to recall who she'd shared the details of that night.

"You know one of my friends, don't you." The dark eyes narrowed and the glare she shot in his direction reminded Galvin of a tiger, ready to pounce on its prey.

"No. I do not know your friends. I know of them because of that night." He paused to let his mind decide how to proceed. "Remember the lightning bolt that came down even though the skies were clear?"

"Mona. I'm going to fucking kill, Mona. This is her idea of funny and you're as sick as she is to go along with it. Both of you can kiss my ass." Isabella jumped off the bed and ran over to an antique dresser in the corner. She pulled on a drawer with such effort it landed on the floor, spilling the contents.

"Damn. See what you made me do."

Right, it's totally his fault her temper created havoc and a mess for them to deal with. Galvin repressed the urge to laugh. He didn't think that would help the situation and bent down to help her put the items back. Their fingers reached for the same garment and touched. If anyone asked, he would have sworn a jolt of electricity passed between them.

She snatched her hand back and he continued to talk as if nothing occurred, but in his soul of souls, he knew something did. They'd connected on another level.

"As I was saying, the lightning bolt almost hit you." He admired the bit of lace he held in his hands; sure this was what she considered underwear. The frilly item disappeared when Isabella grabbed it away and threw it on top of the pile she thrown into the drawer.

"I believe you made a statement to your friends about standing a better chance of being struck by lightning than meeting an immortal." He pushed her aside when she tried to pick up the cumbersome item from the floor to insert back into the dresser. "It would appear you have better luck meeting an immortal than being hit by lightning." He finished the task and looked over at Isabella. The opening and closing of her mouth reminded him of a fish out of water gasping for breath.

"You see after my father hurled the bolt of lightning toward your feet, he then decided I should enter the mortal realm and encounter your acquaintance." By the powers, how easy it was to fall back into the formal speech patterns of Azgard.

"Your...your father?" Isabella wouldn't be too pleased to know her skin matched that of Leif Moultar, Mr. Albino as she called the call the station owner.

"Yes. My father is Thor, the Nordic Thunder God. He is of the world your people refer to as mythology. My mother is the goddess Sif. She dabbles in fertility, but I believe your world delights in her problems with Loki, the Lord of Tricks, when he cut off her beautiful hair." Galvin watched the changing emotions flit across Isabella's face...shock...fear...disbelief and now anger. "Believe me that little incident put what you would call 'a damper on their friendship.'"

"Yeah, right. You should give up on the weather job and focus on your true calling, Galvin. The world could use another Stephen King. Your tales are almost as good as his."

"You doubt me?" He knew to convince her of the truth would take effort, but her mind had closed to the possibility that what he told her was real.

"No, of course not. Then again, my size twelve ass fits into a pair of size two jeans. You believe that, don't you?" Laugher exploded from her perfect lips and tears streamed down her face as she cradled her sides with her arms.

Annoyance put a defensive edge in his voice. "I can prove what I say is true."

*****

Isabella decided she'd fallen asleep when she got home and was dreaming. This was a dream, which contained not only hot sex with the man who stole her heart, but his confession as to his real identity. Of course, the fact the man in her dream turned out to be a pathological liar probably centered on her need to put a stumbling block in the way of her growing feelings for him.

The only way she could accept what was happening here would be if she were dreaming, not really on her way to some mythological world with a guy who claims he is a Nordic god. Her mind just wasn't ready for that.

Yep, her mother would love to hear about this one. She could hear the conversation now. *You see, Ma, I've never fallen for any of the guys you've tried to hook me up with because I fill my nights with a Nordic god traveling into the heavens.*

"Be careful." Galvin caught her before she fell when her heel caught in the crack between blue and green on the rainbow bridge he assured her led to his home. They were off to meet the parents over Bifrost; the rainbow bridge he declared was the only way to access Azgard, the citadel of the gods.

Yeah, right.

When he'd asked her if she'd heard of Azgard, she'd drawn a blank. The mention of Valhalla jiggled a small memory from the mythology she loved in English classes back in her high school and college days. Still, as much as she enjoyed the studies she really didn't have a very good recollection of what was covered and that's what made this dream so odd. Everything she pictured far exceeded the small memories she was able to bring forth.

Before them, a city came into view. Large mansions dominated the valley that spread out below. "Beautiful," she gasped and hugged herself in disbelief at witnessing such beauty.

"The large one on the right," Galvin pointed to an imposing structure that dwarfed the others in comparison, "is Valhalla, where Odin, my father's father resides."

"Impressive." Hell, if she was going to deal with weird dreams they may as well be good ones and this place dwarfed anything she'd seen in the Hamptons. She couldn't envision any of those places having what might have been spears on the roof.

"First we will go to Bilskirnir where my mother and father reside. I think you will like my mother."

Great. He thought she'd like his mother, but didn't voice the same about his father. What was he, an Ogre?

"Here we are." Galvin came to a halt in front of a huge palace.

"Well, it is large." Isabella eyes took in the multi-leveled building in front of them. The special effects in this dream were a little on the over-kill side. She flinched when a flash of lightning lit the sky over the house and the loud booms of thunder shook the ground under her feet.

"Yes. Odin, my grandfather, has said there are five hundred rooms here, but even so it is small compared to the halls of Valhalla where he lives."

"Nothing like outdoing the neighbors, even in the citadel of the gods," Isabella said as she thought of the competition in grandiose homes between some of the celebrities and billionaires on earth.

"Come." They entered through the huge doorway and proceeded down a long hall.

"Lord Galvin, how good to see you again," greeted a stick man.

"Thank you, Thialfi. Can you tell me where I may find my parents?"

"Your mother is in her sitting room doing needlepoint and your father is out in the skies practicing with Mjollnir." Stick Man bowed and faded back through the open door from which he'd appeared.

"Mjollnir?" Galvin didn't mention that name

before. "Is that another one of your relatives?"

"No. Mjollnir is my father's hammer. That's explains why there was so much lightning when we arrived. I should have suspected." He saw Isabella's puzzled frown.

"Thor uses his hammer to create lightning. Less tiring than directing it with his hands, which he does occasionally. Come let us find my mother."

The hike to locate Galvin's mother must have been at least a mile. Isabella regretted her shoe selection by the time they entered a richly furnished room. If she'd known they'd be walking for miles she would have opted for flats.

Various shades of gold and white assaulted her eyes, even down to the woman seated by the window in a flowing white gown with hair the color of pure gold.

Intent on the hoop stretched with material in her hands, Galvin's mother didn't look up. Isabella stood mesmerized watching the needle flow in out of the fabric, pushed and pulled by the elegant, slender fingers.

"Mother." Startled by Galvin's voice, Sif looked up from her work.

"Galvin." The needlepoint dropped on the table beside her. Delight reflected in her face as she came forward to greet her son. Her expression turned to confusion when she saw Isabella standing beside him. "Who do we have here?"

"This is Isabella Girardi, Mother. I have told you of her."

Sif extended her hands with the grace of a queen,

or would that be goddess, Isabella wondered as the golden woman grasped her hot, sweaty palms in her cool, dry ones.

"Isabella, I am delighted to meet you. I have heard of you and your family from Galvin and from Loki."

Alright. I can understand Galvin telling his mother about her, but why the other guy?

"Nice to meet you, too." She felt as awkward as teenager meeting the parents of her first real love. What did one say to a goddess...hey, your son is great in bed. No, if she kept telling herself this was a dream, it didn't matter what she said.

"You have come a long way, my dears. Come, you must join me for tea." Sif clapped her hands and Stick Man materialized at the door. "Thialfi, would you be kind enough to have tea sent in for us."

"Yes, Goddess." The thin man bowed and took flight, reminding Isabella of a dragonfly. All he needed to complete the effect was wings.

"Loki shared with me your family came from the land over which Zeus rules." Sif patted a spot on the white love seat on which she perched where Isabella assumed she wanted for her to sit. Galvin selected a gold and white striped chair, obviously designed for a much larger person because the size was so out of proportion to the other furniture in the room.

The servant retuned with a cart bearing a bone china tea set and a stack of delicious looking goodies. Isabella's mouth watered as she watched him plate éclairs dripping with chocolate frosting. He poured three cups of tea and handed them out and set a plate of baked goods by each person.

"Tell me more about your family," Ignoring her dessert, Sif placed her delicate china teacup on the table in front of the love seat and faced Isabella.

Where to begin? Galvin's mother didn't come across as a one whose only focus in life was to get one of her children married and have them get on with expanding the family tree. The Goddess wouldn't appreciate her son being involved with someone who came across as out to snare her precious boy. No, she didn't want reveal too much information about Angela. Her mother's determination to have her daughter married would terrify the mother of any male, no matter in what realm they lived.

She also couldn't tell the elegant woman sitting next to her about her cross-dressing, gay brother since she was unclear on how the Nordic deities handled that little matter. Gino would appreciate the tasteful décor of the room where they sipped on exotic tea and nibbled on tiny pastries. Though he would probably find Sif's taste in clothes expensive, but non-stylish. Isabella couldn't envision him in the flowing toga style dress the older woman wore. Then come to think of it she'd never imagined him in yards of billowing pink chiffon, either.

No, she'd not even shared these tidbits about her family with Galvin. It would probably be better to disclose information of this sort to him first. Wait and see where things went between them. If got to the point of permanent she'd have to fess up, but she'd cross that bridge when she came to it.

Sif's lovely brow furrowed slightly while she

waited politely for Isabella to speak.

"I come from your average Italian-American family. My parents are both first generation Americans who met when they were very young and produced my brother and me. They came from large families and have lots of brothers and sisters, who in turn have produced lots of children of their own. A family get together with my family is more like a party...a very loud party." God, she sounded like the voice over on a documentary.

"How lovely." Sif's eyes appeared to have glazed over.

"Mother, you can relate if you compare it to one of Odin's events at Valhalla." Galvin sat quietly sipping his tea and listening.

"I see. Yes, that could get very noisy." Understanding illuminated the already glowing skin. "I also believe you have a grandmother who enjoys *Ride of the Valkyrie.*"

How in hell did she find out about Nonna? She and Galvin never discussed her family. "Well, yes. The family finds it a little strange; her favorite piece of music is by a German composer about Nordic gods since she's so adamant everything else in her life be Italian." Then again, most of what Nonna did, Isabella found odd.

"That is also one of my favorites." Sif's guileless blue eyes met Isabella's. "This makes me feel a connection with one member of your family."

Wonderful. Just what she needed. The mother of the man of her dreams making a connection with her loony grandmother. The two of them huddled in a corner at family functions would be a hoot.

"I have yet to meet Isabella's family, Mother. Let us get through that formality before you start making plans to become acquainted." Galvin winked at Isabella in a show of support.

"Tell me about your father." The queenly woman continued her probe, but she hit on a subject that was safe.

Other than herself, Isabella considered her father the only sane one in the family. "My father's a great man. A good husband," his adoring glances at Angela flashed though her mind. "He's also a great father." She would never be able to repay him for all the battles he headed off between her and her mother. "And —"

Loud voices from the hall interrupted her train of thought.

"Thor has returned." Sif sprang from her seat and rushed through the door toward the increasing sound of men talking.

"How lovely you look, my dear." A deep male voice vibrated off the walls.

The murmur of Sif's soft response could be heard, but not loud enough to decipher the words.

"Our youngest son has honored us with a visit." The rumble moved closer to the room in which she and Galvin sat. Relief flooded her heart when he vacated the chair where he lounged and took the place his mother vacated, beside her on the love seat.

"Everything will be fine." Galvin bushed her lips with his and took her hand. "Remember, it is as you mortals like to say, his bark is worse than his bite."

Isabella nodded to let him know she understood

what he tried to tell her. They both rose to their feet when the approaching voices entered the room.

"My husband, come meet Galvin's friend Isabella."

Isabella looked up at the mountain of a man before her. His strong face was covered by a fiery red beard and lightning bolts sparked from the dark blue eyes, Galvin's eyes. He smiled a crooked smile through the forest of hair and cocked a bushy flame tinted-eyebrow. Isabella knew through a flash of intuition that this man didn't approve of her and any relationship with his son would involve a battle of wills. Fear touched her very soul and she glanced at Galvin, wondering if he was worth what lay ahead for her.

Please, please, if she could wake up and find this was a dream, life would be so much easier. A little voice inside her whispered, "This is no dream, Babe."

CHAPTER 12

Galvin admired the ease with which his father drove his chariot. The goats that pulled the Thunder God's favorite mode of transportation, Tranngrisni and Tanngnost, had been in Thor's service for so long they needed little direction.

When Thor made the suggestion after the tea they shared with his mother and Isabella to take a ride, Galvin knew his father was up to something. Now he waited, letting the older deity bring up whatever was on his mind when he felt ready.

"Let us stop here." With a slight tug on the reins Thor commanded the goats to put down on the highest point of Thrudheim, the region in which he, the Thunder God lived and probably knew better than the back of his hand.

Alighting from the chariot Galvin followed behind his father and took a seat on a boulder next to the one chosen by Thor. Together they sat in silence and viewed the mansions below them.

"My son, you have proven your strength and powers with our recent games and I am proud of you."

"Thank you, Father."

"Now, if you will only apply the wisdom you have inherited from your grandfather, Odin and be done with this foolish venture to seek a wife in the mortal world." Thor turned and skewered Galvin with an intense glare.

"Father, I do not feel my desire to marry Isabella foolish."

"*You dare—*" Thor stopped and lowered his voice. "You dare to say marriage with a person beneath your status is not insane."

"You of all people should not throw stones, Father. How would Grandmother feel if she heard your statement? After all, Jord is Mother Earth, mother of all creation. Do you think she would approve that her son thinks her creations are beneath him?"

"I do not feel they are beneath me. I do not look down on them because they do not have our powers and unlimited lifespan, but nor do I do feel they are our equal."

"Their strength lies in the way they use their minds." There were times his father's narrow mindedness made it difficult to control his temper. "Look at the things they have invented to make their lives easier and they have increased their longevity with discoveries in medical research."

"It is granted they have made progress in some ways, but what of the horrible weapons of war and destruction they have created? Never mind." Thor didn't give Galvin opportunity to respond before he continued. "What I am saying here about mortal women is they are for dalliances, not marriage. If you do not believe me, ask your grandfather."

Raised on tales of Odin's exploits into the human world, Galvin didn't think that would be necessary.

Grandfather's promiscuous ways didn't stop with mortal women, either. Look at Thor, the result of a liaison with the Earth Mother, not to mention his various other mistresses in the immortal worlds. Odin's appetite for sex was one of the reasons Zeus didn't invite him to Olympus very often. The Greek god didn't want the competition.

"That will not be necessary." Galvin was ready to end this conversation and collect Isabella for the return trip to her world, but a question did occur to him. "Tell me, Father, why have you not indulged in the salacious activities of your father?"

Thor puffed out his mighty chest. "There have been encounters, but I chose to keep them within our world. Also, I love your mother and find no other female to equal her, in or out of bed."

Love. Yes, he could see that between his parents even now. His mother gentled down the giant man who was quick to anger when things didn't go his way.

"There is a story about your grandfather I wish to share." Thor shifted on the boulder to face Galvin.

"Not really necessary, Father. I have heard the tales of Odin's conquests since I was a child. It is the talk of Azgard when nothing exciting is taking place. The morals Grandfather displays would earn him a title such as Alley Cat in the human world."

"That may be so, but there is one story you need to hear that is not repeated often because few know. Loki shared it with me."

This should be good. Galvin settled back on the boulder, resigned to what was to come. If the Lord of Tricks told a story, it would have his embellishments to it and who knew what would be true.

Once again Thor turned to look out on the valley below and gather his thoughts. "In the not distant pass, Odin made one of his visits to Mount Olympus."

He must have caught the look of disbelief on Galvin's face because he laughed and shook his head. "No, it was not like that. Sometimes Zeus does invite him. On this occasion a council was called of all the head deities of each realm and Odin was included."

Galvin laughed. "You mean Grandfather didn't just show up and invite himself to stay as he's been known to do."

Thor shook his head and continued. "Odin took Loki with him, probably as a source of entertainment because he knows how testy Zeus becomes over his women when Odin takes an interest in one.

'The meeting drew on for several days with the gods arguing among themselves. Poseidon, the sea god took offence to several things and wanted to wage a war of words."

"What upset him to that extent?" Galvin asked.

"It is of no matter now." The Thunder God waved the question away. "After several days of listening to Poseidon and Zeus argue, your grandfather decided he needed a change of scenery and went down from Mount Olympus into the hills outside of the city called Rome, which, though further away, Odin preferred over Athens.

"Loki assumed the form of a falcon and soared in the sky, while Odin took his favorite mortal shape of a Nordic male with a patch to cover his bad eye."

"That reminds me." Galvin shifted his position on

the hard boulder. "How does Grandfather control the blaze from his good eye when he wanders among the mortals?"

"It has something to do with assuming another form," Thor shrugged and then continued with his story.

"While walking through the hills he came upon a young girl. Her beauty took his breath away and he spent the next several days wooing her.

'The council ended, but Odin could not bring himself to leave. He extended his stay on Mount Olympus."

"Zeus probably loved that." Galvin knew the opposite would have been true from what he'd heard about other visits.

"He probably did not care of much. You see, my father spent his time with the woman. They walked the hills outside the city, hand in hand. Odin told her stories of Valhalla and Valkyries. He shared any thought that came to his mind with her.

'The day came when Odin found his new love in tears. When he questioned her to discover the cause, she told him her parents entered her into an engagement with a man formerly from Rome. He went away to America to make his fortune and returned to his home city for a wife. Their wedding was in two days and she was going to America.

"I'm sure Grandfather was relieved in not having to end the romance."

"No. That is the point in sharing the story with you. Your grandfather fell in love with this young woman. Not only was she beautiful and intelligent, but her disposition was sweet and her humor brought him great joy.

'The engagement to one of her own made him realize it was for the best. If he took her back to Azgard it would not matter. She would be a mortal living out of her element and would age and die well before him. He could not bear to have her grow old in front of his eyes and watch her pain when he did not age. He sent her back to her family and the arranged marriage."

"Not to mention that your stepmother, Frigg, would not have been too happy with his keeping a mortal woman in her world." Galvin smiled when he thought of Frigg's reaction to such an event.

"Yes, Frigg can be difficult at times, but she tolerates Father's mistresses. Odin has never forgotten the young woman though. In his heart of hearts he still loves her. Each year on the earth date she married he locks himself away and plays that tune your mother enjoys, *Ride of the Valkyries*."

"What was her name? You did not include that in your story, Father."

"Her name? What does it matter? Loki says Odin calls for Pia when he has consumed too much of the wine of the gods." Thor shrugged his shoulders in dismissal.

"That was a good tale, Father. Thank you for sharing."

"Did you learn nothing from it?" Thor's face flushed, showing signs of temper.

"I learned that possibly Grandfather is not the complete lecher I always assumed he is."

"You were to gain the insight that when you fall in love with a mortal it is best if you leave them and return to your own kind."

"The times are different now. I chose to enjoy as many years with the woman I love as permitted. Her lifespan will be longer than a mortal of so long ago.

"It was the near distant past, not centuries ago." Thor's voice started to rumble.

"How long ago is that?"

"In human terms not many more than sixty years."

Galvin whistled. "Wow, I am impressed. The old man still has it in him."

Thor clenched and unclenched his massive fists. "All of the gods who rule their realms still have their abilities with females. How do you think mortal women would experience great sex? It is a deity's duty to share this gift with them if he so chooses."

*****

Isabella watched the two men closely when they returned. Galvin originally declined his mother's invitation to stay for dinner, but Sif's insistence won out.

Sitting now in the huge room used for dining, Isabella felt dwarfed by the immenseness of the furniture. This room and the other rooms used on a regular basis appeared scaled to Thor's size and taste. Much too masculine for her choice, with all the trophy heads and dark massive furnishing that all the rooms held. The only space in which she was comfortable was the original one in which they met Sif. She would take the goddess' elegant gold and white décor any day over the rest the rest of the place, bursting with testosterone. *Did furniture have testosterone?*

"More mead," Thor demanded of Thialfi as the servant scurried to serve the sixth course of what appeared a never-ending dinner.

Looking at the latest offering placed in front of her, Isabella felt her stomach object. A strange creature stared up at her with one eye. Was this some kind of fish? If so, she had no idea what, with its spinney back and small gills that almost seemed to move. *Damn, this makes sushi look well done.*

She watched the gusto with which Thor consumed each course. How could anyone eat so much? He even asked for seconds on a couple of items. Of course he was a big man, or god, and maybe a huge appetite went with the territory. Though she noticed the portions served to the rest of them, especially Sif, were considerably smaller. Did old deities turn to lard like old football players once their career ended and the only exercise they got was pushing away from the table, Isabella wondered.

Toying with her food, she finally convinced herself to take a bite. The flavor wasn't too bad, but it consistency reminded her of a rubber band.

"Would you care for something else, dear?" Sif smiled encouragingly. "Ladka is a delicacy, but an acquired taste even among the gods."

"No, thank you. The flavor and texture are somewhat like octopus, which I've eaten before. Do we have many more courses to go?" Please say no, Isabella silently pleaded.

"Only another four." Sif indicated with a wave her hand to have her plate removed. "After the last course, we shall retire to my sitting room for an aperitif as I believe you call it in your world."

"Wonderful." A ten course meal, her extended family's idea of a good time, but she decided in her early teens stuffing herself to explosion wasn't for her. Isabella plastered a smile on her lips and motioned to have her plate taken away. Not only would she leave here stuffed to the point of agony, she would be falling down drunk to boot.

"More mead," Thor thundered again and a harried Thialfi hastened to accommodate.

"Mother, mortals do not eat the way we do. They usually stop at five courses when they have a large meal." Galvin stepped in to try to explain why Isabella picked at each course.

She flashed him a grateful smile and inwardly groaned as another plate was placed in front of her. At least this looked familiar and chicken was lighter than another round of beef or wild game.

"Mortal woman, you insult me by not eating the food presented." Thor glared from his end of the table and drained another tankard of brew. He slammed down the empty vessel and this time Thialfi was ready. He removed the pitcher placed on the sideboard only a short while ago and refilled Thor's cup before he made a demand for more.

The urge to tell the deity that he more than made up for her lack of eating appeared out of nowhere. Isabella bit back the retort. "I'm sorry if you feel offended, sir, but I am not able to consume food on the level you do."

"Nor, do you know weather the way I do." Thor's directed his scowl only at her.

"Excuse me, but I have a degree in meteorology which I worked hard to earn. I also have several certifications that can only be obtained by meeting stringent criteria."

The Thunder God waved away her defense with his right hand. "A piece of paper does not mean anything of one's knowledge. Look what you did when I threw a small lightning bolt in your direction the night you and your drunken friends were dancing in the park."

"I jumped. It was totally unexpected as there was not a cloud in sight." Isabella felt her cheeks flame at the memory of the drunken night with her friends that resulted in her being here now. All right, she admitted to herself this wasn't a dream, but she now thought maybe she was losing her mind.

"You ran like a scared rabbit." Thor chugged down more mead. "I cannot understand what my son sees in you, a mere mortal." He twirled the mug in front of him making it impossible for the hovering servant to refill it. A mean smile spread across his face.

That did it. Isabella's back went ramrod straight. "I ran like a scared rabbit because getting hit in the ass with a bolt of lightning is not my idea of a pleasant evening."

Sif cleared her throat and reached across the table to pat her gently on the hand. "Tell me my dear, how will you deal with age?"

"The way anyone else deals with it." Where was

the inebriated idiot going with this? Isabella wondered.

"Is that so? Does everyone wake up and peer in the mirror each morning and see age staring back at them, only to look across the table into the eyes of someone who has not grown a day older?" The grin became evil as he waited for her response.

"Father, enough." Galvin jumped to his feet, knocking over his chair in the process.

"You know what I say is true." Thor stood and faced his son. "She will grow into a wrinkled old crone of which you will have to take care of until the day she dies."

"Do you wish to inflict this on my son?" His glare now focused on Isabella.

She saw Sif hang her head; the curtain of gold hair hid the beautiful face. She obviously chose not to enter into the disagreement between father and son. Well, so be it, but she'd just be damned if she was going to sit here and listen to the old man's abuse.

Enough of this nasty tempered deity's comments. She rose from the table with all the dignity she could muster and tossed her napkin beside her plate. "Galvin, I'm ready to leave… with or without you."

Turning she faced the god. "You. You're a pain in the ass who is definitely too impressed with himself. And you eat like a pig on top of it. I hope I never lay eyes on you again." She felt Galvin's hand on her elbow and it gave her shaking knees the strength to walk toward the door, but she didn't move fast enough to miss Thor's parting words.

"When you die, my son will return to his world and take a wife who is more his equal and they will rule here on Azgard."

*****

"Husband, I feel you may have overstepped your boundary tonight." Sif rose and walked down to the end of the table where Thor sat slouched in his chair.

"I did not say anything that was not the truth."

"Agreed, but you have driven our son that much closer to the mortal." The goddesses' soft blue eyes pooled with unshed tears.

"I only hoped to save him pain." Thor hung his head.

"He loves her. The only way to save him the pain of her loss would be if she is given eternal life." Sif placed her hands on the massive shoulders. "Possibly, we should talk to Odin. He may be able to arrange something."

"The only way my father could grant her life in this realm would be as a Valkyrie."

"What exactly is required in order for one to become a Valkyrie?" She hoped it was something simple, but in her heart knew if that were the case, then becoming one of the formable female warriors would not be such an honor.

"It takes the courage to give up one's life for another and I do not think Galvin's mortal woman has the courage required. Besides, only Odin knows the full requirements, and he's not bestowed that honor in centuries." Thor placed his cup on the table and patted the hand on his left shoulder. "Let us go to bed. There is no need to discuss this with Odin or among ourselves. We can only hope the powers intervene and end our son's foolishness."

CHAPTER 13

Isabella couldn't stop the pounding of her heart and clutched Galvin's hand as they walked up the steps to her parent's house. This would be the first time she'd brought a man home to meet her family since high school. Back then, she followed the rule that any boy she dated needed to come to the door to pick her up and then go through the question and answer session her mother devised.

"Nervous?" She asked Galvin as her hand reached for the door handle.

"No. Are you?"

"Damn straight and you should be shaking in your shoes. Wait until my mother is finished with the inquisition. You'll think your father was a pussycat. Then there's my grandmother. Nonna doesn't approve of anything or anyone who isn't Italian." Isabella rolled her eyes in indication of how much she dreaded what lay ahead.

Her fingers touched the doorknob and the door flew open of its own accord. "Give your mother a hug." Angela held her arms open in greeting and swooped down on Isabella quicker than a bird of prey on its victim.

"And this must be Galvin."

Isabella felt herself released faster than she'd been hugged as her mother turned her attention to the man who stood quietly behind her just inside the entry.

"And you must be Isabella's mother. I can see where she gets her beauty." Galvin flashed the same smile that always took Isabella's breath away and watched her mother's similar response.

"Come, come, and meet the rest of the family." Angela took Galvin's arm and led him toward the living room.

Rest of the family? What the hell was her mother talking about? The only family that was supposed to be here was her parents and Nonna. They couldn't very well exclude the old lady since she lived here, though Isabella would have loved to have done just that.

Following behind Galvin and her mother, who clutched his arm as if he was her new best friend, Isabella saw several of her uncles and their wives. She fought the impulse to strangle her mother. Should have known better, she thought sourly. Angela wasn't able to resist the temptation to show off to her siblings that Isabella actually was interested enough in a man to bring him home.

Thank heavens it was only her mother's siblings and their spouses, not the army that would be waiting to greet them if both sides were included.

Nonna took her duty as family matriarch seriously and sat waiting for homage to be paid. After the aunts and uncles made themselves known, Angela led Galvin over to her mother. It reminded Isabella of a lamb being led to slaughter, but he was a big boy, not to mention a Nordic deity. If he couldn't handle one scrawny Old Italian lady, then he'd better turn in his god like powers.

"Mama, this is Bella's boyfriend." Angela's voice almost trembled with pride at getting to link the boyfriend word to her daughter's name in the same sentence.

Resigned, Isabella stepped forward, mentally prepared to receive an ass chewing in Italian. She knew her grandmother wouldn't appreciate the introduction to a blond Viking god. If the relationship went anywhere it could pose the possibility of diluting the family bloodlines with this new culture.

"*Buono sera, Signora* Piccoli." Galvin bent over and took the hand of the old woman in his and kissed it.

A slight smile tugged at one corner of the normally down turned mouth and the dark pools in her narrow face sparkled. "You be the smooth one, don't you."

"I try." The Viking dropped to one knee.

The light from the lamp by her grandmother's chair picked up the red and copper streaks in the gold hair, causing Isabella to catch her breath. She could understand when Nonna's hand reached out to touch the head of flame with the same reverence she showed her favorite treasures.

Isabella watched something unspoken pass between the man she loved and the old woman she'd feared most of her life. They each nodded their heads slightly as if to confirm a mutual understanding.

The old woman moved to stand and Galvin did a nimble leap to his feet and helped her from the chair. "You done good, Bella." Nonna reached out and patted her cheek.

Shock didn't come close to the feeling that ran through Isabella as she accepted what amounted to her grandmother's blessing. She couldn't remember a time when the old woman approved something she did, so easily.

"Bella, you come help me in the kitchen?"

Repressing the urge to groan, Isabella saw the looks that passed between her mother and aunts and followed Angela into her domain, the aunts hot on their heels.

"Your young man, he's very handsome." Angela started out with the seal of approval on Galvin's eye appeal. The aunts bobbed their heads up and down in concurrence.

"So, tell us more about him." Her mother prodded. "You didn't say much when you called to let us know the two of you wanted to stop by."

Obviously enough that you got on the phone to bring in reinforcements. No, she decided it was probably better not to mention that little detail.

"Where is he from? What's his family like? Have you met them? You need to tell your mother these things." Leave it to Aunt Rose to cut to the chase.

Isabella didn't think her family was ready for the full story here and spent the time on the subway deciding how much to reveal for now. If things led to a long-term relationship and...she swallowed hard...the M word...she'd worry about it then. Sweat pooled in her armpits even thinking the dreaded word, let alone saying...marriage..., caused her heart rate to increase.

"He's not from around here." That wasn't a lie. "He's from further north." Okay, now that fell into the tall tale category.

"Canada?" Her mother piped in.

"Yeah, around there." All right, she'd just moved into complete fabrication.

"Have you met any of his family?" Once again, Aunt Rose stuck her nose into things. If she'd shut up then Isabella would be able to distract her mother from this line of questioning with an abbreviated version without so many lies.

"I've met his parents."

"And?" Angela motioned with a hand for her daughter to continue and not leave the women hanging.

"They're interesting." Now that definitely was an understatement if she ever made one. "His mother is blonde, tall and slender and very elegant." That did cover a fairly accurate description of Sif. "Oh, and she does beautiful needlepoint."

"Sounds kinda boring and snooty to me." Aunt Rose, never one to hold back an opinion, even if it was a wrong one, put in her two cents.

Her mother shot a withering glance toward her sister-in-law before she continued the questioning. "What's the father like?"

"He's big." Try mountain size, Isabella thought. "He has red hair and a full beard."

"Is the beard red too?" Angela's frown told Isabella her mother didn't think too much of the beard idea.

"Yes, the beard is as red as his hair, but it goes

well with his blue eyes."   Eyes that flashed with lightning and intimidated the crap out of her.

"Nice." Angela pasted on her social smile. "When do we get to meet them?"

All right, enough was enough here. Time to get the record set straight. Things would have to get a lot more serious between her and Galvin before they brought the two families together.

"I admit I'm interested in this man, but listen everyone," she scanned the faces that watched her in anticipation; "we're not to the point of bringing the families together. Our relationship's still very fragile and I don't think it would help to introduce the relatives to each other.

From the bewildered look she saw in each pair of eyes staring at her, Isabella decided to change the subject. "Where's Gino? I expected you would have forced him to come tonight, Ma."

"He said he was busy and will meet your friend later." Angela scowled as she ladled meat sauce into a large bowl. "Here, Rose, you take the pitcher and go pour the water for the table." She set the large spoon down and pulled out a large glass water pitcher and shoved the container at her sister-in-law.

"The rest of you make yourselves useful and take the food in." The sisters-in-law scurried to do Angela's bidding, emptying out the kitchen until it was only Isabella and her mother.

"I want to ask you about Gino." Angela placed a hand on her hip and stared at her daughter.

"What about him?" Uh oh, this line of questioning could spell trouble for both her and her brother.

"Has he got a girlfriend?"

Isabella fought to keep a straight face. "Not that I know of, Ma."

"Something's fishy. Every time I call him to come over for dinner, he tells me he can't. He's already got other plans." Angela's lips puckered in distaste. "You think he's getting in deeper with that Joey DeBenedetto? Are your father and me going to get a call in the middle of the night to come get him out of jail, or worse yet telling us he's dead?"

"I don't think things are to that point, really Ma." Damn. Caught in the middle of her brother's secrets wasn't good thing and didn't make her happy. But, she it wasn't her place to break the news to their mother her baby boy was a cross dresser with a new roommate...his gay lover. Angela was going to have an absolute shit fit when she found out. The meddling matchmaker would probably have a heart attack when she discovered she was the one who introduced them. "Ma, I think you just need to ask Gino what he's up to if you want to know so badly."

"I do, but he doesn't answer me. Maybe I'll stop by and see him and we can talk."

"Ma, I think you should give him a call, not just drop in. You know how much he hates that." Wouldn't it be the pits if she stopped in unannounced and received the surprise that greeted Isabella the Sunday she went over without calling first?

Oh well, I'm not going to worry about your brother tonight. I'm just going to focus on my Bella and her young man." Angela pinched her daughter's cheek. "Come on, you're neglecting him. We'll feed him good Italian food and he'll be asking you to marry him before I can get the wedding planned."

"I don't think you need to start planning a wedding yet. I just thought before things went any further Galvin needed to meet the people who are most important to me." If he could handle her crazy family then she could come to terms with his mother whose hair was of spun gold and his father whose idea of a good time was to hurl lightning bolts at unsuspecting mortals. Her situation didn't sound so nuts after all compared to his.

Yes, there were a lot of obstacles for her and Galvin to overcome and she still wasn't completely convinced once the passion died down, the relationship could survive.

*****

Isabella still couldn't believe how well Galvin and her grandmother hit it off. Her mother, she fully expected to fall all over him and her father without doubt would accept him with good humor, but Nonna?

By the end of the evening spent with her immediate family, with the exception of Gino, and some of the extended family it became obvious that Galvin and Nonna were thick as thieves. Galvin spent a lot of time talking with the old lady in her native language.

Okay, she shouldn't have been surprised that a Nordic deity, who spent time on Mount Olympus with Zeus and the Pantheon of gods that lived there, would speak the language of the land over which his godfather ruled.

A surge of relief filled her when she reached her desk and put her purse away. She would be forced to think about something other than her personal life.

"Afternoon, boss. You look glowing today." Sandy arrived and handed her one of the iced mocha frappuccinos she juggled. "Have a good weekend?"

Isabella took the beverage and stuck her tongue out at the perky intern. "It was a good weekend." If only Sandy knew how good, she'd never hear the end of it.

After dinner with her family, she and Galvin spent the rest of the weekend at her place, and most of that time in bed. They were becoming one of those couples she hated. The ones who cooed at each other constantly like a couple of lovebirds, with their own private jokes the rest of the world wasn't privy to, and she loved it.

"Hey, Sweet Cheeks," Kyle came around the corner into the weather pod. "What happened to your Viking stud?"

How she hated the leering smirk on the anchorman's face and nothing would give her more pleasure than to wipe it off with a fist to his row of perfect pearly whites. Then again, being arrested for assault wouldn't help her career or personal life so she fought the temptation.

"Guess it was time for him to move onto greener pastures, Kyle."

"Not what I hear. A little bird told me he got canned...by you. Bet that broke your heart when word came down from the powers above, huh?"

Isabella could imagine the little bird who told him. Damn Joanne. She didn't have to share information her husband would have told her in confidence. The stupid bitch needed to keep business out of the pillow talk she indulged in with her co-anchor after one of their passionate encounters.

"I don't have a heart, remember." If looks could kill, the little worm would be dead. "Sandy, I'm off to do my spots for the radio stations. You know where to find me if you need anything." Isabella gathered the maps and forecasts on her desk. "Excuse me." She none too gently elbowed Kyle out of her path of retreat.

Waiting for the elevator to take her up another floor to the engineering room gave her the opportunity to daydream more about Galvin. A smiled played around her mouth, remembering the confined trip in this very car a few weeks earlier, in which they finally gave into their passion.

Someone slammed into her, waking her from the daydream. "Whoa, Sam. Where are you going in such a rush?"

"Can't talk right now, Isabella. Have you seen my wife or Kyle?"

"I left Kyle over in the weather pod and I haven't see Joanne all day." She looked closer at the station manager. "Are you okay?"

"Yeah, great."

His flushed face didn't support his affirmation, but Isabella thought it probably best not to dig any deeper and continued her journey up another floor to the engineering room.

"Hi, James, did you find the video I wanted?"

The chief engineer reached for a videotape that lay on top of a stack of magazines. "Sure did. Didn't you get enough of tornados last week with what you went through?" James handed her the cassette.

"We lucked out. These poor people didn't and I guess I have survivor's guilt. Watching this can help me focus on how fortunate we were and how little decimation really occurred with our adventure." She had caught glimpses of the devastation on the news, but wanted to fully appreciate her own good fortune and figure out some way to help those less fortunate.

"Thanks, James, I'll get it back to you tomorrow."

"No rush. I got a copy if a need comes up. Let me know if you want anything else."

A wave to the engineer brought a grin and she made her way back downstairs.

The newsroom seemed quieter than usual. It reminded her of an anthill, each of the worker ants going about their business making sure they didn't get in each other's way. No one looked up to check out who entered their space.

"What's going on?" Isabella tilted her head toward the rest of the room and the people hunkered down over computer screens.

"I'm not really sure," Sandy said. "I came back from checking out something in the studio and it was like this. Pretty eerie isn't it?"

She could say that again, Isabella thought. She never heard so much quiet in here, even on weekends there was more activity.

"Isabella." She jumped at hearing her name shouted and turned to find Sam standing in his office doorway. "In here. I want to talk to you now."

"Okay." Dread inched its way through her. Isabella didn't like the sounds of this; afraid of where it was leading.

She shot a questioning glance at Sandy and headed toward Sam's office. Along the way she noticed how people seem to withdraw more into their space as she passed. *Good grief, was she getting the ax today?*

Sam shut the door behind her and closed the blinds. Close inspection told the story of a man who appeared close to the end of his rope. The flushed face that concerned her when they bumped into each other as he came off the elevator was now pale...too pale. His eyes were red rimmed and bloodshot and his mouth looked like it forgot how to smile, the corners pulled tightly down.

The picture of Joanne and her flunky storming through the office flashed in her mind. Did his wife ask for a divorce? Come to think of it, Sandy said Kyle didn't show up for work.

"What's going on Sam? You look like shit." Her efforts to get a smile from her boss only caused more pain on his face. He hung his head for a moment before responding.

"I need to ask you something and I want the truth. From everyone else I get a line of bullshit, but I trust you enough to expect an honest answer."

"Okay, I'll do my best." Dread snaked its way into Isabella's stomach. A part of her knew what was coming and she really didn't want to answer a question that would only cause more hurt.

Sam squared his shoulders and looked her in the eyes. He took a deep breath and then plunged ahead. "Did you know that my wife and Kyle Mason were having an affair?"

CHAPTER 14

The trip over the Rainbow Bridge wasn't intimidating this time. There was no illusion of dreaming and she knew some of what awaited her. Isabella strolled along with her arm linked through Galvin's and allowed herself to appreciate the beauty around her. She loved the glow of colors reflecting up from the path. They gave a hue to whatever passed on that strip of walkway. Glancing in Galvin's direction, she saw he glowed yellow, changing into blue the closer that part of his body came to hers. For the most part, she was blue with shades of red appearing on her left side.

"Did you tell your grandfather we were coming for a visit?" She squeezed his arm in happiness. This time she wouldn't miss out on anything in her attempts to convince her logical mind she walked in a dream as she did on her first visit.

Her senses took over, deeply inhaling the jasmine that bloomed in profusion and she laughed in delight when a butterfly perched on her shoulder, going along for a ride.

"No. I decided after your encounter with Sam you needed a diversion."

He knew her so well. It was as if he could read her

mind at times. When Sam asked if she knew about the relationship between his wife and her co-anchor, she told the truth. Yes, she heard rumors, but never witnessed anything intimate between them.

From the pain in Sam's eyes, he must have caught them in a passionate embrace. Overhearing, a snippet of office gossip didn't create that kind of pain. He'd turned his back then and told her to leave before she could say anything else.

When she left for home later in the evening, she saw lines of light around the closed blinds of his window and knew Sam was still there. She'd hesitated in front of his door and raised her hand to knock and make sure he was all right. Instead, she'd turned and left.

"I know you've seen Valhalla from a distance, but up close you get lost in its splendor." Galvin stopped them in front of the most impressive building she'd ever seen.

"Wow." The word may have been inadequate, but it was the only one that came to mind as her eyes traveled over the various openings and what appeared to be spears jutting from the roof. "How many entrances does this place have?"

Warm breath caressed her ear as Galvin explained. "There are over five hundred doors to various halls. We will enter the one guarded by the wolf."

"Oh." She took a step back as they approached a large entryway. The wolf sat upright on his haunches and pulled his lips back in what looked like a smirk.

"It's okay. He's only trying to intimidate you." Galvin tugged on her arm.

"And a damned good job he's doing too." She allowed her companion to lead her forward until a big blob of something landed with a splat at her feet. Looking up she saw a huge eagle perched over the door.

"Shit, and I do mean shit. That eagle almost got me."

"Another form of intimidation. Come." Galvin pulled her through the opening, pausing only long enough to pat the smiling wolf.

"Good heavens. What goes on in this place? Doesn't anyone ever pick up after themselves?" She tripped over a breastplate and kicked it to the side to join the others scattered over and under the benches that lined the hall.

"This, my love, is where the Valkyries bring those who have earned a position here through their courage."

"Valkyries? I thought they were myths." It occurred to her, until recently she also thought Nordic gods were myths. "Never mind. Dumb comment."

Taking her hand in his, Galvin led her toward a room at the end of the hallway. "Let's go find my grandfather, Odin."

Reaching their destination, Isabella studied her surroundings. Not exactly her taste. Other than the room in Galvin's childhood home his mother claimed for herself, the houses in this realm seemed to consist of large bulky furniture. They must all have the same decorator she mused as she took in the dark wooden chairs and tables. Then again the wood did give warmth to the marble floors and the ceiling...good

Lord...the ceiling consisted of what looked like shields.

"Galvin."

Isabella turned to see a stunning woman enter behind them. This was one of the most beautiful women she'd ever seen. Her beauty equaled or surpassed that of Galvin's mother Sif. Beauty was the only similarity with the gentle blonde goddess. It was obvious with the way this woman moved she enjoyed power and she wouldn't hesitate to use.

"Freya." Galvin bowed from the waist in greeting and took the outstretched hand offered to him. "I did not expect this honor." He applied a kiss to the strong hand he held in his.

Impressed with the ripple of muscles, when Freya extended her arm, Isabella found herself consumed with a fit of jealousy. She'd kill to have biceps like that and even with busting her ass several times a week in the weight room at the gym, hers didn't come close. *Guess there's something to be said for being a goddess.*

"I am sorry to say you have missed your grandfather. Odin received word from Zeus he needed him to come and discuss an issue of some importance and for once he took Frigg with him." Freya fingered the necklace that hung between her breasts and appraised Isabella.

"Who do we have here?"

Under the focused attention of the goddess, chills ran up and down Isabella's spine. Would it be impolite to ask where the bathroom was? She clinched her thighs tightly together in the sudden need to pee. Just nerves. Relax.

Relief flooded through her when it appeared

Galvin sensed her nervousness and came to stand at her side.

"This is Isabella, Freya. Her beauty has captured my heart just as yours captured Odin's when he made you Queen of the Valkyries."

Oh my god. That was the sweetest thing she'd ever heard and if he didn't shut up her tears would flood the place.

"Our Galvin has always been known for his silver tongue among the ladies here in Azgard." Freya tipped her head in acknowledgement of the compliment.

"Freya is my grandfather's favorite Valkyrie. None can compare to her in courage and strength, or beauty."

Nice to meet you seemed an inadequate comment to make to one of this status. Shit, she was as important as the Queen of England and Isabella didn't think she'd feel nearly as nervous meeting the queen. Then again, she wasn't looking to have an on going relationship with any of that queen's sons, but wait, Galvin wasn't Valkyrie Queen's son or grandson. If she remembered correctly the woman was only a mistress of Odin's.

"I'm honored to meet you." There that sounded a little better, she hoped.

Her tense body finally registered the fact that one of Galvin's hands massaged her shoulder. The tight sensation in her neck began to ebb away. She resisted the urge to throw her arms around him in gratitude.

"Galvin, would you do me a favor?" An urn materialized in Freya's hands. "Would you go milk us mead from Odin's goat, Heidrun?"

A slight bow of his head indicated his consent to the assigned task and Galvin took the vessel from the goddess.

"Please remember to bring honey for mine." Freya winked. "You know Valkyries prefer Honeyar to plain mead."

"How could I forget, but for the life of me I shall never understand how such fierce warriors can drink such a sweet brew." Galvin dropped a soft kiss on Isabella's lips and whispered, "Later, my love. I shall return with drink for all of us."

"I, in the meantime, shall show Isabella the halls of Valhalla. She can get a glimpse of how the gods live. Come, my dear."

Following behind, Isabella swore the woman's feet never touched the cold marble. The goddess glided over the floor, which caused her to feel like she was stomping out a forest fire with her plodding steps, as they made their way through the vast building.

Freya picked up the knife that lay on a table and pricked the end of her finger. A nod of her head indicated she found the sharpness to her liking and she smiled at the tiny drop of blood from the wound. "Forgive me, if I am forward."

The tour ended back in the hall where it began and Galvin wasn't back. Isabella wished he was because something told her this conversation was going nowhere fast, at least from her point of view.

"By all means. Speak your mind." *Just remember, two can play this game.*

"I find Galvin's fascination with a mortal most interesting and difficult to understand." The Goddess of War pursed her mouth in distaste. "He has always been a favorite among immortal females in all the realms. What is special about you? I see nothing of importance."

Open-mouthed Isabella stared, unable to respond to such rudeness. Granted, the woman did have a point. There was nothing special about her when compared to women with the powerful abilities that existed here. Still, if rudeness of this level was accepted behavior, then someone better snag an etiquette coach from earth to teach a course on manners.

I'm going to take this bitch out if she says much more and that may create a few issues if I do end up in this family of nuts. Oh hell, who was she kidding? There was no way she'd be able to put a mark on the arrogant bitch.

"There is also the death thing." Freya wrinkled her nose in distaste at the idea of dying. "You will die and he will not. What does committing to each other accomplish, as it will be for him, such a short commitment?"

The two adversaries looked up at the sound of approaching footsteps.

"Of all of Odin's grandchildren, Galvin is my favorite and I do not want to see his pain. Consider what I have told you, my dear." The goddess glided forward to greet her lover's grandson on his return.

"Sorry it took so long. It appears with Odin gone, Heirdrun is not being milked of mead on a regular basis and I felt compelled to relieve her of all she possessed. What did I miss?"

He looked baffled when the two women

exchanged dark glances.

A slight smile played across Freya's lips. "Nothing, dear. As the women of earth would say, just girl talk."

*****

"Ouch, stop it Galvin. That hurts." Isabella pulled away, objecting to the nip he'd given her ear.

"How about this?" He grabbed the retreating woman and laid her across his legs. Without thinking, his hand contacted against her bare bottom. Caressing the smooth skin on the luscious ass before him, he gave into the urge to apply another smack.

"Oh." Isabella wiggled pushing her posterior up, making it more accessible.

"Like that, do you?" His cupped palm came down again. Her skin glowed pink from the administrations of slaps to her shapely derrière and his cock twitched in response. What started as a game to discover the truth of Isabella's conversation with Odin's Valkyrie now became a turn-on for both of them.

Why did he start spanking her? This wasn't play he indulged in with previous lovers, but turning her over his knee was something he'd wanted to do often and not in passion. The woman frustrated the hell out of him at times with her stubbornness and then her quick sense of humor delighted him just as much.

"Are you finished?" She twisted away. "I was beginning to like this game."

"I've only just started." Pulling her beside him, he captured her wrists in one large hand and held them above her head. Looking down at her exposed nakedness he lowered his mouth to claim hers.

"Ouch. What the hell did you do that for?" Galvin pulled back and licked his bottom lip where she'd bitten.

Isabella grinned. "You're not the only one who can play the pain game." She tried to pull her wrists free. "Are we going to continue playing games, or are we going to make love."

Galvin studied her flushed face and leered. "Making love to you is a game. The best of games."

He freed her hands as he lowered his head and kissed the plus point throbbing at the base of her throat. "Ummm, you taste so good." His lips traveled down her heaving chest, licking and nibbling until they reached the hardened peak of a nipple. He rolled the nub between his teeth and suckled gently.

"Yes, oh yes." Her hands dug into his hair and pressed his mouth closer. "More," she demanded when he lifted his head to move to the other side.

The attention to that breast generated the same response of moans and words of encouragement to continue. Heat from her hands seared through his clothes in her efforts to remove them.

Galvin stood and finished the job she'd started, shedding his clothing in a heap beside the bed. His cock throbbed and danced in anticipation of what lay before him. He stopped and admired the woman he loved with all his heart. A finger reached out and played with the patch of hair on the mound above her entry. He enjoyed the lack of hair on the rest of her womanhood and stroked the silky smoothness.

Desire knifed through him when she licked her full lips and then ran her tongue around the outside of her mouth in what he was sure was an invitation. *No.* If he accepted the offer, it would be over in a matter of minutes. Even a deity had limits and she pushed him to his.

"Come." Isabella held out her arms and he moved alongside her.

He was done with games now. All he wanted was to touch, feel and taste the goddess beside him. She may be mortal, but her body deserved worshipping more than any he'd seen in the immortal realms.

Lust consumed him and he lowered his head and kissed her long and deep. The need to slip inside her drove him to push her legs apart. His fingers caressed the slit between her legs and luxuriated in the warm moist heat he discovered. One finger slipped into the opening, then two.

She writhed in response and a low groan told him he succeeded in finding her G-spot and he tapped the rippled area with the tips of his fingers. Muscle spasms clinched his inserted appendages and she screamed out.

"Now, Galvin. Now. Get inside me."

More than happy to accommodate her demand, he plunged his engorged penis deep into her waiting well. Pausing to allow time for his passion to level, he felt her fingernails dig into his butt cheeks. That was all the encouragement needed and his testicles tightened and he exploded as wave after wave of release coursed through his body.

He slid down beside her and pulled Isabella's still

pulsing body against his. "Maybe I should spank you more often." He nuzzled the back of her neck and tightened his hold on her body. The inklings of longing threaded through him and his cock twitched against her backside.

Loving her again would be ideal, but he wanted to know more about what happened when he went to milk the goat for its mead. The return from his realm was not like the fun, relaxed trip to get there.

Isabella was distracted and at times withdrawn. Contrary to what Freya said, he was sure the two discussed something, which upset the woman he loved. He hoped her defenses were down now as she basked in the afterglow of their lovemaking.

"Tell me, what was the girl talk you and Freya didn't choose to share with me?" He felt her stiffen and try to pull away.

"Nothing."

Pulling her closer he inhaled the scent that was uniquely Isabella; sunshine and fruit on a warm summer day. "If it is nothing, why have you become upset?"

"Okay." She tugged away from him, pushing his arms to release her. "It was pointed out to me once again, how different things are in our worlds. You..." her bottom lip trembled "you are an immortal who never ages." A tear slid down one cheek and she pushed his hand away when he tried to wipe it off. "And me, I'm a mortal. Not only is my lifespan short, but I will age before your eyes."

"This does not matter." The speech pattern so ingrained in him surfaced, causing him to sound stiff and formal. "I love you and I know you love me. My life is not forever. Immortals die, too."

"Yeah, just not at the same rate." She gave a sad little smile and stroked his cheek. "I don't want to create more heartbreak for myself when you grow tired of the aging woman you wake up to each morning and go back to your world where the bloom of beauty never fades."

"It will not be like that between us."

"How can you know? Have you ever loved a mortal before?" She kissed him softly and slipped from the bed. "I'm going to take a shower."

"I'll join you."

"No, I'd rather be alone. I need to think." She closed the door behind her and he felt her heart shut down as surely as he heard the click of the door's lock.

CHAPTER 15

"Look, my dear. Our son honors us with his presence. Do you think he has returned to his senses and realized this is where he belongs, not pursuing a woman of earth?"

Thor paused in his chess game with Loki and watched as Galvin walked across the room to greet his mother with a kiss on the cheek. "What makes you think that, Father?

"You come without her. Surely, this is a good sign." The carpet of red that covered the deity's chin jutted out at a stubborn angle.

"Checkmate." Loki's demonic eyebrows lifted and he returned a grin for the glare shot in his direction by the Thunder God.

"How dare you move your piece when I was distracted?" Thor's visible facial skin color now matched the hairs that covered the rest.

Loki spread his hands and shrugged. "It would have made no difference if you were watching, I would have won."

Galvin laughed. "I think he has you there, Father."

"Bah." He pushed up out of the chair. "You did not answer my question. Have you left the woman on earth?"

"I did leave Isabella to go to her work. I will be there when she returns." Galvin delayed in what he came here to tell his parents. Neither of them would be happy with what he was about to say.

"You paid a visit to Freya?" Loki gave up in his attempts to entice Thor into another game of chess.

"Yes. I took Isabella to meet Grandfather, but neither Odin nor Frigg was there. Freya was in charge."

"You did what?" Indignation seeped from every pour of Thor's body. "You did not tell me you planned this. Taking this mortal to meet my father was inappropriate."

"How so, Father?" Galvin knew the only thing wrong with the visit to Valhalla was that he did not seek Thor's approval in consulting Odin.

"Odin has no time to waste on one of your passing fancies." Lightning flashed in the depths of Thor's eyes as he took a menacing step toward his son.

Sif came to her husband's side and placed her hand on his giant arm. "Please. Do not start this battle of wills again."

Looking at his mother's hand on the huge appendage reminded him of a spider's web restraining a bumblebee...one small strand holding back the flight of the larger insect.

"I will not engage in such a battle with my father, Mother. Do not fear." Galvin picked up the needlepoint his mother laid on the table beside her chair. The scene showed Thor in his chariot pulled by the goats and streaks of lightning flashed around them.

How ironic that his mother was so wrapped up in her husband's world it even consumed her needlepoint. He laid the fabric hoop back on the table.

Turning, he faced his parents and saw his mother was now sandwiched between Thor and Loki, the three presenting a united front. "Actually, I have come to tell you of my intentions and to find out how to accomplish something I wish to do."

"With your powers, there is not much you do not know how to do, Galvin.' Loki spoke the thought he saw reflected on the faces of the other deities.

"True. But, I am going to make Isabella my wife. My life is nothing without her." Inhaling he continued. "There is one thing though I have not been exposed to." Galvin met his father's stare. "I wish to know how to renounce my powers. I wish to become a mortal."

*****

Galvin was gone when she woke up. The smell of him lingered on the pillow and she clutched it to her, inhaling his scent.

Not having to go into work until late afternoon, Isabella huddled under the covers, pretending the pillow she snuggled against was Galvin, until the need to go to the bathroom won. Pushing away the comforter she took care of business and plodded her way through the living room, determined to make coffee. Her lethargic body resisted each step but she succeeded in reaching the kitchen.

She watched the coffee brew. If only her life could

be pushed through a filter and cleaned up. Why did she have to fall in love with an immortal? He'd not even bothered to tell her goodbye when he left. Awaking to a kiss would have been a nice way to start the day instead of cuddling a pillow that still held his scent.

It was probably for the best. This gave her aching heart a little longer to avoid the words she knew she needed to say. Their relationship was over. Intense pain knifed its way through her at the thought of never seeing Galvin again.

Good grief, woman, if it hurts this much now think how painful it would be later when he grows tired of you. Why would he want to spend his days watching you age. Face it; you're no spring chicken as it is.

Tears mingled with the coffee she poured into her favorite mug. The splashes of red, purple and yellow on the cup did nothing to lift her spirits as they usually did when she drank from it. The coffee tasted salty, but no wonder given how hard she cried.

The ring of the phone interrupted her pity party. "Hello." Her voice sounded as dead to her ears as she felt inside.

"Bella, is that you."

"Yeah, Ma." She waited for her mother to disclose the reason for the call, not really caring.

"Bella, I need you to come over here...now." The anxious tone in Angela's voice penetrated the fog in Isabella's brain.

"What's wrong, Ma? You sound upset." Her mother spent a great deal of her time being upset, but she learned to tell the difference between a true problem versus the Angela created ones.

"It's best you come over and we talk, Bella. I need to talk to you before Gino gets here."

Biting back a groan, Isabella agreed. Wasn't her life bad enough right now without having to help her brother keep up his front to the family? She wasn't up to Angela's inquisition on what her Gino was up to these days.

"Oh, and Bella. I think it's best if you come alone. This meeting is just for the women."

"No problem, Ma." That presented no problem at all. She'd probably spend the rest of her life going alone to family functions and anywhere else she went.

*****

"That's the story." Angela twisted the shredded tissue in her hands and looked over at her daughter.

Her mother had walked in on Gino and Tom making love. Not a pretty picture for sure and to have Aunt Rose there...well it was safe to assume everyone else in the family knew something strange had happened. Now the speculation was on.

"I'm so sorry, Ma." Isabella never saw this side of her mother. The woman in front of her appeared broken, not the strong force to contend with she usually presented. Was the strength just a front? Could her mother have insecurities and fears like everyone else?

She watched Nonna reach over and squeeze Angela's hand. "It will be okay, Assai. You wait and see."

Life was becoming much too complicated. Angela

didn't fall apart and Nonna didn't express concern. Isabella felt her world turned upside down and on top of that, her mother called her over here to share her pain when Isabella could barely deal with her own.

"Tell me, Bella. Did you know?"

Did she know what? Did she know her brother was really gay? Well, yes. He'd confided in her when she came home for Christmas break her freshman year of college.

Gino waited until he moved out of the family home a few years later, before sharing the news to their parents for the first time. Though that didn't make any impact on their mother, because she considered it a phase he was going through.

Did she know about his relationship with Tom? Well, yes to that one, too. Even afflicted with blindness, she couldn't have missed that there was something between the two of them the day she showed up unannounced. Must be a gene passed along to the females in the family...this showing up unannounced.

"Did you know about Gino and Tom?" Angela's tissue became a ball of tattered pieces, which she rolled around between her hands.

Should she lie? Isabella hated her mother putting her on the spot like this and sifted through her mind for an answer on how much to tell. The doorbell saved her from saying anything.

"That will be Gino." Angela stood and tossed the wad of tissue in the trash on her way to answer the door.

Isabella slumped down in her chair. The makings

of a migraine played around the edges of her vision.

"You got problems, Bella?" She forgot Nonna remained at the table with her and the kindness in the old woman's voice shocked her.

"Yeah." She sighed and knew how bad things were when an almost irresistible urge to lay her head in her grandmother's lap came over her. Saved by the sound of voices coming toward the kitchen Isabella decided a hug for her brother would be the smarter move to make here.

Her mother's face broke her heart when the woman came into the room ahead of Gino and Tom. Good heavens, what was Tom doing here? Gino had really lost his mind bringing his lover.

It was a good thing their father wasn't home. Pop was an easygoing man, but the one thing that got him riled was seeing his wife upset. He worshipped the ground his Precious walked on and anyone who caused her pain, answered to him. That would include his son. She only hoped their mother got herself more under control before Pop arrived.

"Sis." Gino leaned down and buzzed her cheek. "So, you're part of the planning team now."

He looked tired and haggard and even Tom's pink complexion was pasty, causing his freckles to stand out even more.

"No planning team, little brother. Ma just wanted to talk." Part of her felt their mother got what she deserved. It probably was the only way Angela would accept what Gino tried to tell her over and over for the past several years. He is gay.

"Gino. I'm trying to accept this, but it is not easy

for a mother."

He reached across the table and squeezed her hand. "I know, Ma. I only wish you didn't find out this way. I was going to tell you, but I wanted a little time to make sure Tom and me worked out." A sympathetic glance at Tom earned him a crooked smile. "Tom isn't ready to go around broadcasting it either. This is a first for him. His folks don't know."

Angela sucked in her breath at that piece of news. "Your parents don't know you're gay?"

"I'm still adjusting to the idea, myself." Tom laid his hand on top of Gino's and Angela's. "Please, Mrs. Girardi, don't say anything to my dad if you keep the appointment with him next week. Let me tell my parents in my own way."

Pulling back her hand from the two men, she got up and began to move around the kitchen putting cookies on a plate and taking down cups. "Maybe by the time your parents find out, I'll understand better." Her bleak smile didn't relay much promise of that happening.

"Nonna, what about you?" Gino focused on the elderly woman at the end of the table. "Have I brought shame to you, too?"

"Gino, I never said you brought shame to me." Angela set the plate of cookies on the table with a loud plop and cast a glance at her mother.

"Maybe you didn't say the words, Ma, but your actions scream it loud and clear."

Angela hurried back to get the coffee without responding.

"No, grandson, I feel no shame. The path you

have chosen has been a part of our people's history longer than some religions." Nonna's claw like hands reached out and snatched a cookie from the plate. "You must make the life you will be happy with." A little smile played across the old woman's lips. "I ask your mama if she thought all those Roman men used to spend time at those baths just to discuss politics."

Isabella couldn't believe the words coming from the old woman's mouth. Her grandmother never said nice things to either her or Gino and here in less than an hour she'd spoken kind words to both of them, plus made a joke. The world was ending; no other explanation...or hell just froze over.

"Thank you, Nonna." Gino patted the gnarled hand that didn't contain a cookie and then sat up straighter in his chair. "Since we're all together, with the exception of Pop, I want to let you know that Tom and I have decided to live together."

When his eyes connected with Isabella's she flashed him a thumbs up. They both turned to check their mother's reaction to the news.

Angela sat with her eyes downcast, stirring her coffee. The only sound in the room was the hum of the refrigerator and when that stopped the quiet became stifling.

"I'll tell your father." Angela laid her spoon on the table and picked up her cup. "Yes, it will be best if I tell your father."

Squaring her shoulders, she turned and faced her son's lover. "Tom, you're family now so I need to get some information from you. What size shirt do you wear and do you like boxers or briefs?"

Laughter at Angela's questions relaxed the tension and the sunbeams streaming through the window turned the kitchen into a world of light and shadows. The heaviness in Isabella's heart returned now that she no longer focused on a family drama playing out in front of her.

A glance at the clock above the sink told her she also needed to get to work. Losing her job on top of her man would be the finishing touch to her day. "Thanks for the cookies, Ma." She got up and kissed her mother on top of the head.

"Best of luck to you two." A wink across the table at the two men gave her seal of approval.

"Nonna, see you later." Isabella squeezed the old woman's shoulder when she passed her on the way out.

"Bella, wait. I walk with you to the door." The thin body pushed out of the chair and followed her granddaughter.

Great. Now the real Nonna is back. I was beginning to think she'd been replaced by aliens. The old dread came flooding back at the thought of a conversation with her grandmother.

"We talk here." Nonna stopped when they were out of hearing range of the others. "Bella, you sad today. Did something go wrong with your man?"

Shock coursed through her. How did she know? Isabella looked at the bony hand that captured her arm. She couldn't talk about this now. If she did, she'd end up in tears and give the gossips at the station plenty to speculate on when they got a gander at her red-rimmed eyes. Best to say nothing is wrong and get out as quickly as possible.

"It's okay. You no have to tell me. I just want you to know I understand. Love can give both joy and pain."

The sadness in her grandmother's eyes was something she'd never noticed before. "You still miss Grandpa, don't you?"

"Your grandpa was a good man. He did the best he could. We cared for each other in our way." Nonna patted her arm and turned away.

Now that was strange, Isabella thought on her short walk to the subway. She didn't think her grandmother was talking about her deceased husband when she mentioned love. Who then? Her grandparents were married when Pia was a young girl. From all the stories, she heard at family gatherings, her family was very protective until they gave her over to her husband.

Nonna, you little devil, you. What are you not sharing?

CHAPTER 16

"Loki, I think it is time for me to get to know Isabella's family. If my son wishes to give up immortality for this woman, I need to know more about her." Loki watched as the goddess blinked her eyes in an effort to stop the tears pooling in them.

"If you insist, My Lady." Loki bowed from the waist. He needed to delay this visit and give time for him to soften the way. For Sif to show up and announce herself as a goddess would get her laughed out of the Girardi's home. "I will accompany you or possibly it would be best if I go first and lay the ground work for your arrival. My knowledge of the grandmother may help pave the way."

"What are you saying here, Master of Tricks? How do you know the grandmother?" He noted the glint of suspicion when the goddess directed her gaze on him.

"It is of no importance, Beautiful One. Do not concern yourself."

"I shall be the one to decide that. Come tell me of your acquaintance of this woman." As always Sif arranged her gown, careful to smooth out the back when she sat to avoid wrinkles.

Not good, fool. She will demand details. Loki

regretted his slip of tongue alluding to his information of the mortal's family. Honesty was best here. If the golden beauty found out at a later time he withheld information or lied, all of his efforts to again win her trust would be for naught.

"Very well." Loki took a seat and contemplated where to start. The beginning seemed the most logical place. "Remember when Zeus called a meeting of all the realms? Odin took me with him to the gathering and we stayed beyond the scheduled time."

Sif nodded and leaned slightly forward.

Loki's memories of how boring the group was, even now gave him the urge to yawn. How Odin sat through as much of it as he did still amazed the mischief-maker. He looked up from his wool gathering to see Sif waiting patiently for him to continue.

When he finished his story he noted the look of disbelief on his companion's face. "So, you see how I can prepare the way for your arrival. I will remind Nonna Pia Bartolo Piccoli of her youthful indiscretion and let her speak with the family."

Sif shook her head. "You expect me to believe Odin, in all his wisdom, still carries love in his heart for a mortal with whom he had a dalliance?"

"It was not exactly a dalliance. They never...well you know." Why did he feel embarrassed to talk about sex in front of this woman? It was always so and now, more than ever since it involved her husband's father. The only thing worse would have been discussing the minor wanderings of Thor on the rare occasion he strayed from the marital bed.

"Then I definitely do not believe your tale. Odin's lusty appetite is well known in all the worlds. To think he would fall in love with a mortal and pursue her without satisfying his lust is not worthy of belief." Sif stood and shook out her gown, letting the yards of silk fabric flow around her. "I am ready."

Defeated, Loki nodded his preparedness. "I only ask that we appear to the grandmother first and you let me open the conversation."

"As you wish. Let us be gone."

*****

Watching the old woman sleeping in her chair, Sif could not imagine how this could be the great love of Odin's life that Loki purported she was. As if reading her thoughts, the Lord of Pranks handed her a picture frame containing the smiling face of a beautiful young woman.

Realization dawned as she stared at the photo of a curvy body and dimpled cheeks laughing up at her was that of the wrinkled creature who snored softly from the chair brought tears to her eyes. This is what her son would be facing if he insisted on moving forward with his intentions of marriage. Not only would the woman he loved come to this, but so would her gorgeous son when he became a mortal.

"Wh...hmmph...Who there?" The old woman looked around in confusion.

"It is I, Pia Bartolo. That is the name you went by many years ago in Rome, is it not?" Loki's eyebrows rose in question.

"How you know that? What you doing in my house?" Pia pushed up from the chair and stood eye to eye with him. "You get outta my home or I call the police."

"I do not think so." The grin he gave her fit into the satanic category and he laughed when she crossed herself in the Catholic manner.

"What you want, Evil One?"

"It is not what he wants, but I." Sif stepped forward and smiled.

Taken aback by the appearance of another stranger in her home, Pia shuffled over to her chair and collapsed into it again.

"I apologize for our unannounced arrival, but I feel it is important I get to know your family." Tucking a lock of spun gold behind her ear, the goddess knelt beside the chair the old woman occupied. The older female watched her like a hawk, not saying a word.

"Here My Lady." Loki located a footstool and offered it to Sif.

He then perched on the arm of the chair on Pia's other side and decided to enlighten the old woman. "Let me help you recall how we met. You may not remember me at all, I was only a bird in the sky, but I am sure you have not forgotten the man you called your Viking."

The gasp emitted by the human told Sif that Loki accomplished his goal. So the Trickster told her the truth or at least some semblance of it.

"No-no." Pia clutched her heart with one hand. "Nobody, they know nothing about this."

Concerned, the goddess took the limp hand in the human's lap. The rapid heart rate she discovered at the pulse point told Sif how distressed the woman was. "You have nothing to fear from us." Using her powers, she sent soothing energy to calm down her speeding heartbeat.

Pia removed her hand from her heart and pressed the fingers against her trembling lips. "How did you find out?" She asked in Italian.

Switching to the lady's native language presented no problem for Sif. "Loki is the Lord of Tricks and he is a friend of the deity known among your people as Odin. He will share with you what he knows."

"The man…" The stern glance from Sif caused him to stop and start over, changing into the language of Pia's homeland. "The man you encountered on the hillside in Rome was Odin, the chief deity of the Norse kingdom of Azgard."

"You are trying to trick me. He said his name was Huginn." Pia sat up straighter in her chair and cast a disbelieving look at the impish looking man.

Sif watched the smile play around Loki's lips at the mention of one of Odin's ravens. So like her husband's father to take the name of a pet on one of his wanderings in another world.

"No." The immortal's lips twitched again. "He tricked you, even down to the patch he wore over his eye that you thought made him look like a pirate. The fact is, he has a blind eye and no matter what form he chooses to change into, the eye still does not see."

Loki stepped away from the chair to the center of the room. "I too, have the ability to change forms. Do you remember this one?" Suddenly a falcon set on the floor where once the deity stood.

Half rising from her chair, Pia's legs appeared to give out and she fell back with a plop. "You...you, no wonder Huginn...er...Odin watched as you circled above us each day. I did find it unusual for a bird of prey to follow us through the hills."

She sighed and a look of sadness crossed her face. "But, I was young and foolish. I thought was in love."

"Ah, you were in love and so was Odin." Loki changed back and came to sit beside Pia's chair.

"How can that be if what you tell me is true? I was just a young foolish mortal woman."

"Not in his eyes. Or should I say not to his good eye." He peered up at her with an impish grin.

Pia laughed and shook her head. "It seems so long ago and a dream."

"Yes, but you've never stopped loving the golden Viking who you spent those happy hours exploring the hillsides with, have you?"

"No. I have kept him here." She tapped her heart. "Even though he broke it. He sent me away to marry the man my parents selected. 'I do not love you,' he said."

The pain of remembering played across Pia's face and Sif's tender nature ached for the woman. "It was for the best." She squeezed the bony fingers. The agony she must have endured all these years in loving someone who she thought didn't love her may have been minor compared to what might have been. Aging and the end of life were unavoidable in this world. Biting her lip at the thought of what her son proposed to do, she held back the tears burning her eyes.

"My husband was a good man and it wasn't his fault that I could never love him the way he deserved." A single tear slid down Pia's cheek, following a path of wrinkles. "He gave me five handsome sons and a beautiful daughter. What more should a woman want?"

"The love of her life." Sif massaged the age spotted hand she held in hers. "What female, whether she be mortal or immortal, does not wish for her true love?" She received that in Thor. Yes, the Thunder God could be stubborn at times and quick of temper, but she also knew how deeply he loved. Blessed, she was when he selected her.

"Tell me about your family," the goddess encouraged her new friend.

"Why do you want to know about my family? They know nothing of my lost love, only that my parents arranged my marriage to their father." Pia moved to stand and the deities both assisted in her in the effort, exchanging looks as they did so.

"Your granddaughter has a new man in her life, does she not?"

Sif nodded encouragement for Loki to continue.

"Yes, yes. You people know too much. I think this old woman is dreaming." Pia shuffled toward the tiny kitchen. "I'm going to make espresso. You want some?" Not waiting for an answer, she proceeded with the preparations for the strong brew. "If you leave dirty cups then I guess I'll know your visit isn't a dream."

"To answer your question on why we ask about

your family," Loki continued. "Does Galvin remind you of anyone?"

"You look better as a bird," she muttered and pressed the button to start the machine. "Maybe you should stay that way and then you don't ask so many dumb questions."

Sif covered her laugh with a cough into her hand. She liked this feisty individual. Having her in the family would be a source of great amusement and she could see making many trips into this world to share coffee and stories with her.

If Galvin did accomplish his goal of becoming mortal, visits here would be the only way she'd get to see her son as long as he...the lump in her throat choked her and she could no longer let her mind drift down that road.

"Okay, Mister Smarty Pants, who do you think Galvin reminds me of?" Pia placed a mug of brew in front of Loki with a thud, sloshing the contents over the sides.

Wiggling his eyebrows at her, he grinned. "Guess."

"Pia, our friend is playing games with you. You see, I am married to one of Odin's sons and Galvin is from our marriage."

Hooded eyes appraised her and Sif fought a sudden moment of discomfort under the close scrutiny.

"I see. He," she scowled at Loki, "thinks I remember the man of my youth when I look at your son."

"My son has many attributes of his grandfather as

well as his father, Thor."

"Maybe that is why I like him. He does not look so much like the man I remember, but there is something in the way he looks at me...a quality I do not see in the eyes of others."

"Wisdom, maybe," Loki muttered and took a quick sip of coffee. "Ouch, that is hot. I burned my tongue."

"What? You expected something with steam coming off of it to be cold?" Pia shot him a look of disgust.

Turning her back on the sulking male, she focused her attention back to the goddess. "So, my Bella has made the same mistake I made. She has fallen in love with a god." Her chin dropped to her chest.

"There is a difference." Sif saw the grey head pop up and laughed. "My son wants to marry your granddaughter. That is why I came, to get to know more about the family of which he will become a member."

Beady eyes stared, waiting for her to continue.

"You said you have five sons and a daughter. Who is the parent of Isabella?"

"My Angela." Pride sounded in the simple statement and told Sif the daughter was her mother's favorite.

"Do Angela and her husband have other children from their union?" Uncomfortable with the interrogation tactics that came out of her mouth, Sif decided to change how she asked her questions.

"She and Lou were only blessed with two children. My boys, now there are big families. They each have at least six kids." Pia smiled and nodded her head in approval at her sons' virility.

"Angela and Lou, not so lucky, but their two are good kids. They think I'm mean though from my insisting they learn to speak Italian." Lost in her memories, she grew silent for a minute.

"Gino is Bella's younger brother." Once again she paused and Sif watched a display of emotions play across the lined face.

"He has come to realize he is of the Roman persuasion." A quick nod emphasized the old woman's acceptance of the statement.

"Great. Just what the human world needs. More perversion" Loki wrinkled his nose in distaste.

"The Roman persuasion. I am not familiar with that term."

"He prefers men, my goddess."

"I see, and why should you find this so distasteful, Lord of Pranks? You know there are gods who prefer both sexes, especially in the Greek world." Sif used her haughtiest tone to halt the reply she saw him ready to make. If they became family, there was no need to create hard feelings through inconsiderate words.

"Gino is a good boy. His Tom is a good man, too. You will like them and they will like you." Pia smiled at Sif and looked over at Loki. "*You*, I'm not so sure they will like."

A slight nod of head from the goddess when Pia shuffled to the kitchen stopped his response.

Returning with the coffee pot, she poured refills. "I have a question. Does my Bella know what you people are?"

You people. To think, it came down to such a simple term to describe the differences between them. "Yes." Sif returned the penetrating look.

No longer able to tolerate being ignored, Loki took over and Sif sipped from her cup to hide her smile.

"Not only does she know who we are, she has visited our world. Galvin felt it important to help her believe the truth of what he told her about himself." The little deity's chest puffed out reminding Sif of an adder.

"I see. Our Bella is strong willed and with a mind of her own. I wonder where she gets all that stubbornness from."

"I wonder." Loki muttered loud enough to earn a frown from both women.

"Mama, are you home?" Angela Girardi called as she came through the door. "Do you want to walk down to the bakery with me? I thought we could have…" She paused and looked around the room. "I'm sorry; I didn't know you have company."

Pia beamed at her daughter. "Come in Assai. Come meet Galvin's mother and this…"

She paused and frowned when her eyes fell on Loki. A smile broke through the frown. "And this is Galvin's uncle."

CHAPTER 17

"Thanks." Isabella grabbed the triple shot latté and took a swig on her way out the door of her favorite coffee house. "Damn, hot." She burned her tongue on the steaming brew, desperate in her need for all the caffeine she could ingest today.

Exhausted from lack of sleep mulling over the visit with the Valkyrie Queen and all the negatives she pointed out left her mind in turmoil and she'd been unable to get an hour of the needed body recharge, let alone eight.

Then throw in her mother's summons to come over added more anxiety to an already full plate. Angela's discovery of Gino and his lover in a comprising situation left her in hysterics and she needed her daughter to vent on. Yeah right, like she could fix that.

Enough of her family's problems. She needed to focus on her own and decide what to do about her relationship with Galvin Haldor, or was she the only one who thought they were in a relationship? *He was the one who disappeared this morning without even a goodbye.*

"Okay, so she refused to tell him about the conversation with the Warrior Goddess." Isabella bumped into a large man who stopped in front of her. "Excuse me," she mumbled and continued with her thoughts on last night and mumbling to herself.

What started as a silly remark on his part, turned into a game and some of the hottest sex she'd ever experienced. Mostly she preferred her sex vanilla, but the sound of his hand connecting with her flesh and the heated sting of her skin awakened something in her she didn't know existed.

"Yeah, I could get into a little more of that." The woman standing beside her as they waited for the light to change gave her an odd look.

Shrugging her shoulders, she smiled. "Sorry, just thinking out loud.

Afterwards, snuggled against him, his prodding resulted in her spilling her guts on the conversation with Freya and the doubts that slipped into her mind, no matter how hard she resisted them. He laughed and kissed her.

"Don't sweat the small stuff."

Easy for him to say. She'd lain in bed last night beside the man who stole her heart and thought on what Freya pointed out to her during their little chat. Thor said the same thing, but coming from another female and being slapped a second time with the reality of their predicament gave the situation a different perspective.

"What have I got myself into here?"

The facts were there, unable to avoid, as much as she wanted to. She was mortal and human lifespan was but a blink of an eye in Galvin's world. Would he love her more or less in the years to come? That question spun around in her head until the wee hours of the morning and now she was a walking zombie.

Isabella pushed her way though a group of teens blocking the street.

"Hey lady, look where you're going."

Shooting a 'don't mess with me' glare at the skinny, pimple-faced boy, she continued on her way, ignoring the "dumb bitch" remark thrown in her direction.

If Galvin loved her more, how much pain would it create for him when she died? Could his love be blind to her aging? She could see it now...the two of them out for a walk, he pushing her wheel chair and hearing all the comments from passerby's on what a dutiful son...grandson...he is. Her skin crawled at the thought.

Age presented issues for her, too. How would she feel when she looked in the mirror and saw her face growing older and his never changing? Hell, she hated the wrinkles around her eyes now, almost convincing herself they were laugh lines. That illusion would no longer exist thirty years from now, sitting across the table from the unlined face of the man she loved.

And that was the problem. She loved him. It wasn't just the great sex, like she told herself in the beginning. No, she was in love...head over heels in love. Here was the first and only man whose company she enjoyed. His sense of humor delighted her; he showed compassion in little ways, such as with her grandmother. Hell, they even liked the same music.

A gust of fall wind hit her when she turned the last corner on her way to the building that housed the television station offices, bringing back memories of the storm chase. No wonder Galvin kept a low profile during their mad dash through the countryside in search of a tornado. He knew what his father was up to and that he'd be the one to fight the war with the old man over control of the weather.

Nope, she was insane. Way out of her league here. These freaking people were immortal gods. They'd been around so long people considered them myths.

"Okay, decision made." Her relationship with Galvin Haldor had to come to an end for both their sakes.

Dumping her purse in the usual drawer of her desk, a heavy sensation settled in her heart. *Maybe she shouldn't be so hasty. They were two intelligent people who could figure this out.*

"Hello, Earth to Isabella."

Good grief, when did Sandy scoot her chair over to the edge of the desk? "Sorry, didn't see you."

"No shit, Sherlock. You were in another world." The intern flashed a grin and rolled her eyes.

If she only knew how right, she was. "Don't give me crap. You have a few of those moments yourself."

"True." Sandy shrugged. "Just wondered if you were part of whatever weirdness is going on around here?"

"What do you mean?" She'd been so lost in her own problems she'd blocked out Sam's discovery of his wife's affair and how it might affect the station.

"Well, it seems our slimy male anchor is no longer part of the family and the lovely prize winning bee-otch female anchor is nowhere to be seen." Sandy glanced around the room. "And take a look at how everyone has their heads buried. You'd think they were turkeys in a turkey shoot the way they're afraid to raise them."

A quick scan of the room proved the observation was a good one. "See what you mean."

"Where's Sam?" The blinds that covered the station manager's windows along the newsroom were open and the lights in the office were off.

"Haven't seen him either. What did he want to discuss with you yesterday? You were pretty quiet after you came out of his office."

Should she be honest and tell Sandy that Sam found out about the little game being played out right under his nose? Adding her boss's problems to her own made Isabella's head hurt. No, not necessary. Instead, she'd go add a slug of wicked black brew from the employee break room to her cold latté. Maybe if she nosed around in there a little she'd find out about what was going on.

"You know Sam. He goes on about a lot of nothing." Shrugging, she picked up her cup. "Me, I'm going to add some acid producer from the lounge to heat this up. Want me to get you some?"

Sandy shook her head so vehemently her blonde ponytail swung back in forth, hitting her cheeks. "No thanks. The cup I had earlier ate the spoon I used to stir with. God only knows what it's doing to the lining of my stomach."

Back at her desk and depressed by the lack of information obtained from her trip to the break room, Isabella focused on work. She'd finished the calculations for the six o'clock weather broadcast when she saw Sam come in.

He stumbled across the newsroom and disappeared into his office and closed the blinds, not speaking to anyone. The man looked like he needed a friend and she started to go talk to him, when Joanne Kent swept by with a short, heavy-set man trailing behind her.

Everyone in the room kept casting glances at the door over the next half hour. When it opened, Joanne stormed out with the stranger hot on her heels.

Sam's angry face spoke more loudly than words as he faced his staff. "Every fucking one of you is fired. Get the hell out of here now."

"Oh shit, he's drunk." Sandy whispered to Isabella. "What should we do?"

He staggered over to the desk closest to him. "I mean it. Get your shit and get the hell out of my newsroom. I don't need a bunch of back-stabbing traitors working for me." He picked up a book from the desk and threw it across the room and then proceeded to start pitching everything on the desk at anyone close. People scattered in a mad rush for the elevator and stairs.

"Don't you think we should probably go, too?" Sandy pulled on Isabella's arm.

"You go ahead. I'm going to go do some voice-overs and let him cool off. Once he sobers up I'll be able to talk to him. My guess is Joanne and friend set off this little episode." Isabella pulled her arm free and gathered the items she needed.

She slipped into the sound proof recording booth

and began the work on the update of the daily spots for the radio stations they supported with weather information. When she finished, she'd check and see if Sam was sober enough to talk some sense into. The news team would be on the air in less than three hours.

Done. Rolling her shoulders, Isabella tried to work some of the tiredness out of her body. Maybe she'd just put her head down for a few minutes and close her eyes. A glance at the gold watch on her wrist told she'd only been in the sound proof room twenty minutes. Sam needed a little more time to sober up.

The silence lulled her sleep-deprived body into relaxation and weights pulled her eyelids closed. A little nap couldn't hurt and would give her the energy she needed to face her boss. Yawning, she laid her head on her arms and gave in to the lure of sleep.

*****

Strange, it looked like fog outside the window. "Must have slept longer than I thought." Isabella looked at her watch. "Oh shit!" She was due to give the weather for the six o'clock news broadcast and if she didn't hustle her butt, she'd be late. It would be interesting to see who replaced her non-favorite pair of co-anchors.

"Damn, my eyes are still foggy." She rubbed the lids again and blinked. "What the hell?" The grey cloud covering the window was still there. Something strange was happening here. Was Thor up to another of his tricks?

Well, she didn't have time to worry over what a

whacked-out Nordic deity was up to, she had a weather forecast to give and then have a little chat with Sam. Maybe by then the station manager would be sober enough to listen to reason.

Pulling open the door on her way out of the booth, the shrill of the fire alarm and the scent of smoke assaulted her. The dense grey air attacked her nose and stung her eyes. "Oh my God, the place is on fire!"

The soundproof room blanketed her in a protective shell from the noise of the alarm and the smell.

Panic surged through her. She swallowed hard in an effort to gain control and think clearly. "Let's see. Smoke rises. Best to stay close to the floor." The sound of her voice helped her focus. She could talk herself out of this mess.

Crawling along the floor she kept a flow of conversation going. "Sandy, why in hell didn't you come and warn me? Oh yeah, that's right. You left. I told you to leave when Sam…"

Sam. He may still be here. Should I check? She sat back on her heels and tried to see across the room. Blinded by tears and a burning throat from the dense smoke, she placed her face to the floor.

Rest, she needed to regroup. Galvin's face floated in front of her eyes. "I'm sorry I was such a fool to listen to the others and not give us a chance." Squeezing her eyes tighter, she fought back the vision of the man she loved so dearly. No time for that right now. Galvin wasn't here, but given her boss's earlier condition, if he passed out, he was probably still in his office.

A scream tore from Isabella's throat. "Sam, are you here?" She lay listening. The only sound she heard was the crackling of flames as they ate their way through the newsroom.

"Get out of here. You can't save Sam. No way can you get to his office. Find the exit." She slithered along the floor on her stomach in an effort to stay out of as much smoke as possible. "Think, think. Exit. Where is the exit from here?" A picture of the room's layout popped into her mind. "Right, go right."

Her head bumped into something hard and she opened her streaming eyes and made out the pot that contained the palm tree the travel editor kept by her desk. "Okay, the elevators are on your left and the stairs will be another twenty feet beyond." She moved forward.

"What was that?" A coughing spasm drowned out any sound she may have heard. When it subsided, she lay still, listening. "There it is again."

It sounded like someone calling. "Sam. Sam is that you?"

A faint, "Help," reached her ears.

She couldn't be sure it was Sam, but she couldn't just go on and leave whoever it was. They needed help.

"Talk to me. Say something so I can locate you."

"Here. I'm over here." The voice came from the direction of Sam's office. It could be him. She was too scared and tired to know.

Another series of coughs racked her body and her lungs burned from inhaling smoke. Inching her way toward the voice the heat grew more intense. She was close; the voice was almost in her ear. Her hand touched something hard.

"Damn." She tried to push the object out of her way.

"No. No, it's my hat." A hand grabbed hers.

"Hat?" The word registered in her clouded mind, but not the meaning.

"I'm a fireman." The raspy voice paused and Isabella could hear his labored breathing. "My partner and I...pulled a man out...of an office." He stopped in between efforts to talk, to gasp for air. "I tripped...think my leg is broken...twisted the other one...lost my oxygen mask."

"Okay. Let me think." Isabella attempted to bring the floor plan to mind again. "I think we go this way."

How the hell was she going to do this? A man with two bum legs and the smoke so thick standing made breathing next to impossible. Tears of frustration and fear mingled with the ones generated by the polluted air.

"If I pull on your shoulders, do you think you can push with the leg that's not broken?"

"I'll try."

Isabella pushed up into a crawling stance and grasped his shoulders. "Now," she managed to get out before another coughing spasm tore through her lungs.

Inch by inch the worked their way toward what she hoped was the exit. Her foggy brain told her there were more voices in the room, but she had no way to help them. She blocked the sound and continued her efforts to get her and the fireman to the exit. "One more time," she encouraged herself and him after each attempt.

The last one took all her strength and she collapsed on top of her charge. She could swear a voice shouted as blackness descended.

"Here. I've found someone. It's a woman and Pete's with her. Get that oxygen over here, now!"

CHAPTER 18

The doctor shook his head and ran a weary hand through the little hair left on top. "I'm sorry, folks. There's been no change. I suggest you all go home and get some rest."

A sob escaped Angela Girardi and her husband pulled her into his arms. "Shhh, Precious. No change is better than one for the worse." He stroked his wife's hair in an effort to soothe. "Thank you doctor, but we will stay for now."

No, they weren't going anywhere. The past thirty-six hours Galvin huddled with the core group of Angela, Lou, Gino and Nonna in the uncomfortable waiting room with various members of the family floating in and out. Helplessness assaulted him, as well as the rest of the assembled members slumped in the various seating arrangements and perched on any piece of furniture that would support them. This was a new feeling and he didn't care for it. Did mortals feel this way in all difficult situations in their lives? Would he, when he became one of them?

"Nonna, can I get you anything?" He stood behind the old woman's chair and gently massaged the frail shoulders. The feisty Italian lady disappeared, now replaced by this little shrunken shell.

"No. I be okay." She reached up and patted his hand. "You good boy, Galvin."

Gino called from across the room. "Galvin, I'm going down to the cafeteria to get some coffee and snacks. Want to help?"

"Sure." He followed Isabella's brother to the elevator relieved to have something to do instead of watching the pain on her family's faces.

Some brilliant mind situated the hospital food area in the bowels of the building. The décor reflected the other floors, stark and bleak. Nothing cheery to improve the feelings of the patients or visitors who spent time within its walls.

The two men walked down the dingy pea green hallway until they came to the set of swinging double doors that took them into the large open room that severed as the lunchroom. They worked their way through the sterile metal tables with uncomfortable chairs grouped in fours around them to the food line.

"Let's get a cup of coffee and talk for awhile." Gino pulled two white ceramic mugs from the rack stacked by the coffee urns and handed one to Galvin.

Seated with their hot brew in front of them, Gino started the conversation. "Have you heard anything more about how this happened?"

Closing his eyes, Galvin tried to block the pain squeezing his heart. "I talked to the fire chief earlier today." He swirled the black liquid around in the cup, with no intentions of drinking. "The police interviewed Sam. He admitted to being drunk"

Sam's finding out about the affair between his wife and her co-anchor pushed the poor man over the edge.

Mortals seem to take a less liberal view of any dalliances their partners participated in. A lot of the people in his world considered sexual variety a normal happening. Most chose not to comment when their spouses strayed to play in other pastures and yet, some stayed faithful, never needing to test the greener grass theory.

"The Chief thinks Sam was smoking and in his drunken state probably flipped a cigarette butt across the room. It smoldered there while Sam continued to drink himself into oblivion until he passed out in the chair by the door."

"Damn." Gino slapped the table in frustration. "I didn't know the man had a drinking problem. Bella never mentioned it."

"A lot happened in his personal life and I guess he sought escape in alcohol." Galvin didn't think it was his place to share the station manager's problems with the rest of the world, even if it was Isabella's brother.

"How did Bella get caught in this?" Gino scowled.

"Sam kicked everybody out of the newsroom earlier. Isabella went into the soundproof booth to record some info spots for the radio stations they support. The fire alarm in there didn't work for whatever reason, but I'm not sure why she didn't look out and see the smoke."

Why, my darling, did you not notice. Were you that caught up in your work?

"Sam Kent better be glad one of the people he kicked out earlier gathered enough courage to venture back up to the newsroom." Galvin didn't try to keep the anger from his voice. "That's what saved him, but no one knew about Isabella. Two firemen went in to get him out and one tripped over something on the floor and fell as they headed for the exit. He told his partner to keep going with Sam and he'd follow."

Gino shook his head. "Man, my hat's off to those guys. They put their lives on the line everyday."

Galvin nodded in agreement. "The problem with that plan was he'd broken one leg and twisted the other knee. When he took his oxygen mask off for a better look he somehow lost it. Then the heat exploded something and the fire spread rapidly. The fireman was overcome by the smoke and in his condition he wasn't able to move very well."

Galvin's voice shook when he spoke the next words. "That's when Isabella appeared, determined to help him."

The men sat silently, each lost in their own thoughts.

"Galvin."

He looked into Gino's red eyes. "Yes."

"Do you think she's going to make it?"

"I don't know, Gino. I honestly don't know. But if she doesn't, I don't want to live either."

*****

"Here, Ma. Eat something. You haven't eaten anything for two days. You can't live on coffee. Especially the rot-gut stuff they have here."

Galvin watched Gino's attempts to coax his mother into eating with no more success than he was having with Nonna Piccoli. "Pia, you have to eat to keep up your strength. Here, just one bite, for me." He gave her his best smile and received a quiver from one corner of her mouth.

She reached over and took the half of turkey sandwich he held and nibbled at the edge. "You know, Galvin, you are like him."

Puzzled, he watched her play with her food. "Like who, Pia?"

"Ahhh." She looked over his shoulder and instead of answering his question said, "I think you have company."

He turned to see what the old woman was talking about, sure that her lack of eating caused her to see things.

"Loki." Galvin stood. "Excuse me Pia. I'll return shortly." He pointed to the sandwich. "Eat"

She smiled a secretive smile, took a bite of sandwich and nodded.

Grabbing the little man who stood by the entrance of the waiting room by the arm, Galvin steered him around the corner. "Loki, what are you doing here?"

"I came to see how things go with Isabella. Your mother is also concerned."

None of the usual mischief danced in the black eyes and Galvin believed he spoke the truth. "Not well, I'm afraid. The doctors said her lungs were badly damaged."

He bit his lip in an effort not to cry in front of another deity. The urge to shed tears was a new sensation for him and one he wasn't sure he liked. "She is in a coma, the sleep of the undead. They say..." he took a deep breath..."the doctor says she may not come out of it."

"There is nothing the doctors can do? I thought many medical advances have been made in this world." Loki shook his head sadly.

"The things that have been discovered help with a lot of things, but not this. All we can do is wait. Thank you for your concern and thank my mother, also."

Galvin turned and headed back to join the Girardi family, missing Loki's comment.

"Wait if you choose, Galvin. I prefer action."

*****

Loki ignored the snarling wolf when he entered into Valhalla. He didn't understand why Odin kept that nasty tempered animal to guard the entrance to his hall. Stupid beast probably scared off more visitors than those who actually made it through the door.

Watching two young immortals feed grapes to the God of Wisdom and War; Loki considered which approach to take in order to get the needed results.

Should he make his plea based on family ties, love or courage? By Hades, he would use any and all cards available. All was fair in love or war and this was both. He was going to battle for the happiness of Sif's family.

"My Lord." He bowed deeply before Odin's throne.

"Loki." Delight sounded in the god's voice and he pushed away the cluster of fruit dangling before him. "Get up from there, my friend. Since when do you bow before me?"

"When I appear before you on official business, Great One."

Odin's good eye focused on the immortal standing in front of him.

Loki held up his hand to shield his own orbs. "Please, Wise One, could you tone down the eye a little? The glare is killing me here."

"My apologies." The sun glare from Odin's good eye dimmed. "What is this business you wish to discuss, my friend of tricks?"

"I prefer we speak in private." He cast a glance at the group of women lounging around the throne.

The God of Wisdom sighed. "Oh very well, if you insist. Leave us, my dears." The women filed past Loki on their way out, several awarding him glares of venom.

"Now, what is so important?" Odin rose from his seat of gold and walked down the steps.

"I have come to ask you to make someone a Valkyrie."

"You what? This is another of your jokes, right?" The sun started to rise in the god's good eye.

"No. Wait. Hear me out." If he wasn't careful, he would go out of here blind and all from trying to do a good deed.

"Your grandson, Galvin is in love with a mortal. Do you remember how that feels, Great One?"

The sun receded and Odin appeared lost in thought. A smile played across his lips. "Yes, I remember." He nodded his head and sighed. "Galvin is the brightest of my grandchildren and he will find a way far better than we did to deal with his love."

We, what is this, we? I didn't have anything to do with the way you handled your love of Pia.

"Tell me, what does the making of a Valkyrie have to do with my grandson being in love?"

"The woman he loves lies dying. The doctors of earth cannot help her."

Odin directed his full attention to Loki. "How did this happen?"

"She performed a brave act that put her life at risk in her efforts to save another."

"There are many such acts done each day. I cannot make Valkyries of them all."

Time to try another tactic. "Are you aware, Wise One that Galvin's love of this woman is so powerful he wishes to give up immortality?"

"Don't talk foolishness. He would never do that."

"I think he is serious. Ask your son, the Thunder God. Galvin spoke of it to Thor and Sif. His next action will be to come to you." Loki paused. "He would have been here already, but for this tragedy."

"Thank you for telling me of this. I will be prepared when he does approach me. I shall convince him otherwise." Odin walked back up the steps and sat again on his throne, looking every bit the god he was.

"You would condemn your grandson to the pain you have felt the past sixty plus earth years? You denied yourself the love of a mortal woman when you sent Pia Bartolo to wed a man she did not love." Loki played his trump card. "Would you force your grandson and her granddaughter to endure the agony you subjected on the two of you?"

"What is this of which you speak, Twisted Tongue?" Odin's face paled and he stood.

"Your grandson loves the granddaughter of your only true love."

*****

"Galvin, Galvin. Where are you?" Isabella wandered through the darkness shivering with cold. If she could find him, she would take any time they could have together if it wasn't too late. Had she destroyed any chance of happiness because of fear?

"So dark. So cold. Where am I? This feels like I'm trapped in the subway with no lights or trains." Reaching out with her foot, she tried to locate a track. "Oh my God, I'm floating. Am I in space? How did I get here?"

Fire. There was a fire and she'd tried to get out. "Wait, there's more to it. I heard someone and I tried to help him. It was a fireman. We made it to...where? I don't remember."

A pinpoint of white light drew her attention. "I'll go there. Someone can tell me where I am and maybe there'll be heat. I need to get warm." She concentrated on floating through the black void toward the single speck of light. Closer, it beckoned. A soothing sensation filled her, all thoughts of Galvin forgotten. A ship, she was a ship lost in fog and the only way home was the searching beam from the lighthouse showing her the way.

Drawing closer she could see a doorway. The soft illumination encouraged her to enter and she would never know pain again. Allowing herself to drift closer to the promise in the glow, she felt a sudden blockage. Something prevented her from going forward.

A brilliant blaze appeared and she placed one hand over her blinded eyes. Slowly she lowered her hand as her eyes adjusted to the dazzling rays. Someone floated between her and the door. Was it a man with one eye that glowed with the brilliance of the sun? Did he speak to her?

"*No!*" The man shouted the word.

He did speak to her, but why did he shout?

His next words came softer. "No, Isabella. You cannot enter through the door of snowy light. Your courage has earned you something more."

"Courage. What courage?"

"The selflessness you showed when you risked your own life to save that of another. To save the life of one who risked his." The golden orb moved closer and a hand reached out and touched her. "You are mine. I claim you for my army of Valkyries and immortality."

A flow of energy started in her toes and moved upward through her body leaving her elated. She propelled through the darkness, landing with a thud and a loud gasp of breath.

"Miss Girardi. Isabella, how do you feel?"

She opened her eyes and an unknown face floated above her. The man with the sun eye was gone. This one wore a white coat and a concerned look.

"Fine." Her voice sounded scratched and rough from lack of use. She swallowed and tried again. "Fine, really good." One hand attempted to reach out to the doctor. "Except my wrists feel heavy."

"I'll be damned." He shook his head and took her hand. "Where did these gold bracelets come from?"

Isabella raised her arms and looked at the bands of gold encircling her wrists. Looking into the face of the man standing beside her bed, she saw her own shock reflected in the doctor's eyes. "I have absolutely no idea."

CHAPTER 19

"Bella, you need to rest." Angela turned down the covers on the bed and fluffed the pillows. "You should have come home with us so Nonna and I can take care of you." Her mother paused. "Or, I can stay with you for a few days."

"Ma, stop fussing. I don't need anyone taking care of me." Isabella stopped her mother's fluffing and gave her a hug. "Now, you and Pop go home and get some rest like Nonna and Gino are doing. Come on." She put an arm around Angela's shoulders and directed her to the living room. "Pop. Take this woman home and both of you relax."

"I don't know, Bella. Your mother is right. The doctor shouldn't have let you come home so soon. You just came out of a coma this morning."

"The doctor discharged me because I would have walked out if he refused." She kissed her parents and maneuvered them toward the door. "I'm fine. I've never felt better. You two, go."

"You were on your death bed a few hours ago." Angela leaned against the door, stopping Isabella's attempt to open it. "We thought we were going to lose you."

"I'm sorry for the scare, Ma, but as you can see

everything is great now." She pushed her mother aside. "You don't want me to worry about you like that, do you? And I will if you don't take care of yourselves."

"Okay." Angela accepted defeat and allowed her daughter to open the door. "Galvin will be here soon. When we insisted on bringing you home, he said he would run an errand and then come over." A long sigh escaped the lips of the older woman and she stepped out into the fading sunshine. "He has been really good to us. Don't let this one get away, Bella."

Several more hugs from her parents and Isabella closed the door. She stood for a moment enjoying the quiet and thinking of Galvin. Her parents never shut up on the trip home about how wonderful he was. No doubt about it, her mother planned to see this man became a member of the family. Angela couldn't have said it louder with words. "Don't screw up this time."

"If only it were that simple."

She recalled searching for Galvin at some point. Was it during the fire? Memories of the smoke-filled room rushed back. No, that wasn't it. He was on her mind until the smoke forced her to focus on saving herself and then helping the fireman.

The coma? She couldn't possibly remember things that happened while she was in a coma. Could she?

Looking down at the gold bands on her wrists a shiver of fear rippled through her stomach. How did they get there and why couldn't she take them off? They tied in somehow to the man with the blazing sun eye. Maybe one did remember comas. They were basically a deep sleep and no different than recalling dreams. Right?

The desire for a hot bath propelled her to the bathroom. She adjusted the water temperature and poured a half bottle of lavender bubbles under the stream cascading from the facet into the large sunken tub. Watching the bubbles build, she inhaled the perfume the steam released. Shedding her clothes she slipped down into the sea of foam. "Ahhh."

"Now Galvin, it's your turn. What am I going to do about you?" She stroked bubbles over her skin, relishing in the silky sensation. "I love you. If only things were simple and you were the boy from down the street, not an immortal god. Can I take growing old and watching you never age?"

A memory from her coma dream popped into her mind. "What was it the sun-eyed guy said? Oh, yeah. He gave me immortality." She grinned at the idea. "Right."

She pushed up out of the tub and pulled the large fluffy lavender towel around her. Luxuriating in the softness against her skin, she appreciated feeling feminine and delicate.

Her mind returned to what the man said. Immortality. If only that were true. She would have forever, with Galvin instead of a few short years.

The doctor announced to her family she was awake and they all crowded into the room, but everyone faded into the background when she saw Galvin's face. His smile gave her heart a little flip and warmth flooded through her that carried all the way to spot between her legs, creating a heated tingle there. The urge to kick everyone out and pull him into the bed with her almost won out.

Probably a good thing the doctor kept trying to get people to leave, telling them she needed rest. The truth though, she never felt better.

Drying the last bit of moisture from her skin, she dropped the towel. A glance in the mirror on the back of the bathroom door caused her to pause. Moving closer she examined the reflection of her body. Did she look taller and have less flab? She turned sideways for a profile view. Good grief, her tits appeared perkier. Twisting for a look at her backside, she admired her tight ass.

"Hmmm. Comas must play games with vision, too." A dream promise of immortality gave a new vision to the body's flaws. Laughter bubbled over and she moved into the closet to dress.

Looking over her clothing selection, nothing appealed to her. She needed something that would be good for going out to kick ass when the need arose, maybe something in leather. A shopping trip would be in order, but for now a pair of jeans and a t-shirt would have to do the job.

"Kick ass? Where did that come from? I've never been in a fight in my life, why do I feel the need now?"

Are You Lonesome Tonight? pealed throughout the condo. "Got to change that damned door chime. Can't get my useless brother to do it, so I'll frickin' do it myself tomorrow." She worked her way through the condo and didn't pause to check the peephole as she normally did. Flinging open the door she met the grinning face of Galvin Haldor.

"Hello, Handsome." Delight filled her being.

"Hello, Beautiful." He swept her into his arms, tilted her back and planted a kiss that Rhett Butler would envy.

"Aren't we in a good mood?" She asked as he helped her back to her feet and followed behind her, his palms against her ass cheeks generating heat deep in her core.

"How do you feel?" His squeezed through the tight jeans increased her desire.

"Good grief. If I had a dime for every time I'm asked that question, I could retire." Leaning back against him, she sighed. "I feel absolutely frigging fantastic. Never better." She turned around. "You look like a cat that just discovered a big bowl of cream. What's with the smirk on your face?"

"Smirk? I just returned from a visit with my grandfather. Why would I smirk over that? " Galvin leaned in and planted another kiss; his tongue teased the outside of her lips. "Do you remember anything while you were unconscious?"

Puzzled she frowned. "I recall dreams. I think they happened while I was in the coma, but I'm not sure."

"What dreams?"

"I don't want to talk about my dreams right now. I'll tell you later." Her arms snaked around his neck and she pulled him tighter, surprised at her own strength when he gasped. "I want you." She loosened her hold and rubbed her body against his.

"I want you, too." He returned her kiss with the same passion, pressing his erection against her. "But, I want more than sex. I want your love."

Her hand caressed his cheek and her fingers trailed along his jaw. "That you have. I can't deny to you or myself any longer how much I love you." She buried her face in his neck and inhaled, enjoying the scent of him, male and musty.

"I love you more than I can ever tell you," he murmured against her hair.

"Me, too."

Pulling away, she began to wiggle out of the taut denim of her jeans, shedding the rest of her clothes as she made her way to the bedroom. A glance over her shoulder told her Galvin got the idea and pieces of his apparel joined hers.

She tossed the comforter off the bed and settled against the pillows and watched the man of her heart step out of his boxers. His erection pulsed in anticipation of what he knew was coming. Patting the bed, she invited him to join her.

Galvin stretched himself alongside her, pulling her into his arms. His mouth blazed a trail over her shoulders, licking gently at the pulse point of her throat before continuing down to capture a nipple.

A gasp escaped when his tongue traced the areola and his teeth nipped the hardened bud. Heat screamed downward and the moisture pooled between her legs, the ache of desire almost painful. Enough of this. It was her turn and she felt the strength to fulfill a fantasy she'd kept hidden all her sexual life. One she only brought out occasionally when satisfying her own needs.

Moving with a speed that amazed even her, Isabella sat up and reached into the nightstand drawer and pulled out a pair of handcuffs. She secured his wrist to the bed without giving him the opportunity to resist.

"What're you doing?" Galvin pulled against the restraint on his left hand while she secured his right wrist with a scarf.

She sat back and admired her handiwork and the god who lay sprawled before her.

"I'm going to show you what woman on top is all about."

A hand reached out and tickled the cock dancing in front of her. She wrapped it around the circumference below the sensitive head, sliding the skin back and forth. Isabella's lips curled into a leer. "I've always wanted a man at my mercy like this."

His low groan was music to her ears as her fingers toyed with the velvety tip. The desire to feel the smoothness with her mouth sent her head down until her lips touched the quivering organ she grasped in her strong hands.

"My, my. What do we have here?" Her tongue flickered out as quickly as frog reaching for a mosquito, again and again. Galvin twisted, tugging on the restraints that secured his arms above his head.

"Like this, do you?" Isabella felt power course through her and moved her head lower, blowing hot breath against his scrotum and taking a testicle in her mouth, rolling it around. Allowing the ball to slip from her lips, she captured the other one. His moans intensified, encouraging her to continue.

Finished with his testicles, her head moved up again to the rock-hard erection and covered it with wet lips, sucking the entire shaft down her throat. The ability to consume the entire length without gagging startled her. She'd not been able to devour his entire cock in their prior sessions and needed to use her hand at the base.

Her head worked up and down, swallowing the pole before extracting it to the point of release and inhaling it down her wet passageway again.

He wriggled under her administrations and groaned. "Please. No more."

The tightening of his genitals spoke as loudly as his words. If she continued, he would spurt his seed and she wasn't ready for that. She leaned back on her heels and stroked his thighs. Her fingertips delighted in the sensation of his heated skin under the downy covering of hair.

"No, I don't want to waste this." Isabella leaned forward and grasped the twitching cock. Still holding the blood engorged appendage, she moved her hips forward until she positioned her hungry sex over it. Placing her well-lubricated vagina lips against the tip, she slid down. "Oh. That feels wonderful."

He filled her completely and she sat for a moment letting her muscles squeeze the heated flesh buried in her. She began to rock back and forth, tilting forward to allow the base of his penis to rub against her swollen clitoris.

Galvin pushed up with his hips and each demanded more from the other. She felt it building, a burning inferno deep inside, rushing forth and consuming her. Shock waves ripped through her with an intensity she'd never known. "Oh my God." The ripples gradually subsided and her vision cleared.

Looking down at the male under her, a combination of guilt and elation warred in her heart. Guilt over using the man she loved in such a selfish manner; elation over the best orgasm she'd ever experienced.

Leaning down until her lips met his, she kissed him softly. She pulled back and looked into his glazed blue eyes.

"Wow." He shook his head. "That was amazing. Now, if you'll untie me, maybe we can engage in some of that afterglow cuddling and talking you females are always wanting."

Okay, maybe she wasn't completely selfish.

Removing his restraints, Isabella massaged the red marks left on his wrist by the cuffs in his efforts to escape them.

"I don't know what's come over me." She rained little kisses over the damage. "I've never done anything like this."

"It's your first time making love as a Valkyrie." Galvin pushed a curl behind her ear.

"Are you nuts? Me a Valkyrie? Yeah, right and pigs fly."

"In my world they do." He shifted positions and pulled her head to his shoulder and buried his hand in her curls. "I asked you earlier what you remembered from when you were in the coma." His fingers continued to play with her hair.

He was losing his mind. Valkyrie, my ass but then maybe that could be the name of their new game. She did feel strong and powerful when they played it.

She'd explain to him later that here on earth it was called bondage and submission and she definitely liked being the one in control.

The dream, now that was another matter. She wasn't sure how much she wanted to share from her unconscious state. All the drugs they'd pumped into her at the hospital probably accounted for that strange experience.

"You met someone in your dream, didn't you?"

Sitting up as if shot out of a cannon, Isabella whirled around and stared at him. "How did you know?"

"I visited Odin in Valhalla while your parents brought you home." Galvin reached up and stroked her cheek. His thumb caressed her lips as his palm cradled her jaw. "I was afraid of losing you. You pulled away from me after our visit with Freya when she planted the seeds of doubt and I knew you were going to send me away."

He sat up and arranged himself to bring them eye-to-eye. "I paid an earlier visit to my parents to tell them of my plans to become a mortal and to ask them how to accomplish it. They weren't much help. Today, I went to see Odin to seek his help."

Become a mortal! He was insane to assume the problems of a human.

"Your grandfather? I'll bet he was happy to hear about your stupid idea." Isabella's heart pounded like a kettledrum in her chest. He loved her enough to become a mortal.

"I didn't have to disclose my plan to him. Loki already took care of it for me since he went to see Odin at the time of your hospitalization. While you were in the coma with the life seeping from you, he pleaded with the God of Wisdom to make you a Valkyrie." Galvin encircled the gold bracelets on her wrists with his hand. "See. This is your proof."

"Holy shit." She stared in fascination at the gold bands. "I wondered when they were put on and why I can't get them off."

"They are a part of your immortality. Now you no longer have a valid reason to reject me." He turned over her left hand and kissed its palm. "Isabella Girardi, will you marry me."

Tears stung her eyes and she swallowed hard in an attempt to find her voice. "Yes. Yes, yes, yes." Flinging her body into his arms, they tumbled back on the bed laughing.

"We should call your parents. I'm sure your mother will want to get started on wedding plans." Galvin pinned her down and stretched her arms over her head.

"No phone calls with this news. Ma has waited too many years to hear it. I want to see the look on her face when her dream comes true." She wiggled in an attempt to break his hold. "But, she's waited thirty-five plus years, another hour won't kill her."

"True." Galvin leered down. "Look who has the upper hand now."

His mouth claimed hers and Isabella knew they'd have many years to determine who was in control.

CHAPTER 20

"Ma, I'm not wearing that dress."   Isabella wrinkled her nose at the cloud of tulle and lace her mother was trying to foist off on her for a wedding dress. She'd given into her mother's plans for the wedding on just about everything, but she be damned if she'd walk down the aisle in this piece of fluff. She'd look like a blob of meringue.

"Bella, your mother has spent a lot of time looking for the perfect dress." Aunt Rose came with them on the dress hunting expedition.

"And, she hasn't found it. At least, not for me." Isabella crossed her arms determined to win this round. "No way is that going on my body."

Her mother looked at Rose and shrugged. "What can I say?" Her voice quivered with choked back tears. "My daughter doesn't appreciate all the time I'm putting into this wedding."

"Cut the dramatics, Ma. Of course I'm grateful for all the time you've spent on arranging things." God, she hated it when her mother did the almost crying thing, just let the tears flow and be done with it. "I've gone along with you on the number of bridesmaids, even though I think eight is too many. I gave in on the color and style for their gowns and letting you turn the house into a garden." She and half the guests would be lucky not to pass out from the overwhelming scent of all the flowers. *I hope there aren't a lot of people with allergies attending.*

Angela sniffled. "I wanted the wedding in the church."

"And I've always wanted to be married at home. Hell, you got your way with the reception, so let's call it a draw. I still think we could have found a cheaper place than that ritzy hotel."

"Oh, but Bella, the event manager agreed to decorate with the garden theme. The ballroom will be decorated as beautiful as our house."

Sighing, Isabella shook her head. Whose wedding was *this* anyway? At times, she felt her mother was the one getting married the way she stuck her nose in every little detail. But she'd known since she was five years old that when the time came, it would be Ma's show. For the most part, it was easier to go with the flow than go up against Angela's dream.

She picked her battles carefully with her mother. If not, she would end up licking her wounds or at the very least being exhausted. Well, the dress was worth a battle as was the wedding location.

"It's my wedding, Ma." A glance at her aunt let her know she was included in that statement, also. "I have my own ideas about what I'm going to wear."

"What? These crazy outfits you've taken to wearing lately." Angela shuddered when she looked over at her daughter. "Why all the black leather?"

Rose bobbed her head in endorsement of her sister-in-law's question.

Isabella stood in front of the three-way mirror and appraised her outfit. It still wasn't what she wanted. Her mother dragging her all over town to make the final decisions on wedding plans gave her little time to work on the final product. She felt something more warrior-like was needed. The episode she caught of *Xena: Warrior Princess* on cable last night gave her an idea. For now, she'd make do with the leather bustier and vest.

Turning, she considered her refection from the side view. "Hmmm" *Nice tits.*

She glanced over her shoulder to get a better view of the back. The pants fit her like a second skin. Now that she was a Valkyrie, concern about letting her female parts breathe to avoid infections wasn't an issue. *Was it?* Still a skirt was more along the lines of what she wanted for the wedding.

"I like it." She turned for a better view of her backside. Yep, she filled out the black leather nicely. "So, why not?"

"Humph." Rose picked up the rejected wedding dress and stalked out of the dressing room.

"See. You upset your aunt. She thinks you're going to get married in black leather."

"Not black leather, I promise you, Ma." Isabella kissed her mother's cheek. "I'll look around and find something that works for me. You've got all the other details to take care of and I don't want you to wear yourself out before the wedding."

Pausing at the dressing room door, she grinned back at her mother. "By the way, love the darker blue you selected for your dress. Nice contrast to the bridesmaids."

*****

"It's my wedding day." Isabella resisted the urge to pinch herself to make sure it was real. When she hit thirty, husband material became thinner. At thirty-five, she questioned if matrimony was for her. Now, at thirty-eight, she found her soul mate, a part of her still unable to believe it.

"Thank the gods all the fuss will be over in a few hours." The whirlwind of activity over the past three weeks left her exhausted and looking forward to the honeymoon.

"Of course, you're looking forward to the honeymoon. Look who you're sharing it with." She couldn't stop the grin spreading across her face.

Stretching her arms above her head, she swung her feet over the edge of the bed and looked around. Her parents asked her to stay with them last night, in her old room since the wedding would take place here in the home she grew up in. She and her mother talked, instead of arguing, until the wee hours.

Angela still was adjusting to the trauma of walking in on Gino and Tom in the act of making love. Thinking about the pain her mother and brother felt over that experience still made Isabella's heart wrench. Well, maybe Ma learned her lesson about letting herself into her kid's homes unannounced. Lord only knows what she'd discover if she walked in on her and Galvin at sometime in the future.

Doing a couple of side stretches, her mind

returned to her wedding and life changes. When she and Galvin returned from their trip, she planned to go out into the world to work for the good of others. Amazing how easy it was to quit her job at the television station and focus on the new things she wanted to accomplish.

Looking at the reflection in the mirror, she shared her thoughts with it. "You've changed, baby. You gave up a job you considered to be your life. Too bad Sam thought it was because of him, but nothing is further from the truth."

He apologized and asked her to come back to work...no begged her, but she declined. There were no hard feelings about what happened and she was happy to see him on the road to recovery, from the burns he'd received in the fire and his broken marriage.

No, time to move on. Her life changed drastically the last few weeks.

Mentally going over the guest list while waiting for her mother, she was still puzzled over the cryptic messages left by her three best friends. Each said they would try to make it, but didn't offer any reason as to why they couldn't.

Granted her mother put the wedding together quickly, but for the women whom she'd started on this journey with the night of their drunken dance in the park, to not respond was odd. They hadn't responded to her callbacks asking what was up with them, either. Oh well, maybe they were working on their own immortal relationship and who knew what realm they were in.

Taking a deep breath, she tried to calm the

butterflies in her stomach as she appraised her selection to walk down the aisle in. She gave up on finding one ready made and worked with a seamstress to design this creation.

The woman looked at her like she was out of her mind when she told her white leather was the material of choice. Being a professional, after her initial surprise, the seamstress took the sketches Isabella drew up and whipped out her tape measure. After getting, all of the bride's measurements down, she instructed Isabella to come back in a week for the first fitting.

Several adjustments later, Isabella admired the finished product. Her mother's initial reaction should be interesting. Through careful planning, she avoided showing the dress to Angela and today it was too late for changes.

"Knock, knock." Her mother followed the words through the door and stopped so suddenly that Aunt Rose, her shadow these days, ran into her back.

"Dear God in heaven. What is this?" Angela gasped out the words as she and Rose stared.

"This ladies, is my wedding gown." Isabella turned back to the mirror and adjusted the neckline, pulling up one of the off the shoulder straps of the white leather bustier. Her bare abs, now toned and tanned, showed off well. The matching skirt was longer than she originally planned, coming almost to her knees, but the slit up the side allowed her to move around with ease.

"Oh, Bella. How could you?" Angela came forward and fingered the gold studs on the waistband of the skirt. Matching ones adorned the bottom of the bustier and the hem of the skirt.

"I like it, Ma. It fits who I am now."

Angela closed her eyes. When she opened them, she blinked hard to keep the tears pooling in the corners at bay. "You've been so strange since you came out of that coma. I think you got damage to more than just your lungs." She placed a hand up to her mouth. "God forgive me for saying this, but I think you got brain damage." A tear trickled down her cheek.

"Don't cry, Ma, you'll ruin your makeup. I don't have brain damage; it's just that people change. I hear the music starting." She gave a quick hug to both women. "I think you better go get seated. Send Pop in on your way out."

Turning back to the mirror, she slipped gold hoops into her ears. They went well with the cuffs on her wrists and the chain of gold Galvin placed on her neck last night.

The door opened and her father stood behind her, his eyes round with surprise.

"What do you think?" She knew her father would accept her choice with more ease than her mother. He always put a positive spin on everything she did.

"I must say, it is different, but if it's what you want, then I love it." He held out his arm. "Shall we go so I can walk the most beautiful bride in the world down the aisle or in this case stairs?"

"Thanks Pop." She picked up her bouquet and hung on to his arm, fighting back tears. Why didn't she realize how important his approval was on this special day? Getting the nod from Pop always meant a lot to her in every area of her life, but today took on special meaning.

They stood at the top of the stairs and she saw Galvin standing at the end of the living room, waiting. Her mother and aunts did a beautiful job on the decorations. She was glad they decided to keep the wedding small. *The reception will more than make up for the limited people in this intimate setting.*

The first strains of *Ride of the Valkyrie* started to play just like her grandmother insisted and Isabella Girardi took her first steps toward a new life.

*****

Someone clanged their silverware on a glass and the ballroom full of reception guests chanted, "Kiss, kiss,"

Galvin obliged with a passionate tonsil tickling one that left her breathless. After he released her, Isabella adjusted her bustier for what seemed like the hundredth time.

"Darling, you've got to stop with the hand thing."

"Whatever are you talking about?" His fingers traced across the back of the studded bodice.

Pushing his hand away, she snapped, "You know damned well. Stop pushing up my bustier every time the crowd demands a kiss."

"Okay, I'll be good." He sealed the promise with a quick kiss.

Looking out over the several hundred gathered friends and family, she observed a unique blend of individuals. "Do you think we did the right thing in not telling my family the exact truth about yours?"

She saw several questioning looks exchanged as the reception progressed. There would be plenty of talk in the days to come about Galvin's odd group of relatives and friends. Her mother would question her relentlessly at the first opportunity on their strange choice of dress and behavior.

Slipping his arms around her waist, Galvin pulled her against him and joined her in watching the assembled group.

"I still think it's best for now. Give them a chance to get to know my immediate family first. Then, if you feel the need to share with your parents and your brother, we'll do it. It's probably best the rest continue to think I come from a strange background."

They stood quietly on the fringes of their reception and watched, savoring the touch of each other. *Oh my God, there's the girls. They did make it.* Isabella watched as two of her friends worked their way though the crowd towing escorts behind them. She wasn't sure they were going to make it since the major communication the past couple of weeks had been via hurried voice mails.

Raine's date's intent black eyes darted around the room, reminding Isabella of a bird of prey. The glow on her friend's face told her Isabella the dark haired beauty had found happiness.

Holly's arm linked through that of an arrogant looking male whose ears fit right in with some of Galvin's friends. Isabella loved the pale blue silk suit he wore. Now that was one confident man.

"Where's Mona?" The bride wanted to know after

hugs all around.

Holly looked over her shoulder. "She was right behind me. Oh, there she is."

Squeezing between a large man with blue hair and another who could be described as a borderline giant, Mona held tightly to the hand of the man in black trailing behind.

Taking in the black cape draped across his shoulders, Isabella felt a chill run down her spine. His skin and strange eyes gave her the sense he was about to ask to bite her neck. A hand involuntarily reached up to cover her throat.

During the introductions, Isabella caught her friends appraising Galvin with the same curiosity she had about their dates. Had they all found their immortals?

"We need to talk." Mona whispered in her ear as another group of people converged on them. "Meet us at our favorite bar the Friday after you get back from your honeymoon."

"Okay." Isabella had time to give her a quick squeeze before her new husband tugged on her arm.

"There's someone I want you to meet, My Love."

A beautiful Oriental woman approached and bowed deeply to Galvin.

He returned the bow and took the woman's tiny hand. "Kuan-Yin, delighted you chose to honor our marriage with your attendance. May I present my bride, Isabella."

The woman dressed in a blue silk gown with a mandarin collar and lavish embroidery turned her attention to Isabella and studied her with intense black eyes.

"You have done well, Galvin. I have come to give my blessing to your union. Welcome, my dear."

Soft papery lips brushed Isabella's cheek, much like butterfly wings. "Thank you." The woman's spicy oriental scent tickled her nose.

Kaun-Yin bowed and floated away to a group of strangers who were definitely from Galvin's side of the guest list.

"Who was that?"

"Kaun-Yin? My dear, she is the Chinese goddess of fertility. She has blessed us with many children." He kissed her hand and smiled.

"I hope she didn't get too carried away. I don't intend on becoming a broodmare, popping out a kid a year."

Galvin threw back his head and laughed, attracting the attention of the strange band of partiers the fertility goddess stopped to greet. Two men and a woman broke away and started toward them.

"You're in for a treat now," he whispered as they approached.

The woman extended her hand, "Galvin, you have been captured. I do hope this does not stop your visits to my court." She caressed his arm intimately.

Resisting the temptation to tell the beautiful woman to take her hands off her husband, Isabella forced a smile and silently observed the interaction.

No doubt about it, another goddess. Damn, did they all have to be so beautiful? And what was with this flowing dress thing? Was that the 'in dress' in the other realms? Hate the long tumbling hair, too.

"Aphrodite, how nice you graced us with your

presence. I'm sure we will visit from time to time." He removed the hand that played along his arm and kissed it before returning it to its owner's side. "This is my wife, Isabella."

His arm slipped around her waist, drawing her close to him. "Darling, may I present Aphrodite, Goddess of Love and Zeus, her husband."

Isabella noticed the dark glares directed at Galvin and the woman during their flirtatious interplay by the one man at her side. So, the great god Zeus was also a jealous husband. From the stories, she'd heard about him, the old lecher wasn't in much of a position to play the injured one.

"And, this," Galvin indicated the large man standing behind Zeus, "is Poseidon, God of the Sea."

Holy crap. Had Sif invited the entire mythological world? She hoped the dates her friends brought were immortals or they were missing out on a great chance to hook up with one.

Aphrodite blessed her with a tight little smile. "Delighted to meet you. You have stolen a wonderful one here." She reached out to touch Galvin again, only to have the roaming hand captured by her husband.

Yeah, right, she was delighted to meet her. Just what she needed…another sarcastic goddess.

"My dear, I think we need to find Odin and extend our congratulations for the new addition to his family." The Greek god inclined his head toward Isabella. "Your visits will be a great asset to Mount Olympus. You must make sure Galvin brings you."

"As well as to my kingdom under the sea." Poseidon took Isabella's hand in his and placed a lingering kiss on the back of it.

"Wow."   She watched the trio make its way around the room. "How many realms are represented here tonight?"

Galvin shrugged, "A few. My mother didn't want to offend anyone by leaving them off the guest list."

"Between the ruler of Mount Olympus, the God of the Sea and the God of War and Wisdom, we've got most of the world's greatest womanizers here tonight." She laughed up at her husband.

"As long as they don't attempt to seduce you, I have no objection." He kissed her again.

"I feel overwhelmed, so it's probably for the best my mother doesn't know who all these people really are.   She'd have a heart attack."   Isabella looked around the room. "You do realize I still haven't met your grandfather. Did he come?"

"I saw him at the wedding. I'm sure he will show up here, too. It's not like Odin to miss a party."

"Hello, my darlings."   Angela rushed up and buzzed each of them on the cheek. "Galvin dear, I hate to start sounding like a mother-in-law so soon, but why did some of your guests show up in costume?"

Isabella looked to where her mother pointed. "Oh my Lord. How did I miss him?" The goat-man danced around a group of her aunts and uncles playing a flute. His only article of clothing was a loincloth covering his private parts.

"And, what about that other odd little fellow?" Angela pointed to a strange individual by the stage area where the band was taking a break. "He came in costume and has a flute, too. If I'd known so many of your family played musical instruments and insisted on bringing them, I wouldn't have hired a band."

A wince crossed Galvin's face. "I'm sorry, Angela. They're not family, just friends of my parents. I guess you could say they know a rather eclectic group of individuals."

"So it would seem." A frown winkled her brow. "Bella, what about your friends? What's their excuse for bringing such strange dates?"

"You know how it is, Ma. Once you hit the downside of thirty, selection becomes slim."

"Hmmm, if you say so, but I expected better of them." Angela squinted across the room. "Oh dear, what now?" Rose was signaling for Angela to come to the cake table. "Don't go anywhere. We cut the cake in a few minutes." She rushed off to see what new problem needed her attention.

"So, who are they?" Isabella indicated toward the two individuals her mother thought came in costume.

"The goat-looking guy is Pan. He's the son of Hermés or I think you may know him as Mercury, the messenger of the gods." Galvin shook his head as he watched Pan move from group to group playing his pipe. "We should be glad he made an attempt to cover himself. He usually wears nothing. Let's hope he and Loki don't hook up or there'll be mischief to play for sure."

"And the other one?" She indicated the lone figure playing the haunting music. His headgear bobbed up and down as his thin body hunched over, intent on the sounds coming from his flute.

"That's Kokopelli." He sighed. "A Native

American fertility god. I think my mother didn't want to take any chances on us not having lots of children from all the deities here that handle that area."

"She can kiss that goodbye. Two's the limit." Both of their mothers would find out that rule was etched in stone.

Looking around, she agreed with her mother. There were a lot of people here who looked more like they were attending a Costume Ball.

"You know, my family is beginning to feel normal, compared to them." The band was back from break and rocking. Gino and Tom were the first couple out on the dance floor and it was obvious they were enjoying themselves.

"I'm glad Tom told his family. They seem pretty accepting of their son's new living arrangements." She wished her mother was as easy, but it took a war of words to bend their stubborn mother. Finally, Angela now accepted only one of her children would give her the coveted grandchildren and she told everyone, "better the glass half full than half empty." '

"Who's the big guy over there?" She pointed to yet another drop-dead gorgeous male who could only be a god.

Her husband peered around a couple that walked in front of where she pointed. "That's Apollo. He's the Greek god of prophecy. I'm sure we could get him to tell our future."

"No thanks. I'd rather live it a day at a time and enjoy the surprises." Isabella paled. "Good heavens, who's that?"

Galvin looked in the direction she stared. "Oh,

that's Odin."

"He could be your double, if there was more red in his hair and he lost the eye patch."

"Come. I'll introduce you to my grandfather." He grinned down at her. "Good looking devil, isn't he?"

The clanging of glass stopped their progress across the room.

"Okay, everybody, it's time to cut the cake." Angela glowed at being the center of attention. "Make way for the bride and groom."

The crowd parted like the Red Sea and made a path for them to get to the cake table.

"Here, cut this layer." Aunt Rose placed the cake knife in Isabella's hand and pointed to the second layer of the opulently decorated cake. "You put your hand over hers and smile at the camera," she instructed the groom

"Yes ma'am," they said together and did as instructed.

Galvin fed her the bite of cake without squishing it her face, which was a good thing. She didn't want to have to kick his ass in front of a room full of people. Returning the favor, she resisted the urge to smear frosting all over his mouth and lick it off.

Odin stepped out of the crowd and came up to them. Turning to face the gathering his deep voiced silenced them when he spoke.

"As the head of our little group, I speak for all of us in saying that Galvin could not have selected a more beautiful or courageous wife. Grandson, bring forth my new granddaughter so I may get to know her."

Little group my ass, Isabella thought as she looked

out on the sea of faces, not recognizing a lot of them.

"I'm delighted to meet you in the mortal world, my dear." Odin lowered his voice and the one good eye gleamed giving a hint of the brilliance it concealed. "I am Odin, Galvin's grandfather." He spoke softly and took her hand in his, bowing over it and kissed her fingers.

"You. I remember you from my dream. You stopped me from going to the light." She might not recognize the physical form, but she could never forget the voice and the eye. The eye that almost blinded her with the glare now focused on her in a normal way.

"I told you it was not your time to enter the door of white. I claimed you for my army of warriors and for my grandson."

Odin bowed again and raised his voice for the assembled audience to hear. "It is a tradition in our family to select a special gift for the bride. For this bride I have chosen well, I think." He gave a wave of an arm. "Bring forth the gift."

A man wearing a winged hat and sandals floated across the floor. From Galvin's description earlier, she knew it could only be Hermés. He led the biggest, blackest horse she'd ever seen. Horses terrified her when they were normal size, let alone this gigantic beast.

The buzz from the crowd told her most of the guests were just as confused as she was.

"I...I...uh." She was at a loss on what to say. Get that creature away from me seemed a good place to start as Odin held out the reins toward her. What the hell was she supposed to do with horse? If he wanted to give her something, why not a new BMW or Mercedes?

"See, even a change doesn't make a mouse into a lion." Thor laughed and whispered something to the man at his side.

Isabella saw the challenge in her father-in-law's eyes and squared her shoulders. She was no longer a timid mortal woman. Instead, she was a proud Valkyrie and deserved to have a magnificent steed such as this one to ride. Taking the reins from Odin, she stepped forward and scratched the head of the mighty beast. Slipping around to its side, she flung her left leg into the stirrup and threw her right one across the wide back, grateful for the long slit in her skirt.

Someone jumped up behind her and her husband whispered in her ear. "Don't worry, Odin will take him back to Valhalla. You can get him from there anytime the need arises."

Laughing she kicked the sides of her new transportation and they rode out of the ballroom to the excited murmurs of the wedding guests.

*****

Loki hovered around the fringes of the gathering, bored. The fun he could have if he connected with Pan. Instead, he made it a point to avoid the goat-man and his pipe, knowing they would not have refrained from creating mischief and Sif's disapproval.

Between them, they could have livened up the dull relatives of the bride. If they only knew the truth about the clan their precious Isabella has married into

He rubbed his hands in glee at the thought of implanting the facts about the bride's new family in their twisted, narrow minds. The idea appealed tremendously until Sif caught his eye. She seemed to know what he was thinking and gave a slight shake of her head, which stopped him from following through on the impulse.

Well, at least the presentation of the wedding gift created some excitement. He'd skulked around earlier and listened in on some of the conversations by guests and knew the Girardi family and friends were also confused over the guests who thought this was a costume ball.

"What is this?" He spied Odin and Nonna Pia making their way along the far side of the ballroom.

Not being one to miss out on opportunity, he quickly made his way in the direction he'd seen them go. No way could they evade him as slowly as the old woman walked. Did they leave? He stood before the closed door debating if he should check outside when a soft giggle from behind a curtain caught his attention.

Slipping behind a stack of boxes he heard voices and made his way to the corner. Sure enough, there they were. Odin discovered a glider swing and the two sat side-by-side rocking in a back and forth motion while engrossed in conversation.

"The Devil One told me who you really are," he heard Pia say.

Odin threw back his head and laughed. "I have heard Loki called many things. That is a new name for him. He is a trickster, I admit."

They grew quiet for a few minutes; each appeared

lost in their own thoughts and memories of that time so many years ago.

"It is best things happened as they did." Pia twisted her arthritic hands in her lap and tried to hide them under the folds of her skirt.

"No, do not be ashamed of aging." Odin took her hands in his. "You are right, it is for the best, but not for the reason you think." He massaged her palms. "I was then and am now married. My wife allows me a lot of latitude in certain things. Bringing the woman I love to live in our home would not have been one she would have condoned."

"I didn't know you were married, then again, I didn't know you were a Nordic god either."

She pulled a hand free and touched his face and then placed her fingers to hers. "You've not aged at all and me...I've grown old and wrinkled."

"You are still beautiful to me." Odin's knuckles grazed her chin. "In my mind's eye you are still the young, sweet Pia who loved to dance on the hills."

"Thank you. Your good eye must be as blind as the one you wear a patch over." She smiled. "It's okay. Now, I worry about my Bella. She has married one of you and will grow old like me. What will Galvin do then? Break her heart?"

"That has been taken care of. Isabella risked her life to save that of a fireman and I have made her a Valkyrie. She is one of us now. Not a god...an immortal and a proud warrior."

"Thank you."

Loki saw tears slide down the wrinkled cheeks and she took Odin's hand and brought it to her lips, allowing them to linger there for a moment.

Wiping her face with the back of her hand, she stood. "Come, we'd best go back to the party. All the talk will be about what an old woman like me is doing with a young buck."

Loki ducked down behind another group of containers and allowed them to pass. He stayed put, thinking about what he'd seen and heard. It was obvious Pia still loved her Viking.

The Lord of Mischief was sure the young Italian woman Odin fell in love with still held his heart, too. It would have taken more than his plea alone to make Isabella a Valkyrie for the God of War to have followed through.

"Enough of this boredom. I do believe I saw Crow earlier." Connecting with the animal god could result in some fun. They could educate these mortals in animal rights and even Sif wouldn't find fault with that...would she?

CHAPTER 21

Squeezing the white convertible into the small parking spot, Isabella thanked the heavens once again that Odin agreed a car was more practical in this realm than the horse.

She grumbled to herself about inconsiderate people with huge vehicles hogging space. "If this idiot puts one ding on my car, I'll break him in half." Her ways of finding out things these days left no doubt she'd know within the hour if she put out the call to find the owner.

Time to worry about that later if the need was there. Excitement at seeing her friends surged through her and she checked her hair in the mirror. Sighing in frustration, she ran her fingers through the mass of curls. Some things didn't change, Valkyrie or no, and her hair fell into that category.

Straightening her short black leather skirt and adjusting the matching bustier, she slung her bag over her shoulder before entering the bar where she agreed to meet Raine, Monica and Holly.

Thank heavens they'd made it to the wedding even though she'd not been able to spend time catching up on what was happening with them or share her story. Mona had been smart enough to arrange this meeting when Isabella had been pulled away to meet other guests. Now she looked forward to the show and tell that was bound to happen.

Slapping her hand on the counter she called out to the man behind the bar filling the cooler. "Barkeep, a tankard of Honeyar." She developed a real appreciation for this concoction.

"Huh?" The bartended turned from his task and glared at her. "What are you some kind nut case?"

How dare he? Straightening to her full height, she met his glare. "No. I only asked for a drink."

"Well, we've got beer on tap or in the bottle. Take your choice."

Obviously, this dolt didn't know what she was talking about when she requested her favorite beverage. "Do you have mead?"

"Look, lady. I told you we have beer. Now do you want a draft or a bottle? I don't have all day to screw with someone who lost their way to a Halloween Party." Crossing his arms, he waited for her order.

"Very well. You don't have to get in such a snit about it. Give me a tankard of your strongest ale…excuse me, I mean beer."

"We got pints and half pints. You definitely look like the pint type." He slapped down a glass of brew in front of her, slopping it over onto the bar.

"Fine." She threw a wad of bills in his direction and turned to survey the room.

"Isabella, over here." Mona waved from a darkened corner.

"Love the new outfit," Holly commented as she approached the table.

Raine tossed a lock of long dark hair back over her shoulder and frowned. "The white leather for the wedding was okay. This one's a little too masculine for my taste, but whatever."

"Gosh, I haven't seen you in a skirt this short since college. You've still got great legs." Mona looked more closely. "In fact, I think you've got better muscle tone than ever." She reached over and ran her hand over Isabella's thigh. "I'm envious."

"So what are you supposed to be and since when do you drink beer? You never used to dress like this and you said beer made you gag." Raine continued to frown.

Smiling, Isabella sat down in the empty chair. "Ladies, since we really didn't get a chance to talk at the wedding, do I have a story to tell you." She took a long drink of ale from her glass. "And Raine, I prefer mead, but a girl's gotta do what a girl's gotta do."

"Anyway, let me tell you all that's happened." Isabella took a long swig of ale and faced her friends. "But since you asked, Raine, it's not what I'm supposed to be, but what I am. I'm a Valkyrie." She sat back, enjoying the looks of disbelief on her friend's faces. "You see, it all started the night we last got together and indulged in a little too much vodka before we went...

Finished with updating her friends on how her life had changed since they last had a chance to really talk, Isabella sat back and surveyed their faces. Raine and Holly, both had a smug look about them and poor Mona stared open mouthed.

"Oh, by the way, before I forget, Mona. Let me

give you back that book you left at my place when you helped me get home that night."

Mona's brow wrinkled in confusion. "Book, what book?"

Catching the look that passed between Raine and Holly, Isabella was a little confused herself. "You know, *The Still Sexy Ladies Guide to Dating Immortals.*" Mona still didn't seem to get what she was talking about, but Holly bit on her lower lip in what looked like an attempt to keep from laughing and Raine stared into her drink as if it had become a crystal ball.

"Oh come on guys. I can tell you all know what I'm talking about. I admit I didn't dig it out from behind the dresser where it fell until Galvin and I were making room for his stuff. Maybe if I read it before all this happened in my life, things might have gone a little smoother."

Okay, so Mona still wants to play dumb. Maybe I need to refresher her memory, though I still don't know how she came up with the book to leave it that night. Must have been something she'd picked up earlier and saw that as the opportune time to have a little fun. I was so wasted I didn't notice.

"Let's see, there's the section on how to meet and seduce a shapeshifter." Isabella drummed her fingers on the table as she recalled some of the tips. "Watch out when you're in the heat of passion and your lover loses control to the point he starts to change shapes on you." Raine giggled into her drink and avoided Isabella's eyes.

"Then you have the chapter on elves. I didn't realize their ears were so sensitive." Holly squirmed in her seat and blushed.

"Oh yeah, I especially liked the section on vampires. You really have to be careful kissing one to avoid cutting your tongue on their teeth."

"Really?" Mona leaned forward in interested.

Guess I was wrong about Mona's date at the wedding. If she'd hooked up with her immortal, she'd know that. Maybe he was just one of the weird Goth types she's so attracted to. Still she doesn't have to keep playing dumb about the book.

"Okay, enough of the joke, ladies. Here it is." Isabella reached for the bag she'd dropped on the floor beside her. The book wasn't there. Did she forget to put it in before she left the house? No, she distinctly remembered sticking it in her bag.

"Uh, sorry, but it seems to have disappeared."

Mona laughed and shook her head. "Yeah, right. You really had us going there. I'm sure it was a great book." She winked at the other two women at the table. "Maybe our Isabella is going to add author to her list of accomplishments and this is the book she intends to write. After all, she does have the experience, now."

"Stop with the joking Mona. Didn't you read it before you left it at my place?" Isabella glared at her friend. "Remember the chapter about werewolves? Good grief, after reading that, didn't you have the urge to get out and run with the pack and howl at the moon?"

Looking around the table at her friend's faces, she felt the need to defend herself. "I'm not crazy, you know. Besides, Valkyries don't lie."

Raine cleared her throat. "I think we need to order another round of drinks and then Holly and I can share a few things.

Relief flooded Isabella as she watched Raine's face. Maybe she wasn't the only one to receive a copy of the mysterious book.

*****

Galvin paced in the giant hallway of Valhalla, listening to his wife and grandfather argue. Odin insisted they stay in Azgard as Isabella's due date drew near.

"One of my Valkyries is ready to deliver a baby and this one is even more special as it is the child of my grandson. I will bode no arguments on the matter." The God of Wisdom turned his back, indicating the subject closed.

Leave it to his wife to see things differently. Isabella would argue with a tree if the wind shook its leaves when she passed.

Odin seemed to enjoy the confrontations, at times generating one for amusement.

If only the same could be said of her relationship with Thor. He and his mother spent many a dinner trying to divert a battle between his wife and his father.

"Excuse me, Oh Wise One."

Ouch. He wished she wouldn't use that sarcastic tone when addressing the old man.

"Babies. I'm having twins, according to Apollo. He's fixated on a multiple-birth." She rubbed the small of her back and continued. "I still don't know why I let you talk me into having my pregnancy monitored in this realm." The petulant tone continued. "This is my first time in childbirth and I want my mother with me."

Thank the heavens they'd told her parents and brother about Galvin's family's true identity. It took some convincing for Angela to accept, which Isabella told him not to worry about since that was just her mother.

She admitted to shock when Nonna accepted Galvin's heritage so easily and intervened on their behalf to help Angela come to terms with the fact their family now was also comprised of immortals. Isabella attributed the miracle to an earlier visit Sif and Loki paid the old woman, enlightening her of the true situation and allowing time for her to adjust to the idea.

Odin turned around. "We shall have her come here then."

"And what about my father, my brother and my grandmother?" Both hands now supported her back as she waddled toward the deity.

Isabella's stomach was enormous, but given how much she ate these days, Galvin thought it should not come as a surprise to him or anyone who watched her indulge in a meal. Her appetite was insatiable   She even challenged Thor to eating contests on a regular basis...and won.

"By the heavens, woman. You try my patience." A reluctant smile played at one corner of Odin's mouth. "Very well. You shall have the whole family."

"Good, now that's settled, I'm hungry.   Sif's expecting me for dinner." She started toward the door and stopped.

A strange look played across her face and she rubbed her large stomach. Galvin rushed to her side.

"Is something wrong, Love?"

"No, not really." She took another step and clutched her belly, bending over. "Oh dear. I think I'm in labor."

"What? Oh my stars." Odin changed from an all-powerful deity into a male intimidated by the prospect of childbirth. "Get the women. Get the women." He rushed out to summon someone.

Galvin helped Isabella stand up. He placed a hand over the large bulge. "Feels like a party going on in there." He kissed her gently. "What do you need from me?"

"I—"her response was cut short by the return of Odin with Freya at his heels.

Not many people could say their midwife was the Mother of Childbirth. "We shall get her to the room I have prepared for her." Freya slipped an arm around Isabella. "Come, my dear. Let us leave the men to do what males do best. Worry and brag."

Isabella's laugh turned into a groan as another contraction hit. Galvin moved to follow and Odin placed a hand on his arm.

"No, the women will take it from here. Get her family and yours. This is her first birth and it may take awhile."

*****

His ears ached from the strain of trying to hear what went on behind the closed doors. All of the women from both families were on the other side, even Odin's wife, Frigg and Thor's mother, Jord. He, the husband of the woman in labor, was shut out here with his father and grandfather as well as the men of Isabella's family.

Gino joined him in pacing. They passed each other every few minutes, as they chose opposite directions to work off their nervous energy.

"I brought cigars," Gino stopped and pulled a handful of stogies from his pocket.

"Good." Galvin wondered what was so wonderful about that. The mortals' strange traditions amused him, but rather than expose his ignorance of this one he let it go. Isabella would explain it to him later.

Did he hear a sound? He headed toward the door, but Odin beat him to it, already with his ear pressed against the wood in an attempt to determine what happened on other side.

"What do you hear, Grandfather?" The other men congregated around them waiting for his report.

"I thought I heard a cry." Odin pressed his face tighter against the wood.

The door opened and the deity went sprawling forward, landing at Frigg's feet. "Love you on your knees, but I don't have time to for that now, dear." She stepped around him and turned to Galvin. "Your wife would like to see you."

He rushed to the side of the large bed on which his wife rested, very pale and tired. "How are you, Izzy?" The use of the hated nickname got the smile he was after.

"Well, all things considered, good." She accepted the kiss he placed on her mouth and teased. "Have you met your children?"

That's right. That's what this was all about. In his concern for Isabella, he forgot he was now a father. Someone placed a small bundle in his arms.

"This is your son." Isabella's fingers stroked the downy blonde covering the top of his head. She turned toward the sound of a small wail. "His sisters want their turn."

"Sisters?" He looked around at the adults circling the bed. Four women held bundles similar to the one in his arms and the men hovered over them.

"Yes, sisters. We have quintuplets. Enough babies to keep all the grandmothers happy." She smiled a tired smile and lay back against the pillow.

The roar in his head drowned out the rest of what his wife said. Five babies. The words whirled in his mind leaving no room to focus on anything else.

His wife's voice came back into focus, "And, we need to come up with names. I know we only picked out two girl and two boy names, but we need to expand our list."

Each of the women gathered around him, presenting the tiny pile of blankets each held for him to see. He touched each soft cheek, marveling at the perfection of all five. All were fair of skin and similar look. The differences lay in their hair. Pale duck-down puffs covered the heads of three. A thatch of dark curls framed the face of the fourth, delighting her Italian grandparents and the fifth one sported a crown of red equal to her grandfather's red mane. No doubt about who would spoil her. The Thunder God cooed above the infant, a smile lighting the usually serious face.

"Well, My Love, I think it is safe to say the fertility gods heard your statement and chose to override your wishes."

A confused look played across the tired face. "What?"

"The wedding reception...don't you remember. You swore not to have a child every year and two was your limit."

"I did, didn't I?"

He laughed. "It appears they have struck a compromise. We have their fertility blessing for lots of children and your wish for only two pregnancies."

"I think fulfilling their blessing will keep them happy, and I for one, am delighted to settle for one pregnancy." Isabella giggled, "Why push fate? After all, I've been struck by lightning."

Galvin laughed and thanked the heavens. He leaned over and planted a soft kiss on her lips before whispering, "That makes two of us, My Love.

To read an excerpt from the next

Still Sexy Ladies Guide to Dating Immortals

DANCIN' IN THE MOONLIGHT

by
Beverly Rae

Turn the page

Chapter One

"Five."

"No way. He's not even a four."

"Okay. So how about that guy?"

Two of her friends questioned Carly at the same time. "Which one?"

Carly rolled her eyes at the other women and shook her head. "The lean, mean-looking one by the bar. The one staring at Tala."

Tala darted her eyes toward the bar, found the object of their discussion, and whipped her gaze back to her Cosmopolitan. "Figures."

"Just because he looks mean, doesn't mean he is mean, Tala. Besides," Sara licked sugar off the rim of her glass, "I like 'em a bit rough around the edges."

"Sara, don't razz Tala. She's just being cautious." Carly managed to appear delicate nibbling on a piece of sushi. "You know what she's been through."

Oh, crap. Pity from her friends was worse than suffering through an abusive relationship with Mark Winston. Well, almost. "You know, ladies, I booted Mark to the curb over four months ago. Can we give the pity party a rest now?"

She glanced around the table at her three closest friends. Carly, the oldest one of their thirty-something group, leaned against the back of her stool and regarded Tala with cool eyes almost the same gray-blue as her own. Sara caught the unspoken communication between the two women and tucked her head, giving her silent agreement to keep the conversation light. Yet Melinda, normally the quietest one of them all, decided to add her two cents.

"I mean, damn, how long can you last, girl? Four months and counting without any sex? How the hell do you keep from going insane?"

"She spends a lot of money on batteries."

Tala started to laugh at Carly's impromptu response, "Hey, I can have a different fantasy every night. One night I can savage Brad and the next night I'm licking up and down Clooney's body." Figures the quiet one in the group was the most sexually active. "Actually, Mel, four months isn't very long. I mean, for most of us."

Mel adopted a perfect coquettish smile and nodded. "I guess. But if you ask me, I'd rather die than go four long, lonely months without male companionship. Much less without the Big O. Still—"

"Still, no man is better than an asshole, right?" Tala flicked back a loose strand of hair. "Okay, here's the deal. I broke up with Mark because he hit me. So maybe I'm not ready to leap into the pond again. It's a sad fact, but all the guys I meet up with aren't worth the time of day anyway."

Carly opened her mouth to speak, "Honey, we've all been there. Not the violent part, but the lack of quality fish in this pond.

"That's what I'm talking about." Tala jumped in and headed her off. "Besides, I'm good to go, at least until my vibrator dies." She winked at Carly when her friend snorted at her joke.

Tala gulped in a breath of much needed relief, released the air, and relaxed. Now maybe their *Girls' Night Out* tradition would get back to normal. This was the first time she'd gone out with the ladies since· Mark, and she didn't want anything spoiling the night. "But hey, don't mind me. If you want to search for your perfect man," she added finger quotes to the description, "then, by all means, don't let my self-imposed celibacy stop you."

"Uh-oh, Tala. Don't look now, but Man-At-The-Bar is headed your way." Carly's warning barely made it out of her mouth before the "lean, mean-looking" man appeared at Tala's side.

The stench of alcohol and smoke smothered the atmosphere around Tala and she had to shift her head to the side to gasp in semi-clean air. His hand slid behind her, stopping to rest on the top of her stool. "Hey, beautiful one. Tala, right? Name's Fred. How about you excuse yourself from these other gorgeous ladies and join me for a nice, private drink?"

Oh, shit. A fan. He must have recognized her from the zoo's public service and promotional spots, *Tala's Animal Facts.* Just what she needed. Not. She tilted her head up and batted her eyes at him. "Wow, Fred, I haven't had such an enticing invitation in a really, long time. How can I refuse?"

His stained, toothy leer didn't do anything for his bloodshot eyes. "You can't." He snaked his hand around her arm and tugged, "Come on, babe, let's go back to my place and you can show me what you've learned from all those wild animals. In fact, I bet you're the wild animal. You know. In bed. With Fred?"

Tala slipped her thumb under his fingers and ran her fingers over the top of his hand. Putting on her best air-head voice, she tossed her hair away from her shoulders in a perfect imitation of the stereotypical blonde bimbo. "Oh. My. God. You're a poet and don't even know it."

Fred blinked, her barb slipping straight over his head. "Huh?"

"Poet? Know it? Get it?" When he clearly didn't get it, she shook her head, trying not to let her jaw drop to the ground. Was this guy genetically stupid? Or drunk stupid? "Never mind. Don't strain your brain."

His face lit up as her joke finally hit home. "Oh, I get it now. Bed and Fred. Strain and brain." His loud horse-laugh echoed through the room, stopping conversations and swiveling heads in their direction.

"Let me give you a little tip, Fred. Unless you want a broken hand, back off. Now."

Sara giggled and nodded. "She's been taking karate."

Carly chuckled, "Isn't it tae kwon do?"

Fred got a little green around the gills, "Aw, but she wouldn't hurt me." Yet, he carefully withdrew his hand before adding, "Would you, babe?"

Damn, how she hated anyone calling her "babe." But before she could open her mouth, Carly twisted on her stool, knocking over her drink. The cool liquid splashed onto Fred's bright orange shirt and green pants, a dark stain spreading over his crotch.

"Oh, I'm so, so sorry!" Carly feigned a contrite expression while winking at Tala.

Fred's curse only added to the ladies' enjoyment, although they all tried to go along with Carly's ruse.

With a groan of disgust, Fred flicked drops of drink off his hands. "You bitches are crazy." Adding a few more choice expletives, he slinked back to his hole at the bar.

Giggles erupted from all four ladies as Tala high-fived Carly. "Thanks, girlfriend. Fred doesn't realize he got off easy."

Carly grabbed the rag from the waitress who'd arrived to clean up the spill. "I'll take care of this." She nodded toward Tala. "You can get the drink my friend here is buying me."

Tala sipped a little of her Cosmopolitan and echoed Carly's nod. "You bet. You deserve it."

Sara pointed an accusing finger at Tala. "You need to let yourself go. Free your inner goddess. Run naked through the woods. Do something and get over it."

Tala tried to control her infamous temper, but some sneaked out anyway. "Well, you know what you can do, don't you, Sara?"

"No. What?"

"Bite me."

"Ooh, Tala. I didn't know you got into women."

Leave it to Sara to turn a jab into a joke. Of course, that was part of the reason she loved these women so much. Sure, they were tough, yet they were loving, too. After all, they'd had to be strong to rise to the top of their professions, but they cared about her. Accepting Sara's lead, she quipped, "I don't usually swing that way, but for you, Beautiful, I might."

Sara batted her eyes, ran her tongue over her lips, and wiggled her fingers in a come-and-get-me gesture.

Tala faked a lecherous smirk at Sara just as a couple of good-looking men passed by them, shooting them a disgusted look. The two friends reached out for the men, pretending to pull them to the table.

"Hey, don't go. We're only kidding!"

Tala crossed her heart. "Yeah, really. We love men."

Carly slapped her hand down on the table. "Will you two cut it out? Do you want gossip getting around the bar that we're lesbians? Which would be okay if it were true, but when you're trolling for men that's the last message you want to send."

Mel sipped at her wine cooler and agreed. "Right. Besides, let's not lose focus. Keep your eyes peeled for the perfect man." She copied Tala's earlier use of finger quotes. "This is the hottest club in Denver."

Tala's sarcastic laugh turned heads in her direction again. Lowering her voice, she explained. "There's no such thing as the perfect man. It's an oxymoron, not to mention an impossibility. Especially for women our age. And especially for successful women like us."

"Maybe we *should* become lesbians. I wonder if the whole sex thing and finding the perfect partner would be easier if we eliminated men altogether." Tala, Mel, and Carly raised their eyebrows at each other. When Sara caught their reaction, she held up her hands and backpedaled. "Hey, I'm only wondering. I love men, too, you know."

Mollified, Mel picked up where they'd left off. "I agree with Tala. I don't think a perfect man exists. To be perfect, a guy would have to be half man, half god. Like Hercules, or Zeus, or whichever mythical hunk you can think of." Mel sighed. "You know, someone with major brawn."

"Yeah, but he'd have to have brain power, too. I don't want a pretty boy toy. If I wanted a handsome dead-head, I could take home half the men in this bar."

Carly's assessment rang true to Tala. "As long as the head that's dead is on the shoulders instead of in his pants, then at least he'd provide some fun for a little while. But she's right. The perfect man has to possess all the right traits. Looks, intelligence and a—"

"A wild side." Mel ripped tears into the edge of a napkin. "Your definition of the perfect man would include animalistic qualities. Probably need a hairy chest, too."

"Ewww, I like mine smooth."

Tala blushed, hating the heat spreading across her cheeks. Yet she couldn't help telling them more. "Well, if you want to know the truth, I think the perfect man would be like a wolf."

Sara sputtered into her drink. "A wolf?"

"Told you, hairy chest. Never mind Tala. She's always had a thing for wolves. I think she wants to make it with an animal. Personally, I think she's worked at the zoo a little too long for her own good."

Tala's hair stood up on her neck and she fought the urge to change the subject. "You know what I mean, Mel. I want a man to be *like* a wolf. Beautiful, with muscles and endurance. And loyal to his woman."

"His woman? You make 'woman' sound like female. Or bitch." Sara tilted her head back and gave a teeny howl.

"Yeah. I've heard wolves mate for life." Carly sipped her Chocotini and waved at Tala to go on.

Tala let her mind envision the ideal mate. "Hey, go with it for a sec. I mean who wouldn't want a guy like this? Wolves are tough when times call for tough, but they're also loving and playful, too. And they're rarely cruel."

"You'd have to make monthly appointments for him."

"For his shots?"

"Nah, the groomer."

Tala smacked Carly in the arm. "I'd take him where I get my bikini wax done, thank you very much."

"Forget the grooming. Think about the dough she'd have to shell out for training. I mean, he's got to be housebroken. Not to mention taught to sit up and beg. Or should I say, lie down and beg."

Sara was the only one not laughing, immersed in her own thoughts. "*Immortal.*" Sara played with the swizzle stick, tapping on the table in rhythm to the music blaring through the speakers on the dance floor.

"Immortal?" Sometimes Sara came up with some good ideas. Tala squinted at her in the dim light of the bar and waited.

"Yeah, immortal. Forever young and virile. Forever hunky. Forever mine."

"Yuck. If he's immortal, then you'd grow old while he stayed yummy. I'm not sure even an immortal would stay with some dried up old prune." Leave it to Carly to pop up with the negative in the situation.

"What if loving him made you immortal, too?" Sara winked, enjoying her dream.

"Okay, I guess we're going deep into this fantasy, aren't we?" Carly raised her glass to Sara. "But I do like the way you think."

The ladies stopped for a moment, letting the thought sink in.

Immortal, huh? The word "immortal" jogged Tala's memory of her cousin's recent visit. Would her friends think she'd gone nuts if she brought up the idea? She checked their faces and decided to risk it. Besides, she could always blame it on the booze later.

"Funny we're on this subject." She hesitated, then took the plunge. "Because my cousin brought up the same subject not long ago. In fact, she and her friends had a similar discussion."

She searched her memory, dredging up all the details she could remember. "They're like us. Thirty-something, successful, and manless. So they brought up the plan of summoning an immortal man."

Mel leaned forward. "You mean, like Hercules? Or Adonis? Or Zeus?"

"Okay, we get it. You want a Greek god." Carly downed the rest of her drink and motioned for the waitress. "Or are those guys Roman?"

"Who cares? I don't care if they built Rome or Athens. I just want *them* built." Mel followed Sara in ordering another drink.

"Maybe mine would be part elf. Like the cute one in the movie we saw last week." Sara grinned and ran her tongue over her lips. "No wait. I've changed my mind. Maybe I'd prefer—"

Carly's sarcastic tone interrupted Sara's musings and brought them back to reality. "And did they have any luck finding their immortal men?"

Sometimes Carly could be a real kill-joy. Tala scowled at her, unhappy with her negativity. Which made the truth even better. "Come to think of it, I think they did. Well, at least they found love. I can't say about the immortal part. But here's the really weird part. They did some kind of ceremony to call their men to them."

Carly Kill-Joy smacked down the others' exuberant reactions. "Now we're getting silly. A ceremony to attract an immortal lover? Get real, Tala."

A stab of embarrassment for letting her whimsy run wild zipped through Tala. Until Sara spoke up, keeping the dream alive. "Let's do it."

Carly sputtered into her drink. Dabbing her chin dry, she threw an exasperated look at the others. "Do what?"

All eyes squared on Sara.

"Let's summon our immortal men."

"Are you kidding?"

"Carly, shut up. Sara, are you serious?" The excitement in Mel's voice mimicked the shiver running through Tala.

"Yeah, I am. I mean, what's the harm in trying? Besides, it'll be fun."

The conversation stalled as the waitress returned with fresh drinks. Once she'd left, Sara took up where she'd left off. "What exactly did they do, Tala?"

Are they seriously considering summoning their perfect men? She tried to recall how they'd ended up on this topic, but the alcohol fogging her brain kept her memory out on a leave of absence. Just how desperate could they get? Tala bit her lip and shook her head. "I'm not sure."

Sara clapped her hands. "Hey, I have an idea. Since Tala's perfect man is a wolf," She paused at Tala's warning glare, "uh, wolf-like, then how about we do something under a full moon?"

Mel gasped and slapped her hand over her mouth. Lowering her hand slowly, she whispered, "I think the moon's full tonight." She checked her watch, and met their eyes with wonder in her own. "In fact, the moon should be high in the sky by now."

Without finishing their drinks, the ladies pushed away from the table, grabbed their purses, and headed outside.

******

"This is so ridiculous. I hope nobody sees us."

Carly stood with her arms crossed, tapping her foot, and glaring at the other women standing in the middle of the bar's parking lot. "Are you all actually going to do this?" Nonetheless, she clasped Tala's hand in her own and reached for Sara's hand.

Ignoring Carly's outstretched hand, Sara giggled, spun around, and let the cool breeze of the summer night ruffle her hair. "Come on, Carly. Let yourself have some fun. And who knows? Maybe we'll get lucky and it'll work."

"Yeah." Mel grabbed Sara's arm to keep her from toppling over. Acting like teenage girls, they hugged, squealed, and hopped up and down, giggling.

"Look, Tala." Mel pointed toward the heavens. "A full moon. Talk about your premium conditions. Perfect for calling up your wolfie, don't you think?"

Tala grinned at them and tapped Carly on the shoulder. "Lighten up and stop worrying. If anyone sees us, we can always claim we were drunk out of our minds. Besides, who's going to care?"

Carly shrugged and linked hands with Mel to start forming a circle. After Mel pulled Sara to her side, Tala grabbed Sara's other hand. Once in place, all eyes fell on Tala.

"Okay, Tala. So how do we do this?" Sara squeezed Tala's hand and scanned the faces around her. "Do we make a silent wish like when you blow out candles on a birthday cake? Or chant something about immortal men?"

Tala paused, trying to recall her cousin's description of the process. But, when she couldn't remember any details, she flung caution to the wind and guessed. "Uh, how about we, one by one, speak our wish out loud? How else are we supposed to know what everyone wants? And I'm dying to hear everyone's wish. Especially Carly's."

Sara shook her head, an intense determination creasing her forehead. "We need to do something more dramatic along with our wishes." She scanned her friends' faces, searching for suggestions. "Like maybe a dance after we're through describing them?"

"Sure. Why not? If we're going to do this nutty thing, then let's go all out." Carly fixed her steely-eyed glower on Tala, making her squirm, but she held her ground. "Any volunteers to go first?"

Mel nodded toward the horizon. "Better hurry. We want to catch the moon at its highest peak. So I'll go first." Staring into the night sky, Mel took a huge breath and described her perfect man. "My Immortal One—"

"Now there's a title to live up to."

"Shush." Tala nudged Carly into silence. "Go on, Mel."

Mel's description went on for several minutes with exact details given to every aspect of her man. From eye color to length, Mel left nothing to the imagination.

"Wow." Sara's whisper spoke for the group as they all nodded in awe. "Something tells me you've given this some real thought."

"I hope you get him, Mel. He sounds incredible."

Heads turned at Carly's warm declaration and she scowled at them. "What? Just because I think this is stupid doesn't mean I don't want the best for my friends. Sheesh." She tossed back her hair in defiance. "So here's my immortal hunk. He'd be tanned, dark, rippling with muscles, impeccably dressed and..."

Tala stared at the moon above her, allowing her mind to drift away from the sound of Carly's voice. Wouldn't it be great if she really could summon her dream man? Her half-wolf, half-man stud? A punch in the arm broke her out of her reverie.

Catching Sara watching her quizzically, she wiggled her hand for encouragement. "Okay, Sara. You go next."

Taking a deep breath, Sara spread her lips wider, unable to hide her excitement. "Well, let's see. My Immortal One would be a man like no other."

As Sara continued to describe her version of the faultless male, Tala's mind drifted off again, letting the image form in her mind's eye. Within seconds, the form appeared, drawing her deeper into her trance.

His long, toned body, sleek and glistening in the moonlight, slowly rose from a crouched position. Muscles rippled across his chest, highlighting the broad expanse while large, brown nipples accented his hardened pecs. A sprinkling of silky black hair running from his six-pack abs led to the full, curly patch below and Tala wetted her mouth at the sight of his richly endowed self. Yet more magnificent than his body, his face drew Tala's attention away from his torso. Straight, black hair teased the tips of his shoulders and flowed around his angular face, while his strong, square jaw beckoned for a woman's touch.

And then she saw his eyes.

Amber eyes. Golden, compelling, magnetic eyes drawing her to him. Commanding her to be his, promising to be hers. Eyes she recognized from pleasurable nights of lustful dreams.

Her breaths shortened with the ache, the need clutching at her heart. Could he exist? Even as she wondered, he bent, inching back into a crouch. His image morphed, blurring the lines of his physique while outlining another. She blinked, trying to see him better but, instead, lost the vision for a moment. She whimpered, a small, tortured sound.

Blinking again, Tala saw the new image. The eyes were the same. Amber eyes. Golden, compelling, magnetic eyes. She blinked again and stared into the eyes of a black wolf.

"Tala?"

"Hel-lo? Tala? Are you okay?"

She jerked to awareness to find the others gawking at her. All three of her friends had their cell phones pointed at her, snapping pictures. Then she noticed why. She was down on the pavement, on all fours, gravel digging into her knees and palms. She must've fallen over from too much alcohol. "What's going on?"

Sara reached over and helped her to her feet. "Well, for one thing, you're sweating like a pig. Gross!" Releasing Tala's hand, she wiped her palm on her jeans. "Having hot flashes already?"

Tala shook her head to both answer the question and to clear the remnants of the dream lingering inside. "Excuse me?" She lifted her hand, noted the clamminess and copied Sara's gesture. "I, uh, guess I'm a little hot. Probably just the alcohol."

"Yeah. Sure." Mel's tone left no doubt of her disbelief.

She glanced around her, clarity forming again, and tried to make a joke. "What's the big deal? I zoned out for a minute and fell over. Too much drink, I guess. No biggie."

The ladies dropped their hands, but remained focused on Tala. Unnerved by the intense scrutiny, she tried to pick up where she thought they'd left off. "So Sara's finished, right?"

When no one nodded, she swallowed and continued anyway. "Carly, I think it's your turn. It's Carly's turn, right?" Uneasiness crawled down her spine at their lack of response. "Cut the crap, would you? Or are you trying to scare me?"

Carly patted Tala's arm, bringing her into a hug in the process. "I already took my turn, remember? You haven't been ill lately, have you, Tala? I mean, with a fever or anything?"

Tala broke free and stepped away from the group. "Will you stop? You're acting like I've done something crazy. Haven't you ever gotten a little tipsy before? Damn it all to hell and back, knock it off."

The three women glanced at each other and back to Tala. Mel dropped her head while chewing on her bottom lip, but Sara and Carly returned Tala's glare. Carly flipped open her cell phone.

"What is the matter with you guys?" Tala's nerves strung tighter and she tried hard not to fidget. Was this a joke? Or did she have a problem? She gritted her teeth and asked the question she didn't want to ask, but had to. "You're acting like I've gone over the edge. What the hell did I do to make you act this odd?"

Several tense moments passed until Carly broke the silence. "We're not the ones acting strangely, Tala. You are."

"Yeah? So what strange thing did I do, huh? And didn't all of you do something just as weird?"

Turning the cell phone to face Tala, she revealed the snapshot. "Just look at the picture." Again her friends exchanged telling looks. Taking a deep breath, Carly gave her an unexpected answer. "You howled."

Tala's mouth dropped. "I did what? You're kidding."

From the expressions on their faces, joking was the last thing on their minds. In fact, Mel still couldn't meet Tala's eyes.

"You lifted your head, stared at the full moon, and howled."

"I did not." No way could she believe such an outlandish accusation. She'd daydreamed, sure. But howled?

Carly lifted an eyebrow at her. "Take a look at the picture, honey. Head thrown back, baying at the moon in full color."

Tala shook her head, but held out hope for a better explanation. "No, but—"

Carly dipped her chin and raised both eyebrows. "I swear, girl. I am not lying to you. You stood there and let loose with an actual throw-your-head-back, no-holds-barred, canine-loving howl. Hell, I thought we'd have a wolf pack on us before the sound died out."

Sara nodded. "It's true, Tala. You bayed at the moon."

"I did?" Had she really howled? If she had, she needed to come up with a good explanation and quick. "Hey, I was just kidding around." She forced out a laugh. "And you all fell for it."

"Looked real enough to me."

"Yeah. Too real."

Needing a major diversion, Tala hopped a few feet away, gyrating to an unheard rhythm. "Come on, ladies, let's dance." When the others eventually joined her, she grabbed Carly by the hand, pulling her into a spin. "Dance. Now."

Whooping and shouting, the other ladies stretched out their arms and began twirling in circles. Sara bumped into Mel, sending the two crashing to the ground in a fit of hilarity while Tala and Carly skipped around them.

Exhausted, Tala and Carly pulled the two women to their feet and hugged each other. "Well, if nothing else, dancin' in the moonlight was fun."

Sara's silly smile reinforced Tala's statement. "Yeah, it was."

Mel stumbled to a stop and blew out a long breath. "I don't know about you girls, but I've had enough excitement for one day. But I gotta say I thoroughly enjoyed everyone's performance. Whew! I'm danced out."

Carly caught Tala's eye and rolled her eyes. "Especially Tala's. She proved she deserves her wolfman."

Sara leaned against Tala and nudged her in the arm. "Yeah, who knew you could howl?"